HAMBURG NOIR

HAMBURG NOIR

EDITED BY
JAN KARSTEN

Translated by Noah Harley,
Geoffrey C. Howes, and Paul David Young

BROOKLYN, NEW YORK
Publishing books since 1997

Published by Akashic Books
©2025 Akashic Books
Copyright to the individual stories is retained by the authors.

Series concept by Tim McLoughlin and Johnny Temple
Map of Hamburg by Sohrab Habibion

ISBN: 978-1-63614-115-2
Library of Congress Control Number: 2024949338

EU Authorized Representative details:
Easy Access System Europe
Mustamäe tee 50, 10621 Tallinn, Estonia
gpsr.request@easproject.com

Akashic Books
Brooklyn, New York
Instagram, X, Facebook: AkashicBooks
info@akashicbooks.com
www.akashicbooks.com

ALSO IN THE AKASHIC NOIR SERIES

FORTHCOMING

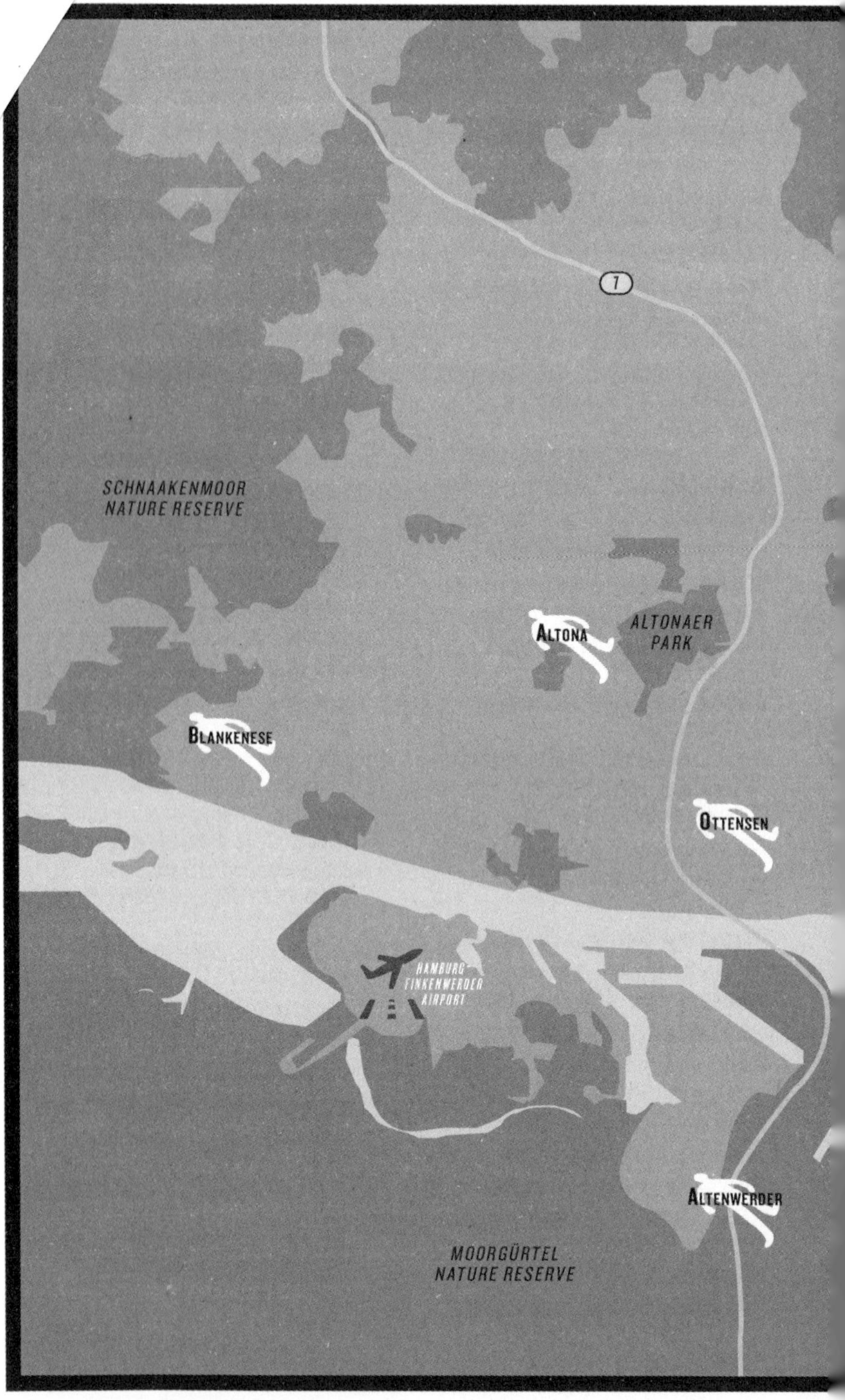

7
SCHNAAKENMOOR
NATURE RESERVE
ALTONA
ALTONAER
PARK
BLANKENESE
OTTENSEN
HAMBURG-
FINKENWERDER
AIRPORT
ALTENWERDER
MOORGÜRTEL
NATURE RESERVE

NIENDORF
HAMBURG AIRPORT
OHLSDORF CEMETERY
HAMBURG
WINTERHUDE
HOHELUFT
EIMSBÜTTEL
24
HEILIGENGEISTFELD
HORN
ST. PAULI
REEPERBAHN
ROTHENBURGSORT
BILLWERDER
1

TABLE OF CONTENTS

PART III: POWER & OBLIVION

INTRODUCTION
A Port for the Stranded

Translated by Noah Harley

" Hamburg is a giant counting house by day, a giant brothel by night," satirist Heinrich Heine quipped a good two hundred years ago, in a mordant description of the Hanseatic city's two defining poles: its free trade and its permissive nightlife. Behind any ridicule lies the reality of the city as a place of economic, moral, and social contrast, one that persists into the present day. Or as Ingvar Ambjørnsen once wrote, "Buying and selling, I thought. That's what it all revolved around. And I thought of all the people who had nothing to sell and therefore nothing to buy, but who kept their grip nonetheless, neuroses blossoming and psychoses vivid as ever" (*The Mechanical Woman*, 1991).

When Saxon settlers built the Hammaburg fortification at the edge of the known world in the eighth century CE, they did so in a prime geographical location nestled in between the Alster and Bille rivers, with the Central Eastern European hinterland behind and the Elbe in front—the powerful river that would prove the lifeblood of the city and guarantor of its rise.

Soon a busy trading center, the town developed slowly at first, then with increasing speed throughout the Middle Ages. With the founding of Neustadt in 1188 and the construction of the port, Hamburg became the engine of the Hanseatic

League alongside Lübeck, the primary outlet to the North Sea and Western Europe. By the end of the eighteenth century it was Europe's trading post, a critical center of maritime commerce linking every corner of the earth.

In an era before commercial air travel, Hamburg was quite literally Europe's gateway to the world. Anyone from Northern Europe looking to strike out for distant lands or the New World on the far side of the Atlantic had to start from Hamburg, creating a cosmopolitan melting pot of different cultures and lifestyles from early on. Today, nearly 40 percent of Hamburg residents trace their roots back to one of more than 170 countries.

The Port of Hamburg continues today as one of the world's busiest; the ships and cranes, teeming crowds and shrieking gulls, and the sounds and smells of the shipyards, unloading docks, and warehouses have always been a fixture of the city's identity. It is a location that has undergone one incarnation after the next, from the cog ships of the Hanseatic League to the tall ships and general cargo vessels of yesteryear, to the monstrous container ships of our time. At present, a new chapter in the city's history is being written with the HafenCity project, built around the €866 million Elbphilharmonie.

That is one side of the city, at least as it appears in the glossy tourist brochures: the panoramic view of the harbor from the landing piers; the distinctive Kontorhaus district, a UNESCO World Heritage Site along with the adjacent Speicherstadt district; the gaudy department stores around Binnenalster, the glittering lake in the heart of the city; and the red-light clichés of St. Pauli.

Hamburg Noir prefers to explore some of the city's less illuminated districts, out beyond the superlatives like the "most beautiful city in the world" that Hamburg likes to pin on its lapel.

It isn't that Hamburg has an exorbitantly high crime rate; the index lies somewhere in between Chennai, Melbourne, Bangkok, and San Diego. Yet crime has never been the exception to the rule, but an integral, and perennial, element of the city's history. There is the callous reckoning of the city's power brokers; the black market activity and countless sorts of smuggling one would only expect from a city of trade (as recently as 2021, sixteen tons of cocaine with a street value of nearly €3 billion were discovered here, in Europe's all-time largest haul); and last but certainly not least, the everyday crime that typically plays out below the threshold of public perception, whether related to drug trade and procurement or the turf wars of organized crime—not only in the red-light district.

Then, of course, there are the all-too familiar companions to a human life: the obsessions and fateful decisions we arrive at out of love, greed, jealousy, misery, necessity, despair, hatred, or anger.

For Hamburg has always been a place for the stranded—sailors no longer in service, lost souls, failed soldiers of fortune, windmill chasers. By the Middle Ages the city had already come to be defined by social contrasts: wealthy ship-owning dynasties and affluent merchants on the one hand; mass poverty, hunger, and misery on the other. The divide meant the wars and disasters of the early modern era hit the poor especially hard, as in 1806, when the French occupation forced any city resident unable to demonstrate at least four months of provisions to leave, ultimately halving the city's population through flight or death. Or in 1892, when a cholera outbreak claimed more than 8,500 victims in what was then Europe's largest slum district, the Gängevierteln, where people lured to the city in the hopes of a better life subsisted under medieval conditions.

Still, amid all the crass inequality Hamburg has largely responded to its disasters with a mixture of pragmatism and resilience. When the Great Fire of 1842 destroyed a third of the city center, including the town hall and St. Nicholas Church, the resulting push for modernization brought the wide streets and modern construction that help define the city center to this day.

It would take all of the city's powers of resilience and determination to survive and rebuild in the wake of the devastating bombing raids of World War II. Over the course of ten days during the summer of 1943, more than 34,000 people died in an unparalleled series of attacks from British and US planes. The firestorm that resulted from "Operation Gomorrha" obliterated half of Hamburg's housing stock, reducing entire neighborhoods to apocalyptic, rubble-strewn scenes; only the tower of St. Michael's Church emerged unscathed. Anyone looking at the pictures from the era would hardly believe that in just fifteen years Hamburg would have reestablished itself as a bustling metropolis. Yet throughout all the demolition, rebuilding, and construction, Hamburg retained its unmistakable character. Now as then, the spires of the city's five chapter churches still mark the city skyline, in part since hardly anything has been built that's taller than the 132-meter spire of St. Michael's, following an unwritten but ironclad rule.

Today Hamburg's industry and economy still place it among Germany's richest regions, the place where the greatest number of the country's millionaires call home. The distribution of that wealth is disproportionate in the extreme, as is visible from the sea of faces the city presents: the sea captains' homes and the villas looking out onto the Elbe in

Blankenese; nearly rural suburbs; socially restive areas south of the Elbe and to the northeast, in parts of which every other child lives below the poverty line; the crowded urban scenes of Altona, St. Georg, and St. Pauli.

The many facets of Hamburg's ambivalent identity, forged over centuries, are on full display in the stories collected in this anthology. Here, we have assembled some of the city's finest and best-known writers, luminaries in the world of crime fiction and German literature, featuring multiple recipients of the German Crime Fiction Award and the Hubert Fichte Prize, among others. Relative newcomers rub shoulders with established authors, some of whose work now spans decades, like Ingvar Ambjørnsen, who first came to Hamburg from Norway in the mideighties. Many of Ambjørnsen's novels give voice to societal dropouts and petty criminals, the prostitutes and the drunks, depicting their worlds as empathetically as they do unsparingly. Writers like Frank Göhre, a towering figure in German-language crime fiction whose work condenses reality and fiction into rapid-fire, highly associative, dialogue-rich studies of society. Taken as a whole, Göhre's evocative settings provide a sort of counterchronicle to the Hanseatic city that spans decades, laying bare time and again how tightly political and economic power are interwoven, and petty criminality with more organized crime.

Nora Luttmer walks us through Rothenburgsort, a diverse, industrial area in the city where Auntie Lien runs her small Vietnamese restaurant—until a bull-necked extortionist threatens the intricate social web that exists between Ghanian traders and Senegalese day laborers, between the Afghan market and snack bars and the Lebanese import-export shop.

Jasmin Ramadan shows Hamburg's immigration as a process of daily arrivals. Fresh from Sudan on an art stipend and searching for the vanished woman whose apartment she's been allowed to stay in, Ramadan's protagonist discovers family in an unexpected place: a local bar in Eimsbüttel.

As a port town, it's no surprise that pubs are a mainstay in Hamburg; the bars and hot spots, notorious dives and drinking dens, are often open along the piers or on the block around the clock, at times providing the only constant in the lives of their patrons. As in Tina Uebel's requiem for the Clochard, a neighborhood institution where people with nowhere else to call home find one, but which didn't survive lockdown during the pandemic.

It isn't bars alone that set the pace and rhythm of the neighborhoods. Aside from its parties, Hamburg has long had a thriving music scene, home to Johannes Brahms and the Beatles and now featuring the world's third-largest concert hall, drawing massive crowds. Yet over recent decades it's been the many small clubs (not just around the Reeperbahn) that have largely set the tone for the musical underground, whether swing—under mortal danger during the Nazi era— jazz, rock and roll, punk, avant-garde pop, or hip-hop.

Fittingly, two contributors to this volume have been well-known as musicians for decades. Bela B Felsenheimer delivers a tale full of gallows humor about small-time dealers and bouncers in St. Pauli, with a problematic character named "Rocken Roll" leading the charge. Timo Blunck stages a "Grusical" deeply rooted in the city's history, parodying Hamburg's reputation for musicals, serial-killer novels, and the middle class's new fetishization of cooking, all in the same breath.

Brigitte Helbling explores the ways in which seemingly harmless encounters can mushroom into greater and greater threats, introducing us to aikido as an art form for dealing with danger, even in completely unexpected ways. In Kai Hensel's coming-of-age story, set against Hamburg's triannual carnival, an encounter between two teens leads to the unnerving discovery that it isn't always wrong to commit a crime.

In "The Assignment," Katrin Seddig sets out to capture the city's essence by literary means, having her heroine stroll through an almost expressionist cityscape of hellishly loud arterial roads, disrepair, and vast construction sites. As the "new, shiny, and clean" blots out and overwrites the "old, boggy, and overgrown," it echoes the ruins of the past: the "essence" of the city is "lethal." Seddig's story is also a clear-eyed chronicle of gentrification as the constant companion to a city forever at war with itself over who should get to determine a neighborhood's profile: the people who live there or the investors and real-estate speculators yet again.

Till Raether cooly narrates the demise of a captain of modern finance who runs his private equity firm aground gambling on crypto currency. The sharp turn in fortune leads the loser of the bet south of the Elbe, to the less glamorous corners of the industrial port behind Europe's most modern shipping-container terminal, where people live in condemned warehouses, in the forgotten, in-between sections of the city.

The water is never far off in Hamburg, no matter where you end up in the city. Matthias Wittekindt's protagonist Manz, a young police officer in the 1970s, is charged with investigating an attack on a young woman found dead in a small branch of the Elbe east of the city center. The trail leads to a nearby hang-gliding club, where the old guard of the Hanseatic elite spend their weekends.

Robert Brack takes us even farther back into the past, to the Altona of a hundred years ago. Still an independent borough at the time, Altona was a bedroom community for the workers who toiled in Hamburg's factories under difficult conditions to process the tobacco and other wares that flooded unceasingly into the city through trade. In vivid, concrete prose, Brack writes about cigar rollers and cigarette stuffers, an ill-fated romance in patriarchal times, and a restive worker population who finally get enough of the daily drills on the "parade grounds of capitalism."

The degree to which class tensions still determine individual fates in the present day is on glaring display in Zoë Beck's contribution. Against the backdrop of the exclusive Elbchaussee and Hamburg's yacht marina, Beck shows us the corruption of Hamburg's modern business elite, as superficial as they are debased, in a sparkling minidrama that wickedly but casually brings home money's perennial ability to make every last problem disappear and destroy entire lives.

The fourteen stories in this collection all look to where good (crime) fiction has always looked: toward lesser-known settings and living situations, repeatedly drawing our attention to lives overlooked, the lost souls and the powerless who have slipped through the cracks of commerce. The perspectives on the metropolis are as diverse as the writers' backgrounds, resulting in a varied depiction of Hamburg as a colorful hodgepodge of people inhabiting a lively city of millions. Between water and spirits, between power and oblivion, between dream and reality.

Jan Karsten
Hamburg, Germany
April 2025

PART I

Water & Schnapps

ANT STREET

BY NORA LUTTMER

Rothenburgsort

Translated by Noah Harley

The scent of cinnamon and star anise filled the air. Today's lunch special was *phở bò*, rice noodle soup served with thin strips of beef. It was just about all anyone ordered—and that in spite of the heat. It was ninety-five degrees outside, unusual for Hamburg, and hot air crowded into the small restaurant with each new arrival or departure.

Lien stood behind the counter mixing fruit drinks, dressed like always in a tight-fitting black top with a stiff collar, her hair pulled into a neat bun. There was hardly an empty seat in the house. Closing her eyes for a moment, she took in the murmur of voices, an unintelligible whirl of languages whose sounds she loved.

Last year she had moved her restaurant out of Hamburg's downtown to Bill Strasse, in the heart of the industrial Rothenburgsort neighborhood. Onto a cobblestone street with pockmarked asphalt, where tractor trailers double-parked overnight. The wholesale dealers who had set up shop in the run-down buildings and factories had something for everyone: old washing machines, mattresses, hi-fi systems, bikes, antique TV sets, refrigerators, chandeliers, all sorts of junk. Then there were the things that had been discarded long ago as useless in Germany, most of which were shipped to Africa.

Everyone had called her crazy when she abandoned her restaurant's choice location behind the Deichtorhallen for Rothenburgsort, a forgotten corner of the city known for its industry, harbor offshoots that ended in piers and scrapyards, and the Elbe and its tributaries.

Downtown, Lien had been able to charge twelve euros for a bowl of *phở*, here just 5.90.

But she was sixty-six now, and no longer had the patience for the anxious crowds, hip creative types, and frustrated office workers of the city center. It had all grown to be too much. Here on the outskirts, just twelve minutes by bus but a whole world removed from downtown, things were more relaxed, calmer. She felt at ease.

Lien had taken the business over from a Polish man. The dining area wasn't very big but had a large window looking out onto a commercial courtyard. Across the way from Lien stood Mohammed's Import-Export-Lebanon, with every last product announcing itself as "Made in China." Rocking horses, washtubs, buckets, rolls of artificial turf sold by the meter, toilet brushes . . . all plastic. In loud, bright colors.

Lien had left the restaurant the way she found it: open kitchen behind the counter, white walls, laminated tabletops, plain seating. All that mattered to her mind was the food, not some clever interior-decoration scheme. The small shrine bearing the figures of Thần Tài and Thổ Địa, the gods of prosperity and the soil, was the only hint that the restaurant was Vietnamese, or at least Asian. The shrine was set up on the ground by the entrance.

Lunch hour had finished, slowly the tables emptied. The guests paid, thanked Lien with a nod, and left. Lien reached for one of the green mangoes she had bought that morning, walked around the counter, and set it down at the shrine. She poured Thần Tài and Thổ Địa a small shot of schnapps each and lit some incense.

Standing back up, she spied a squat, bull-necked man through the window. He stood on the other side of the courtyard, smoking and looking in her direction.

Ma quỷ, Lien swore to herself, demons and ghosts. She felt her hands grow clammy and blood began to pound in her veins. An uneasy feeling spread through her—uneasiness and rage. The man out there was only waiting for the last guest to leave the restaurant. Then he would come over and make his demands. Name the amount she would have to give him.

The racketeers had been troubling the area for weeks now, demanding protection money. They worked in twos. She hadn't seen this man outside before, only the other, who had been by just last week. He had called himself Erik, although he almost certainly had a different name.

Just days ago, the bike shop down the street had burned down. Emergency rescue had barely managed to stop it from spreading to neighboring buildings. Nobody knew for sure whether the fire was the work of the two men. Not that it mattered anyway—as long as everyone believed it was, it shored up their power.

Lien looked over at the man, answering his gaze. Her eyes flashed angrily, though there was no way the man could see that from his distance. Her first choice would simply have been to lock up shop. But that wasn't a solution either, sadly.

She sighed, snatched the rice straw broom leaning in the corner next to the shrine, and, as her last guest finished up, began as ever to sweep up the scraps of lunch fallen to the floor. The bristles made a harsh scraping sound as they moved over the plastic floor of the dining area. In the process, Lien swept up a number of ants who scurried back and forth frantically, as if they had lost their way and could no longer find their associates.

And then, just as she had known would happen, the man stepped inside the restaurant. Right as the last guest left.

He stood before her, legs apart, arms folded across his chest. She could smell the cigarettes on his breath, cut with the acrid air of strongly scented soap. Lien guessed he was twenty-five, thirty at most. His face was wide and pudgy. He wore white running shoes like everyone these days, with jeans and a black T-shirt that outlined his muscles. Muscles trained at a gym, Lien thought, which might look like something but didn't serve for anything except lifting weights. A snake tattoo wound its way under his arm. His blond hair was plastered down with sweat, and pearls of moisture hung off his upper lip. His skin gave off a reddish glow.

The heat doesn't suit him.

"We're closed," Lien said in passing, as though unaware of the real reason for his being there.

"You owe me eight hundred euros, for last month," he rasped, his voice harsh, raw. You could hear that he smoked too much.

"Oh, so you're Erik's partner?" she replied, speaking as though Erik were a friend.

"Partner?" the man snorted. "I'm Erik's boss."

"I gave Erik the money," Lien said. "Just last week." She smiled the way she thought the man might expect her to. Asian women were always smiling like that, weren't they? Even when an extortionist showed up. *What bullshit.*

The man shifted from one leg to the other, grinding his teeth. "I didn't get it."

"But that's impossible. Ask him! I definitely gave it to him."

The man shook his head. "You give *me* the money. Eight hundred, not a cent less."

"But I . . . I can't pay twice."

"That's *your* problem."

"It's too much," Lien said, still trying to work her way out of the demand. Or at least lower it. "I don't have it."

"Then get it. I'm giving you two days."

She nodded vaguely. "I'll see what I can do."

He drew air in loudly through his nose and his shoulders lifted, his chest expanding. *Puffing himself up*, she thought.

"Eight hundred euros. Day after tomorrow." Then he turned and left her standing there.

Lien watched the man stroll back across the courtyard. He turned for another look at her restaurant. Was he already mulling over the best way to set it on fire? *How many generations of shit-eaters did it take to make that asshole?*

This restaurant was Lien's domain, it was her life. Couldn't anything ever go smoothly?

That was all she wanted after all: to run her shop in peace. Without outside help. Without depending on others. And definitely without some goddamn self-appointed racketeer breathing down her neck.

Barely had the man disappeared when her next-door neighbor Mohammed came crashing into the restaurant through the back storage room. An unpleasant odor trailed in behind him. Stagnant water, algae . . . at least that's what Lien told everyone; the storage room opened out onto the Bille canal, which was capable of producing truly breathtaking smells in the heat. It was why Lien always made sure to keep all windows and doors shut.

"Close the door," she called out.

But Mohammed, whose bulky figure and friendly round

face always reminded Lien of a bear—a bear who wouldn't bite—was far too upset to react. "Auntie Lien," he stammered, almost out of breath. Though only a year or two younger than Lien, he called her *Auntie* out of respect. "So he was over here too?"

It was a rhetorical question; Mohammed had obviously seen who had been hanging around outside her shop.

"He threatened he . . . would do something to my daughter," Mohammed pressed on, so quickly that Lien had a hard time catching the words as they tumbled out. "If I don't pay. But I . . . so much . . . again . . . it . . . How am I supposed to get it all together?"

His eyes closed, and Lien guessed at the scenes running through his mind. Images of what would happen. Her hand came to rest on Mohammed's arm.

"They're all talk," she said, not believing her own words. Still, she had to calm him down somehow. She liked Mohammed, and felt sorry for him.

He pursed his lips, face pale. Eyes full of fear. "P-paying twice? H-h-how are *we* the ones responsible if Erik just took off with our money?"

"Did he say that?" Lien asked. "That Erik took off?"

Mohammed shrugged. "It's just what I heard . . . it's what everyone's saying . . ."

Of course. As far as rumors went, it was like living in a little village around here.

"But what am I supposed to do?"

"There's nothing you can do. Just make sure you get the money together," Lien said. "For your daughter's sake." *What pathetic advice: just bend over backward, subordinate yourself, give up.* But what else was she supposed to tell Mohammed? That everything would turn out all right?

Mohammed trudged out head hung low, again without closing the storage room door behind him. She really would have to air out the restaurant before she opened for dinner. Not yet though, it was still too hot. The heat would only make the stench worse.

Lien picked up the broom and continued sweeping. It was almost meditative, the act of moving the broom across the floor, the same scratching sound repeating itself over and over.

When she had finished with the front of the restaurant, Lien moved on to the storage room, which had become another part of her daily routine. There among the sacks of rice, boxes of noodles, ten-liter bottles of fish sauce, and other kitchen supplies marched an army of small black ants. Here a column, there a column, all arranged in neat lines.

She swept across the lines of insects, which scattered immediately. She managed to brush a number into the dustpan, using the one with the long handle so she wouldn't have to bend over. The remaining ants reassembled and continued marching as if nothing had happened. Lien repeated the trick. But there were too many. These damned ants would be her undoing.

She had tried stopping up the holes they got in through, to no avail. Once they showed up, the ants always found a way. Around the sacks, beneath the crates, past the bottles, even under the heavy freezer cabinet. Straight to their target. *I might be a little like an ant myself*, Lien reflected. *I definitely go straight to the target.* The only difference was she didn't march in a column, but alone. Always alone.

She had read somewhere that ants are among the first to colonize corpses, feeding on the keratin in eyelashes, eyebrows, and the surface layers of the skin. What an image.

* * *

It was quiet at the restaurant the next morning. Once in a while someone dropped in to order takeout. By noon the thermometer had crept past eighty-five; it had only cooled off a little by evening. Lien still hadn't managed to get the ants under control.

Dark had long since fallen by the time she closed up. She would have to watch out not to twist her ankle on the uneven cobblestones.

She set off for home on foot, like she did every evening. Lien had moved to the area herself since relocating the restaurant into a newly built apartment block, somewhat soulless if you asked her. They had painted the building pink, as if in some desperate attempt to breathe life into it. Yet it also put her right next door to the Elbe, not a thousand feet from the river. By night she could hear the heavy chugging of cargo ship engines and the metallic shriek of trains as they passed over the bridges spanning the river. That she was very fond of.

Nearly all the metal shutters to the stores on Bill Strasse were still rolled up despite the late hour. Good weather was rare in Hamburg and it had to be enjoyed, even if that meant setting up a folding chair outside one's shop. No one wanted to return to the confines of their own four walls. Nor did Lien for that matter, but she was tired and had to be at the wholesale market by five a.m. at the latest, or the best produce would already be gone.

Senegalese day laborers stood around the German-Chinese Kitchen food stand, eating rice with sauce and drinking beer after work. "Hey Lien," they called out to her. Every now and then they came to her restaurant, too. Lien waved back.

Several doors down, a group of women were tidying up

after an evening church service in a warehouse owned by Jakobus, a Ghanian man. They pushed store counters back into place and stacked the chairs in a corner. They also greeted Lien. Though she wasn't Christian, Lien would still attend services from time to time. It gave her a sense of belonging, but without the risk of people trying to involve her too closely, as might happen at a Vietnamese pagoda. That wasn't something she wanted. In every aspect of her life, Lien was a lone wolf. Another reason why she ran the restaurant on her own, without any help, who she would have to chase around too much anyway for them to make things any easier. She was welcome at the Ghanian services, but she was also an outsider who they left in peace.

She turned left onto Ausschläger Billdeich at the Afghan Bazaar, then left again onto Billhorner Deich. What few streetlamps there were threw more shadows than light. It was far darker and deader here than on Bill Strasse at this hour, though a tingling in her neck told her that she wasn't alone. Someone was following her.

She straightened up and kept walking, head erect, without turning around. A muted reflection in a kiosk window was enough to confirm her suspicions. Behind her came a squat, bull-necked figure—the nameless racketeer. Not that she was all that surprised; Lien had figured that he would follow up on his demand. Just for the fun of intimidating others, of spreading fear.

He moved lightly, and with a stealth Lien had possessed herself at one point but since surrendered to age. Still, she had noticed his presence. This fact alone brought her a certain satisfaction.

She passed a group of teens on a bench—they ignored Lien and her pursuer. He was close behind her now, though he didn't draw any nearer. It was clear to Lien that this wouldn't last.

Even wearing well-cushioned orthopedic shoes, Lien's hips hurt when she walked. An old injury. She tried to ignore it. *Whatever you do, don't show weakness.* It wasn't far now. Just through the park with the bunker, then to the right.

The bunker walls were coated in lichen, fungus, and moss. A streetlamp revealed a rat running along the side of the building. Two crows hopped about a city trash can, jabbing at a plastic bag filled with god knows what, their talons scraping against the metal. The path ahead was littered with empty cans and decaying banana peels. Lien took a big step over the trash and almost screamed. The movement had sent a stabbing pain shooting through her hip; she had to take several deep breaths before it became bearable. She continued, hobbling now, one hand braced against her back to ward off the pain.

Evidently, her pursuer saw his chance and stepped up to her side. "Hurts?" he asked. It sounded mocking.

She ignored him and kept hobbling.

He grabbed her by the arm and whipped her around so they were face-to-face. The whites of his eyes were red; they reminded her of a sick bull terrier's. His mouth twisted in an amused smile. He really was the sort who got pleasure from causing others fear, Lien thought. In that sense he was like her brother Hung, who everyone called The Merciful, though he was anything but. In the former East Germany Hung had a job as a foreign contract worker at a light bulb factory in Karl Marx City, now Chemnitz. After the Wall came down, he sold smuggled cigarettes in Berlin like so many others. But Hung had risen quickly in the hierarchy. By 1992 he was one of the top bosses. In the late nineties, when the Berlin police stepped up their actions against the Vietnamese gangs, he had relocated to the Czech Republic, establishing himself there as a respectable businessman: market stalls, little restaurants, the import-export trade. But he still had his hands in all kinds of illegal ventures.

Lien had pondered asking for her brother's help with the protection money. But even with his own sister, Hung's assistance worked like a lifelong franchise—she would never be done paying it back. And that wasn't something she wanted.

She would have to deal with it on her own.

"I'll have the money," she said, twisting her arm out of his clutch. There would be a fat bruise there tomorrow.

"Twenty-four hours," the man responded, drawing back unhurriedly.

Lien stood there trembling, her hip aching. Her hands balled up in fists trying to contain her emotions. Who in the hell did this guy think he was? Messing with the entire social fabric of the neighborhood, thinking he could rile everyone up with his blustering and threats. She was beside herself with anger. She couldn't go home now in the state she was in. She had to calm down first, catch her breath.

She continued past the bunker to the Entenwerder ferry house, a small timber-framed building that made her think of a witch's lair with all of its little additions and outbuildings. Directly behind it lay the Elbe.

The willows along the embankment sketched black silhouettes against the moonlit sky as a cargo ship plowed down the shipping channel. The drone of the engine reverberated across the way toward her. Water sloshed, a dog yapped in the distance. Seagulls cried. Even they couldn't sleep in the heat. Over on the other side of the river, amber lights from the industrial plants illuminated chimney smoke as it spiraled into the sky in thick columns, before fading off in the darkness. A smaller vessel made its way down the river just a few meters from shore. Little more than a flickering shadow in the night.

Lien breathed in deeply, absorbing the familiar, slightly musty smell of the silt. Gradually her sense of calm returned. The Elbe had that effect on her. How stoically the river moved along. An unstoppable force that lay hidden beneath its dark surface, but was still plain to feel.

It was nearly midnight the following day and Lien was by herself in the restaurant when he came in.

"Time's up," he said. The words could have come out of a movie script.

Lien nodded. She had been waiting for him. She opened the register, lifted out the cashbox, and removed a bank envelope, handing it to the man.

He took it and sat down across from her at the counter. As he counted, Lien switched on a burner holding a pot of beef broth that she had set aside especially for him. She brought some meat out from the fridge and took a knife down off the magnetic strip on the wall.

She closed her eyes, concentrating entirely on the knife in her hand. She loved the moment of the blade sliding through the beef with practically no resistance. Lien had carried the knife with her from Vietnam years ago. It was handwrought, the wooden handle black and worn from use.

She looked back up at the man and pictured the smooth steel gliding through his neck like butter. He wouldn't scream—he wouldn't have the air to with his throat slit.

"With a good amount of meat," the man said. It sounded like an order.

"Of course," she answered as meekly as possible. Let him wallow in his self-satisfaction.

As if he had even the slightest clue who she was.

Lien had arrived in 1972, to what at the time was East Germany. She had been chosen for a course of study—as a demobilized soldier. It turned out that the Communists had been quite forward-thinking even in Lien's day. That or pragmatic, depending on how you looked at it; they had accepted anybody who supported their cause, young women included.

Lien had joined the women's youth brigade and traveled to the front to motivate soldiers, to "sing louder than the bombs." After three weeks she was the only member of her troop still alive. So she had switched to weapons. She was a quick study in killing. Without hesitation or pity. Although when she thought back on it now, it hadn't ever been difficult for her, right from the start. Her goal had been to survive; nothing else mattered. That's how it had been during the war, and that's how it was today.

She cut off several more slices of beef and then, with a trace of regret, set the knife aside. She was too old, he was too young. She wouldn't be quick enough, he would put up a fight.

She took a bowl off the shelf, dropped in a handful of cooked rice noodles and some bean sprouts, then laid the fresh meat on top still raw. Using a large ladle, she spooned steaming broth into the bowl, instantly cooking the thin strips of beef. She sprinkled scallions, more bean sprouts, and small Vietnamese coriander leaves on the dish, then added a splash of garlic vinegar and squeezed a quarter lemon over the bowl before setting it on the counter.

The man picked up his spoon and took a careful sip of broth. He nodded appreciatively. So it did taste good.

Now it was Lien whose lips twisted in an amused smile. She set down two glasses and a bottle of *rượu thuốc* between them. "Homemade herbal schnapps, an old family recipe. Can't hurt," she said, pouring them each a shot.

The man looked down at the glass, back up at her, then back down at the glass. He paused. He was clearly wondering what was in it. He was suspicious. That was smart of him. But it was too late.

Lien raised her glass. "To your health!" she said, and drank. The liquor was strong, it burned at the back of the throat.

The man reached for his own glass, but it slipped from his hand before he could bring it to his lips. It burst into pieces on the floor. He might have done better to be suspicious of the *phở* instead of the schnapps.

Another old family recipe, the poison—quick and extremely effective.

The man's eyes widened in surprise as he swayed in his seat. Then he understood. A final split second of panic before his pupils rolled back in his head, leaving only the whites of his eyes visible. Foam inched out of his mouth. He slumped, then his upper body fell across the counter, his head slamming down into the *phở*. The bowl shattered.

What a mess.

Lien leaned in close to the man and laid a finger on his throat, feeling for a pulse. It had already grown faint. "Greed always leads to misery," she whispered in his ear, then poured herself another shot.

She came around the counter and pushed the man—dead by now—off his stool. The body hit the floor with a dull thud.

Lien grabbed hold of the feet and dragged the man toward the back the restaurant. The body was horribly heavy; it was even heavier than Erik's. Her hip throbbed painfully. Each breath stabbed at her lungs. Damnit, she really was getting too old for this sort of thing.

In the storage room she finally had to stop and catch her breath. She stood there bent over, hands clutching her knees. There were the ants, scuttling around her feet. This time they weren't as orderly.

Could it be that they could smell death? Whatever the case, they had veered off their usual path and were scrambling toward the fresh corpse.

Lien waited until her breathing had steadied, then braced both hands against the freezer cabinet and pushed. Her arms broke out in goose bumps as the metal scraped against the concrete. *Scrreeech, scrreeech*. A bit more, just a little bit more, and then it was over.

The floor hatch lay there, exposed.

Directly beneath the storage room there ran a stone-wall drain, about three feet wide, that sloped slightly downward, diverting rainwater from the street into the canal. Whenever Lien sprayed down the storage room with a hose, the drain allowed water to flow down through a grill in the floor hatch. Quite useful, really.

Using an iron rod bent slightly at the tip especially for this purpose, Lien lifted up the cover, then immediately brought her arm up against her nose and mouth. The stench was truly awful. She would probably have to stop up the grill as a first step. Plaster, silicone, concrete—she'd think of something. The sodium bicarbonate she had ordered in bulk still hadn't been delivered. And the small packages she had bought in the supermarket clearly didn't come anywhere close to neutralizing the smell.

Stagnant water and algae, my ass. It was the sweet smell

of decay. It was astounding that nobody had recognized it yet, that everyone had swallowed her story about the canal just like that. Then again, if you had never dealt with death before . . .

She peered down into the drain but couldn't make out anything in the darkness. It was only when she switched her phone's flashlight on that she saw the ants. And then Erik. She swore. The decay hadn't actually progressed very far. And the position of Erik's body didn't leave any space for his dead compatriot. Lien fetched her broom, stuck the handle down into the drain, and pressed. She could feel the bloated flesh giving way. But it kept slipping, and now dozens of ants came clambering up the wooden handle toward her. She brushed them off—the last thing she needed now was for the little creatures to climb up and piss on her too.

She brought an oversized soup ladle with a long handle in from the kitchen. It had a wider surface area, but it also meant Lien had to kneel down on the floor to get closer to the body. Really, at her age. The pain in her hips had spread now, down into the tips of her toes. She tried her best to ignore it. The second body had damned well better fit in the drain, come hell or high water.

The next time an extortionist showed up on Bill Strasse threatening her and her neighbors, she would have to shoot him out in the woods, Lien thought, ideally by some marsh he would sink into immediately. Something that didn't require feats of strength. She was exhausted. She was also soaked in sweat, Lien of all people, who was rarely even damp.

Using the ladle, she finally managed to move Erik a bit off to the side and farther down in the drainpipe. Far enough that only his shoulders and head were still visible. That would have to do. Erik's chiseled boss would fit right in.

Somehow Lien managed to get herself off the ground, then drag the second body the final stretch over to the hatch and shove him in feet first. For a moment his shoulders caught, and she was afraid she would have to pull him back out, but a few good kicks made the body drop down the bit that she needed to close the hatch over him.

Now she just had to hope that by the time the first heavy rains threatened in the fall, the two had decayed far enough in their drainpipe that the rainwater would be able to flow out into the canal. Not that anybody would be stopping by to make an official inspection of a clogged pipe.

Before sliding the freezer back over the hatch, Lien swept the ants into the grate. So they could reach their keratin more easily. For whatever reason, she sort of liked the minute creatures. They were quite helpful, even if they could give her away. Follow the ants and you'll find the bodies.

And now for a *rượu thuốc*. She had certainly earned it.

I'LL BE GONE IN A MINUTE

BY TILL RAETHER

Altenwerder

Translated by Noah Harley

S tickler has lost everything, right down to the five hundred–euro bill. He has a vague notion of a gun and how he would use it on the man who now owns everything that used to be Stickler's. The wife, the company. The house. The dog. The car. The house out on the North Sea. The kids.

There had been the times before, they went like this: A bill arrived, five hundred euros, a lilac note all fresh and crisp with a couple of lines from his dad's widow, *Do something nice for yourselves*. A hundred a head. And then the bill wandered off into one drawer or another. The kids ordered something off the Internet and he and his wife gave up on the idea, they already had everything anyway. A card went out to his father's widow far too late, *Thanks, we spoiled ourselves rotten*. But Stickler had a private equity company that was in the black and the kids had the Internet, so nobody gave another thought to the bill that his son had dubbed "the purple moolah" out of mock respect, and which simply kept its place in the drawer.

Now he stands out in a drizzle, on a street corner at the edge of Othmarschen, tennis courts, an old folks' home, a school. Hand in his coat pocket, crinkling and uncrinkling the bill that he just pulled from the junk drawer on his way to the living room, while Jutta was in the closet getting him the cashmere coat. A diversionary tactic so that Stickler could get to the drawer. I only came because I need the coat. I'll leave in a second. I know, I know I'm not allowed to come near the house. But you can see I'm completely soaked. My other coat is at Jürgen's, but he won't let me in anymore. Because of the money. Thanks. Yes, I'll wait here. I'll be gone in a minute.

It's true that all his things are at Jürgen's apartment. Stay here until everything blows over, Jürgen had told him at first. Then Jürgen realized that Stickler had lost his money, too. Return the hundred and forty thousand, you're not getting a single thing back until then. Not one suitcase. Look, I don't give a fuck if you're standing out in the rain. I've had enough. Jutta sees it exactly the same way, by the way. Maybe a hundred and forty thousand is just a joke to you. But I need it. That's my money. That's all my money. I really think you have to hit rock bottom first.

Jürgen had said it all through the intercom system. A radio drama for the entire neighborhood.

In his other pocket Stickler is carrying a broken telephone, which also came from the junk drawer. It was totally dead. But maybe he could palm it off on someone. Jürgen had held on to his real one "as a deposit."

Realizing that he has nothing left save the purple moolah, a dead phone, and the cashmere coat, something lifts. Hope is a ballast. Now it doesn't matter what happens. It feels like progress.

He senses hunger and goes in search of a cheesecake bar and a can of Red Bull at the gas station on Bernadotte Strasse. The cashier waves the purple moolah away, he doesn't take anything over a hundred. Stickler's briefcase is in Jürgen's apartment; all his cards are locked anyway, the accounts cleared out. For some creditors. Whose money he put in the wrong place. The wrong place? Momentary, fleeting impressions. It could have been a revolution after all—Stickler, the first investor in Hamburg to go into crypto with private equity. Though not the first person to make money that had been entrusted to him vanish into thin air. If you do that I'm out, Jutta had told him. Tell people that you're in blue-chip stocks then go into crypto. His mistake had been to tell her his plans. If he hadn't said anything, there wouldn't have been any ultimatum. He was well acquainted with her love of ultimatums. If you can't decide between Xandy and me, I'm gone. That was twenty-five years ago. If you don't want kids, I'll find someone else. Twenty years ago. And on and on. At the time Stickler found it motivating. He had come to think of it as blackmail. Jürgen and Jutta both agreed: Stickler had only himself to blame. It had been right for him to turn himself in to the prosecutor, they said. Wrong to ignore the meetings that followed. To just up and leave. To hide out at Jürgen's. To lie, then keep lying. Jürgen, you'll get your money. Jutta, I have it under control. Soon it was Jürgen leading the negotiations between the bankruptcy managers and Stickler's lawyers. And now all that's left of the company belongs to Jürgen, and Stickler's lawyers have discontinued their case because Stickler can't pay them any more. And now Jutta belongs to Jürgen, because everything belongs to Jürgen.

Do you know anything about welfare? Jutta's question. She'll need it. She hasn't worked a day in her life.

Stickler leaves the cheesecake bar and the can of Red Bull lying on the counter. He boards the bus toward the train station in Altona, riding without a ticket for the first time in thirty years. He crosses the pedestrian zone to a pawnshop, cash for his cashmere. No luck, they don't take textiles. Has he tried one of the boutique stores that sell vintage fashion? But all he gets there for the coat are sympathetic glances. Vintage, maybe. Fashion, not so much. Does he know the Goodwill over behind the station?

Screw cash, Stickler decides. The purple moolah will have to do.

Do what? Let him get his hands on a gun. Now that the only person he has to talk to is himself, snatches of old conversations come flying through his head. Somebody who once said, This or that person might have a gun. To show off.

A gun? Where? Stickler had asked.

Out on the streets. You just ask around. It doesn't take long.

It's early evening as he gets off at the Reeperbahn station and emerges from below ground. Two bars toss him out when he asks about guns. The women working at the first give him a look that sends him packing; at the second it's the bouncer, someone must have ratted him out. That, or it's because he didn't order anything. Stickler knows how dumb he looks: just taking a seat, looking around to make eye contact, leaning in, then asking.

It's embarrassing.

But you get used to it. In the third bar, a couple of streets farther back in the shadows, there's simply no response. When they finally do ask Stickler to order, he leaves as though something just occurred to him. Broken phone up to his ear, something to hold on to.

At the next street corner he notices a woman trailing him. You can't tell her age—unlike his. What's he looking for? He stands there and explains to the woman, who's dressed in a hoodie and ancient Doc Martens, he would use the phrase *migrant background* in quotes if he still had anybody to talk to. She names her price: sixteen hundred. Stickler groans. Sure, but it comes without a serial number, without anything. Clean. Single-use. He could leave it right where he uses it, she says.

Stickler tells her he has five hundred. He's running out of time. And patience. And he's running low on small talk.

She reflects, then says: Two hours at the pond.

Which pond?

In Altenwerder. The wooden bench on the north side. He has a vague idea of where that might be, and looks down instinctively at his phone for Google Maps. The phone is still dead, the screen blank and black as coal. When Stickler looks back up, the woman is gone.

He's ready to move on to the next bar and keep asking, but he knows he won't get any closer. Closer to what? To pointing a gun at Jürgen. To doing something really insane in other words, starting some real shit, like they used to say before as a sign of respect. But also something manly. An ultimatum, something definitive. Something that would bring everything to a halt. And since there's nothing to lose, what happens is all the same now anyway. He'll point the gun at Jürgen and say, Give it all back. Jürgen will get a scare, then he'll laugh and say, Cute toy. Or something like that. And then Stickler will shoot. One shot would be enough. Into the wall or the ceiling, or Jürgen's leg. Spur of the moment, depending on the mood. It's true, maybe there's nothing left to lose. But at least for a moment, there would be a feeling of respect again. Even if only for a split second. Stickler hopes that moment will feel like an eternity. Besides, Jürgen might even shit his pants. Bonus points.

He pauses at a bus stop to study a city map—it looks like there's even a bus that goes there, Süderelbe, the main street in Altenwerder. An industrial area on the far side of the harbor. A bus door hisses open and he asks the driver. Stickler barely manages to catch the names of the two lines before the driver asks for his ticket. He drops back off the bus, landing with both feet in a puddle.

He waits until all the taxis that witnessed the scene have come and gone, then hails one with the tails of his cashmere. The second taxi lets him in; the driver looks even older than he does. Altenwerder Pond, Stickler tells him.

At this time of night? But there's nobody there. He's instantly suspicious.

Stickler takes out his dead phone and looks down at the coal-black screen as if to check an appointment. That's the one. He casually flashes the five hundred–euro note. The taxi heads off. König Strasse, back already on Bernadotte Strasse, Stickler didn't make it that far, then Kreuzkirche, highway on-ramp, Othmarschen, Elbe tunnel, traffic traffic traffic. Stickler's breathing is shallow, the driver is listening to Udo Jürgens. There are white fingerprints on the door to the glove compartment. Stickler's heart jolts. He knows those marks. From where? From his father. It's only after the A7 has passed through the Elbe tunnel and is headed back up that the picture comes into focus. The lemon bonbons his father would suck on, an English company made them and they came in a bronze tin with a green label. They were only for the car, and were covered in some form of powdered sugar, maybe so they wouldn't stick together. You couldn't have one without leaving white prints. On the dark lacquer finish inside the Benz, on the pleated flannel trousers. On the Jinglers brand jeans with the knee patches.

Does Stickler want one? Just before the exit for Waltershof, the driver lifts the handle to the glove compartment of the old E-Class Mercedes and hands Stickler the tin. Stickler is painfully hungry. He tries to take two and manages one, he pops it in his mouth. He glimpses white powder on his lips in the rearview mirror.

It's finally getting dark. The Altenwerder horizon reveals silhouettes of warehouses, windmills, and shipping cranes. To Stickler's right are rows of shipping containers and stockpiled cars. To his left logistics centers with few windows, behind them unrolled mattresses stacked thirty or forty feet high. There are tractor trailers parked on the shoulder, not a soul in sight. The taxi stops at a curve in the road, where the gloomy maw of a nature reserve opens out beyond the abandoned sidewalk. Shapeless reflections on murky water.

That'll be twenty-seven eighty.

Make it thirty-two, with a receipt, Stickler replies.

The taxi driver leans over for his receipt booklet, while Stickler pretends to reach into his pocket for money. And just like that he is out of the backseat and onto the embankment. To his left is the pond, behind a dark-green metal fence about six feet high. To his right a dirt path, matted reeds, a stream springing from somewhere beyond a weir, torn-up shrubs. After three or four steps Stickler has practically lost all sense of direction. Sounds from the A7, maybe a thousand feet off, louder now than in the cab. He slips onto his side, feeling a stab of regret for his cashmere jacket. The ground offers no resistance, Stickler's entire right side is covered in muck. He hears the car door and tired cries of protest: What are you doing, etc. Stickler hopes the taxi driver hasn't made an emergency call. There must be over an hour still until the woman turns up with the gun. Why doesn't the driver give

up? Won't he lose more money running around here or waiting for the police than by just going back to work? Stickler
retreats deeper into the gloom and mire. Tighten your core
muscles, pull your navel in, like those yoga classes with the
Canadian trainer when he could still afford that sort of thing.
The tension in his body causes him to slip even farther off
the path and down the small embankment; first his feet are
in the water, then his lower legs, now his knees. This must be
the feeder stream for the pond.

The driver's footsteps on the path. Huffing and panting.
The final shadow from the day falls on Stickler. He lowers his
head even more, his nose nearly in the grass now, as though
the driver won't be able to find Stickler so long as Stickler
can't see him. But he can feel the shadow. Then the pant
legs of the driver appear in his field of vision, his sensible
footwear.

Stickler lunges and yanks the driver by the legs. The
driver topples over him, slipping down into the mud and
clinging to Stickler's ankles. As they slide together deeper
into the stream, Stickler loses all sense of time. He keeps
kicking because it bothers him to feel someone pulling on
his legs. He is in water now over his hips. Another kick. He
wishes the driver would just stop with all the pulling and tugging. Stickler needs a moment to think. The water is cold,
unrelenting. His lower abdomen contracts. He finds something solid to stand on, maybe the chest or head of the driver.
After a while things grow quieter beneath the surface. Then
it's only Stickler splashing about, or making little waves as
he tries to keep his balance on the driver's torso or face. He
gives up and hauls himself up the slope to the path with fist-
fuls of reeds. The reeds are dry and cut into his hands. His
mouth tastes like the lemon bonbons. The taxi driver won't

be coming back up. Stickler studies the surface of the stream, broken up by trash and old vegetation, until he is entirely certain of it. He returns to the taxi, shoes squelching, frozen up to his midriff, as though he were entering another universe. He finds a proper parking spot and takes the key, but can't find the driver's wallet. It must be on him still. Stickler doesn't want to go back into the water. He takes a handful of lemon bonbons and shoves them in his mouth, powdery and tart. He slams the door shut. A peeping sound then a blinking light, the power-lock system. He sits down on the bench, chewing lemon bonbons to drown out the sounds of the A7 and the thoughts running through his mind. Nobody lives out here, only machines. Switch tracks and train bumpers stand between him and the highway. Shipping containers piled on tractor trailers, shipping containers on freight trains. He's sorry the taxi driver is dead. He realizes with some relief that it isn't the worst he's ever felt. In the end it was kind of an accident. Like everything else, you might say.

The woman arrives from the other direction, where a train switching tracks lends a steady pulse to the darkness. Stickler is a little startled; when he asks how she settled on the pond as a meeting place, she replies that she lives here. He gestures with his chin toward the pond, a fenced-off hectare of stagnant water in a no-man's-land that used to be a village green. Of course not, not the pond. In one of the warehouses. In a decommissioned area. Most goods hit the streets directly these days. It's cheaper to let the unused warehouses stand empty than tear them down.

Stickler really doesn't need a lecture about urban development.

She hands him an object wrapped in cloth. He reaches

for it, but cloth and object both vanish back into the darkness of her silhouette.

First the money.

He hands her the damp five hundred. He is amazed to see her take out a marker and a UV light the size of a laser pointer. She knows her stuff. In the artificial blue light he can see that she must be around forty, her eyes black, or quite dark. Once she's convinced that the purple moolah is genuine, Stickler receives the iron piece wrapped in cloth. He unpacks it, and can already feel that the pistol is completely rusted over, its surface rough as though it had lain submerged in water for years.

You can't be serious, he says.

I made you an offer for sixteen hundred. That's what you get for five.

She has a point.

Stickler has the weapon near enough to his face that the air smells like stale water, rust, and the highway. Like dirty oil. Like his unwashed hands, like bloody reeds. Something rustles. The ghost of the taxi driver. But it's just a wild goose breaking out of the underbrush and, against all odds, swinging up into the evening sky. Followed by a second. Stickler lets the weapon sink down into his lap. The woman sits beside him, as though curious about what will happen next. That makes two of them.

Stickler finds the safety with his thumb and releases it, then raises the pistol, a Walther by the looks of it, the sort of thing people used to keep as a toy. They used to be a hundred times lighter. He sticks the rusted muzzle against his temple, away from the woman, who could have left long ago by now. He has a hard time pressing down; the trigger resists with everything it's got—its spring is all resistance. He feels the click more than he hears it. Stickler lets the weapon fall back down again.

You didn't say that you wanted bullets too, the woman says.

No, I didn't, Stickler replies. It's all right.

WAY DOWN BELOW

BY Ingvar Ambjørnsen
Hoheluft

Translated by Geoffrey C. Howes

Sometimes when I don't feel like sitting in the Finken
pub with Konrad or Lotte, when I don't want to talk
to anyone, when I just want to drink by myself in quiet
gloom like some tortured animal at a dark forest stream, then
I go to the Muny up on Ring Road 2. It's the kind of place you
can pass by for fifteen years before you realize that alcoholic
beverages are being served in a tiny hole in the row of buildings. On one side there's an old-fashioned record store, and
on the other a defunct tailor shop. Out on the street, Ring
2, heavy traffic rumbles past day and night, rattling the windowpanes in the old buildings. Like weather and digestion, it
rumbles along on its way. That's how life's road to death is,
and when you reach death, a new failure of a life is born—
that's just how it is.

Everything that goes wrong ends up here at the Muny.
Nobody here basked in the schoolyard while someone of one
sex or another proffered a juicy mouth or firm ass cheeks.
The teachers didn't show up at all. Neither did employers
with encouraging words. You might as well forget all that and
think about the transparent pricing of the whores and thugs,
if you can still think—and before you know it, you're standing there all alone, and it doesn't matter whether you come
from Germany or the steppes of Eastern Europe, from Kurdis-

tan or Eritrea. And now you're standing here, and even here, hate and self-loathing are the order of the day, and you have no business within these four walls unless you've already lost, or you're a spy like me.

There are thousands of disagreeable neighborhood bars in Germany. They're of no interest to anybody but the people who dawdle their lives away there, day in and day out, with crap games and bullshit from the back lots and stairwells of the city, with flat beer and cheap schnapps. They're depressing enough, but not totally hopeless. Quite often there are roars of laughter late in the evening—the people talk to each other, and even if what gets said is not terribly intelligent or uplifting, these joints are still not totally devoid of hope. There's gambling, and dirty nails scraping scratch-off tickets. There's some sort of an idea of something else, maybe something better, and the TV usually works when there's a soccer match on. It's not a given that no one cares who wins. There might be someone who does.

But places like the Muny are different. Here the half-dead green plants in the filthy windows have given way to faded plastic flowers, toughened by nicotine and human sweat, or they've simply been replaced by piles of dead insects, empty shells lying in the dust with legs sticking up in the air. Down in the Muny it's dark and damp even on summer mornings. There are no seasons here, only an unrelenting flow of leaden minutes. Time that gets dragged across the grungy wooden floor, where the knots stick out like black warts. The kind of warts you have to be a little careful of, if like me you're here as an emissary of the living, of the life being lived outside of this bar and similar basement windows in other cities, ones that have not totally given up hope. Because what we have here are graves with liquor licenses that like to stay open 24/7 so the dying can come in anytime and sit for a little while by themselves, together with others who likewise have no interest in chatter, music, or TV movies. These are people who can tell that death is taking their pulse, and they come from rooms and apartments that are the spitting image of this bar. The only difference is that at home the bottles are lying around on the floor, empty or broken, whereas at the Muny they get piled up behind the bar in red bins with *Astra* printed on them. Here there are no beer taps, there's not even a refrigerator, there's only a listless *fssss* every time the man behind the bar—nobody knows who he is and he has no personality at all—pops the cap of one more lukewarm pilsner, or a *glug-glug* when a shot glass gets filled up so far that the surface bulges like an eye staring up at the flypaper hanging there like forgotten New Year's streamers from 1958. That was the year when it's possible a murder happened in the outdoor privy. It's been a long time since anybody's talked about that, or anything else for that matter.

In Norway, where I'm from, there are no places like the Muny. There's not even anything remotely similar. Bars like this one that are so unpolished you'd think they must have been imported from distant galaxies. When I go downstairs and sit at the bar in the Muny, nine out of ten times the same thing happens. The bar is transformed into the bottom of a beleaguered little pond, a polluted spot not far from a freeway, a place where people dump all kinds of crap. They drop it in the pond and get on with their lives. This impression is amplified by the green light of a neon sign over a gambling establishment across the street. The light falls through the moss-covered windowpanes and settles on the inventory like noxious water and oil and gasoline, a sort of sick daylight that penetrates the layer of algae above us, and back in the corner sits a woman with no teeth, picking her nose like a half-blind goby. The bottle glints in its own lonesomeness. The glow of cigarettes, like luminous tadpoles. Down here, everything is the way it was before rules and regulations were introduced. Here there are no deals or agreements, and with every gulp I take, it's like breathing underwater. You grow gills when you sit here. Lonesome pike glide through the room or hover threateningly at the curtain of garish glass beads hanging in the doorway to the back room with its appalling bathroom. When the man behind the bar yawns and runs his fingers through the green growth on his head, anyone who wants to can see the eel that's ensconced itself where this man's tongue once was. The cancer patients, over by the stairs leading up to the world of others, have given up. They're lying half on their sides and look like broken chairs someone has hurled off a truck bed at high speed.

From my wristwatch, tiny little bubbles float up to the surface and deposit themselves in clusters in the bacterial membrane beneath the sickly sun. Like captured time. Outside, the night is starry and bitterly cold. Or maybe it's a hot summer evening, with the sound of throbbing techno from a car waiting for green. I follow the tracks between the houses to the remnants of the sheds where long ago the streetcars took their beauty sleep, much to the joy of the city's citizens the next morning.

Everything is so different. How is it possible to move from one world to another in such a short time? It's as if the space below the earth existed only as a brief dream vision. It's like that every time. I walk here thinking such thoughts. And then one more thought: *Who is the spy in my own life?*

I feel like I'm under surveillance. Every time I've been in the Muny having a drink with myself, I've had the feeling there's someone behind the windows of the dilapidated tenements up there on Ring 2, that someone's standing there in the darkness on the sixth or seventh floor, someone familiar with this swimming pool down in the basement, this vision of hell that I've just disturbed by my uninvited presence.

The black squares on the wall. The lights turned off, or never turned on. I imagine there are halls up there behind the plaster and bricks that no one knows of, where a secret life unfolds like it does in novels I've never even thought of, maybe even with sequences of dreamed events way above my level, beyond my capabilities. One evening I'm moving through the neighborhood and thinking these kinds of thoughts, so I'm walking and I sense a foreignness that always overcomes me after an encounter with the old specters at the Muny. It's an evening that contains multiple seasons. I remember it exactly: it's snowing, a cold wind is blowing with the fragrance of lilac, car exhaust, and meadow flowers, and my coat reeks of past benders, but life is still good enough that it seems natural to me to thrust a fist into each coat pocket and whistle some happy tune.

Anyone following me?

Anything plaguing me?

I don't mean that seriously. It's only a little game I like to play, especially when I'm sinking into crapulence. I walk along and whistle to myself and savor the fear a little, while seeing life stand still in front of me, the near-death up there at the Muny. Or maybe the zombies do wake up as soon as

I've left the premises? Maybe dancing and joy fill the place the instant the echo of my heartbeat fades away into the shadows behind the old tram sheds? No. Then it's easier to imagine that the Muny simply ceases to exist, as soon as I've climbed the stairs, that the Muny lives only in a secret chamber within myself.

I wander through Hoheluft with confused thoughts and savor the aftertaste of stale beer and cheap schnapps. I go to the Poletto and knock back good wine for two hours. A totally different form of alienation prevails here, a different kind of absence. Down here among the neighborhood's relatively young and absolutely rich folks, I'm the one who's in closest contact with dissolution and death. I can tell by their eyes, by the exaggerated cheerfulness of the young woman with candy-apple cheeks who feeds me cheese and crackers, and who brings glass after glass full of the fantastic, fantastic stuff from Corsica. I feel it in the sidelong glances and the disdain concealed behind the snappy repartee, and maybe that too is nothing but nonsense, conceit, and paranoia. But no. Surely they see me for who I am. The messenger from the front. The walking hotbed of infection. The guy with ketchup on his coat after the abortive visit to the lunch stand, like an unexpected orgasm.

I drink eight glasses of the fantastic stuff, but I can't shake the feeling that something is crouching under a table here and watching me. A shadow I brought along from the Muny.

And when I get home, I immediately see that someone has broken open the lock. The door is swinging back and forth in the draft. A strange, sweetish odor, actually not unpleasant, but odd. Once again, I think of the echo of my heartbeats, which fade as soon as I leave the Muny behind me, or which make the Muny disappear. Now my heart is beating against my Adam's apple, and the echo reverberates in my mouth.

I push the door open with the toe of my shoe. Stand stock-still and listen. Nothing. Only the distant swish of the traffic down on the street. Is he standing there inside, just as petrified as I am? There's no way he didn't hear the rattling of the elevator.

I take the bunch of keys in my hand and let four of them protrude between my fingers. Clench my fist.

Then I go inside.

He's lying in the kitchen. He's taken off his coat and laid it over himself like a blanket. He's eaten practically the whole package of cooked country ham, and the fingers on his right hand are yellow and shiny with mayonnaise. The jar is upside down on the floor behind his back. He's sleeping deeply, without a sound. Only his chest is rising and falling.

I carefully close the refrigerator door, go into the living room, and lie down on the sofa. I can see his legs on the filthy floor. A man of about my age. I've never seen him before. I think about the long path he has taken to get here. The long path I myself have taken to get here. Two strangers.

I feel nothing. I doze, and in my mind I picture the subterranean room up there on Ring 2, in multiple versions and variations. The walls glow as if from inner embers. Or everything is in ice-cold darkness. Whispering voices. Laughter. And the whole time there's my own heart, which beats and beats a rhythmic countdown. And the cosmos that rolls over us in its utter brutal boundlessness.

At some point in the gray dawn: a sobbing whimper, and the apartment door being cautiously closed.

The sound of furtive steps disappearing down the stairwell.

UNDER BLACKTHORN

BY MATTHIAS WITTEKINDT

Billwerder

Translated by Noah Harley

Bergedorf, November 1, 1972

A sultry, mustard-yellow room, ten by ten with twelve-foot ceilings. Crossbars divide the windows, which are so fogged over that water droplets leave long trails as they trickle downward. At nearly eighty-five degrees, the room is palpably overheated. Add to that the inescapable odor of french fries mixed with frying fat that has been seeping through the floorboards for decades.

In short, a love nest.

"It was on purpose!" Christine Manz's voice rings out like a dare.

"Let's hope," her husband replies lightly. He's bleeding. Red drops splatter against white ceramic. He looks down at the basin. He exudes an air of satisfaction as he watches the blood. He's naked. His penis is only half-visible, concealed by the bronze shadow of his front thigh.

"You *hope* I bit you on purpose?" Christine now wants to know. At twenty-nine, she's three years older than him. "Darling, what are you thinking about?"

"I'm wondering how they make this kind of basin."

"I don't believe you."

Christine Manz lies on the bed, naked. Legs spread. A thin turquoise bedspread—no, that's not right, it's . . . an imitation-silk scarf . . . overly long. It's wrapped itself around one of her thighs, partially covering her nether regions before trailing off to the right. It brings to mind the image of a slow-moving current, flowing over the churning bedsheets in small waves that shimmer like natural silk before crashing down over the edge of the bed onto the blackberry-colored floor, where the fabric fans out in a delta that dissolves into a dark eternity amid the shadows. A painter might talk about a reclining nude with a shawl.

A look, a look back, a reflection. Christine regards her bronze husband as he stands at the washbasin, illuminated by a dangling twenty-five-watt bulb. He gazes into an ancient, clouded mirror mounted from the side, trying to stop the bleeding on his lower lip. In the spotty reflection he can make out not only his lip but his wife lying on the bed.

So Manz's lower lip was bit, most likely in a moment of raised passion. It's still too soon to talk any more about the city. Behind closed doors other things matter, in this damp boudoir for instance, done up in the style of the early thirties. We don't have to talk about the body lying in the water either, her red-orange hair floating freely among the blackthorn, because . . .

"You've got a nice ass."

No response, he's occupied with his bottom lip.

"If I put you up for sale" she continues, her voice husky, "I think I just might turn a profit."

They've been married for four years, two kids, she earns more than he does because . . . she works with her mind. He's with the police. *Still with criminal investigations!*

"And a nice stomach . . ."

A slight turn. Not just with his head. His penis, the same bronze color but with a dark-blue tinge, also comes into view. A question mark in a thought bubble.

"Which means you don't have a stomach," she elaborates.

"How much do you think you'd make if you put me up for sale?"

"A hundred? Two hundred?"

"For a night?"

"Oh no—for a whole night I'd charge more."

Time slips by without any further activity. They're still in their Bergedorf boudoir, Hamburg-Bergedorf. At least that's what the enamel sign in the center of the gray train platform nearby reads. Clanking and clanging sounds from a poorly constructed train bridge come in regularly. This isn't Christine's first time visiting her husband. She loves it when he takes her to places like this before they go dancing. Hamburg-Bergedorf, to give an idea, is made up of worn red bricks tossed together into houses. An architecture of daily use, which nobody could accuse of a coherent aesthetic plan.

Berlin investigations loaned Manz's services to Hamburg. The police do that sort of thing—lend out people. He hasn't worked his way toward a senior position yet, he's still young. Powerfully built, muscular too, but still young.

Christine already has her sights set on him training for a higher rank. She's got the necessary connections. Knows people. She'd like his worth to increase.

"Well? What are you working on now?" she asks, searching for a new topic.

"An investigation out in Boberg. Two boys found a body in a fishing pond."

"And the file?"

"Huh?"

"You always give your cases such funny names . . ."

"Blackthorn."

"Black thorn."

"Uh-huh. But they're never cases—always operations. Things are in motion."

"Do you have a suspect yet?"

"I'm going back tomorrow to interview some witnesses at a glider plane club again. They spin in circles there over the ponds in Boberg."

"Speaking of which—are we going dancing?"

A cold fall wind. The bridge overhead shudders in rhythm to the train. Manz keeps a close hold of his wife as he guides her to the car. She climbs in the passenger side of a Ford Taunus 12M, beige, with a dark-gray roof.

Operation Blackthorn began with a mother's phone call. Her son and his cousin had found a body. Yet Uwe Börnsen and his cousin Till from Ratzeburg were considered notorious liars in the family, and generally as lacking in character.

"When Till starts spouting his mouth, I immediately discount 90 percent of what comes out," Uwe's grandmother had volunteered. They had gathered at the farm of Uwe's parents, where Manz's superior, Commissioner Böll, had asked the boys to meet. The farm was in Billwerder, along Billwerder Billdeich in the Elbe river valley. They found themselves in a large room with a low ceiling, beneath timber beams that resembled bacon rind.

"We thought best in the parlor," Uwe's mother said, gesturing with long, lithe fingers toward a grandiose room that was the very image of agrarian prosperity. It was a cold Monday, and birch logs and pine cones whirred and popped in a scorching-hot woodstove.

Commissioner Böll asked the questions, Manz kept his silence. "Let's have it, boys."

"Till and I went out for pike. This morning. Over in the fishing ponds in Boberg. In the notch."

"The notch?" Böll repeated.

"That's what everyone calls the inlet. Because it's narrow and long, like a canal. It isn't far by bike."

"Got your fishing permits?" Böll asked. Manz couldn't see where he was headed.

"We don't need fishing permits, we live here. If you live here, you don't need one."

"Is that so?"

"Pretty sure."

Till smirked at Uwe's response.

"All right, keep going."

"So we had a spoon lure on the line because—"

"Pike," Böll cut in. The two witnesses bobbed their heads in unison. Commissioner Böll knew about pike fishing. He was a dedicated fisher himself and sat on the executive board overseeing Hamburg's fishing clubs—where he was responsible for dealing with unlicensed activity.

"We were at it for half an hour," Uwe went on, "in the fog. That was around eight." A quick look over, Till nodded. "Then Till's lure got stuck when he was reeling it in. He cast it out too far over to the right and I told him right away. 'Way too far right,' I said. 'Can't wait to see how you plan on getting that out.' I had already spotted a strange clump of bushes over there. It was blackthorn, it turned out."

The fire flared in the stove. It almost sounded like an explosion. Uwe's mother glanced over briefly. Her face framed dark eyes, and sweat glistened on her brow as her long fingers fidgeted in the pit of her apron because . . . well, because of her kid, a dead woman, and now two cops in the house. It was enough to unravel nerves that were already frayed to begin with.

"So Till's lure was caught," Uwe said. "To the right of the inlet where we were standing."

"You stand in the water when you fish?"

"Well, we had rubber boots."

"A lure like that costs money," Böll said.

"Yeah, we knew that if we tugged on it the lure would snap off. So we took off our boots and socks and pants, and we went in."

"How deep?"

"To the top of our underwear. That's when I saw the hair. Under the blackthorn. When they trim branches, what do you call that . . . ?"

"You mean cuttings," Böll responded.

"I thought it was a wig. A lot of people throw garbage in the pond, sometimes trash from their yard. I thought maybe I could sell the wig or give it for Secret Santa if I got a girl. I got both arms all scratched up on the thorns of . . . what's it called again?"

"On the blackthorn cuttings."

"And when I finally got to the wig and tried to pull it out, it came up. The face. Right away I knew it was a body. So I got out."

Till nodded, his face covered in red blotches, still-unwashed hands trembling.

"How old are you two?" Böll asked.

"Thirteen."

"A fishing license only costs three marks a year for someone your age."

"That's not bad actually," Uwe said. Now he, too, had red blotches on his face.

"You have to pass a test. But the advantage is that then you're in the club, you'll get tips and learn something about protecting waterways."

"I think we know who the dead person is," Uwe countered. "It could be Mrs. Böge's daughter. Her name's Nerine and she's seventeen. She hangs around. With three guys from Mümmelmannsberg. They might be construction workers, because one of them usually has concrete on his pants and . . ."

". . . they're building something big over in Mümmelmannsberg right now," Till finished in a thick voice.

"Mrs. Böge was at the bus stop yesterday and asked if we had seen Nerine. She often stays out for a couple days at a time. And Nerine has red hair."

"That's right, and the three guys who were always picking Nerine up drove a red Ford Capri. Two antennas. One had a fox tail. If they're the killers . . ." Till's voice got lost in mucus, and he looked as though he were going to choke. Then he lost it. His young chest heaving, tears, suddenly afraid, as if . . . well, as if it were finally dawning on him what had happened.

His fellow fisherman Uwe didn't fare any better. His mother's hands flew from the apron, fingers stretching out toward her child. It was clear that Commissioner Böll had nothing more to say here. She gathered up the boys and brought them back into the cinnamon-scented kitchen, where she fed them bread with marmalade and cake. Wrapped in her broad, white angel's hands and trembling in fear, the kids looked four years younger. Evidently they were just now coming to grips with the situation.

It only took twenty minutes for Manz and Böll to reach the discovery site.

The forensics team was still at work. A giant pile of neatly trimmed blackthorn branches lay dripping along the water's edge. A medic sat with one leg dangling out of the open door of a dark-blue Ford Granada. He jotted something down on a clipboard.

"A blow to the head. The parietal bone."

"Meaning?"

"It came from above. Like some giant did it."

White: the fog as it began to clear.

Black: the car that came to carry the corpse away.

There was little sense of excitement.

Commissioners Böll and Manz stood awhile in silence by the water, which hinted at fall. Golden leaves floated atop the thin white-blue surface, while two black coots, white markings over their beaks, cautiously returned to their territory.

Manz felt a chill and looked at his watch.

"Anything case-related yet?" Böll asked a member of the forensics team who was inspecting a rust-brown object riddled with holes.

"Nothing yet."

Above they could already see that the lifting fog would reveal a bitterly cold, pale-blue autumn sky. Then Manz heard a . . . a buzzing . . . mixed with a sort of rumble. He turned and thought to himself, *Blinding white and straight as an arrow.*

Led by a steel cable, the glider plane rolled down an airstrip of light sand that ran between patches of short, tawny grass.

And off it goes.

The glider bounced twice at the tug of the steel cable, its wings parallel to the ground, before it caught the wind and veered sharply upward.

"I'm going back to talk with Kollmann," Böll said. Kollmann was the coroner in the dark-blue Granada.

"I'll take a look around then," muttered Manz, still looking up. High, higher, higher still, and then . . . released. The hook was attached to a small parachute; Manz had never seen anything like it. In 1972, gliding was still restricted in Berlin. It had something to do with the unpredictability of the winds and thermodynamics—that and the Russians.

A winch, or something like it, was pulling the parachute, which the wind now carried sideways along with the hook, off to somewhere hidden from Manz by a small birch stand with light-yellow foliage. The hook must have had some weight to it; there was a slight shudder as it made impact behind the trees.

Once Manz crossed through the grove, he spied a vehicle at the start of the runway. Massive. It could have been the first truck ever built, painted in the exact same matte-red color as the lightship *Elbe 1*. Was it a tow truck or something from the fire department?

A gigantic motorized winch was set up on the back of the truck, while on a doorless, equally old VW Bug, two strong-looking men were busy loading the hook and the miniature parachute onto a sort of frame. Before long the Bug raced off, carting the hook to the next glider in queue.

Manz's gaze swung slowly to the right, and there it was in all its glory: A barracks of untreated wood—gray, though a choice gray, and while the building looked aged, it was a very refined age. A spacious, covered terrace with railings completed the setting. The building reminded Manz of old Westerns. The kind where the set designers had a generous budget to work with.

Men and women stood leaning against the railings. The women were all dressed in flared, cream-colored pants, one opting for a bright-yellow silk scarf, a second for red, while a third seemed to prefer turquoise. The men wore colorful shirts, saffron-yellow, poppy-red, sky-blue, grass-green. All shimmering like silk. The sort of clothes jockeys wore riding horses.

Six lawn chairs had been arranged in a neat row next to the barracks, all facing the sun and the starting line. In each chair a woman sat in the same position. Thin, long-legged, their gleaming aviator glasses pushed up. All wearing eggshell-colored, tightly girdled flared pants. Along with white fur jackets. Along with green leather English boots with oversized brass heels, along with tobacco-colored silk blouses, along with strikingly large scarves in solid colors. Every one of the reclining women had also armed herself with a set of heavy black binoculars. *Form follows function*—that's how architects of a bygone generation might have described the sight.

Manz counted thirty people. Two blond giants in traditional Danish dress moved about serving sparkling champagne and light snacks from trays. The general impression was of a sandy-hued scene with fine ladies, a stand of birch trees shimmering yellow, a gray barracks, and people resembling pure dashes of color. Manz kept his initial impression that the image had something *American* about it.

And why wouldn't it? In 1972, Hamburg was a city with an international flair and a host of dark corners. There was more there than just the port, where waving day visitors traversed the crisscrossing waves of the Elbe on small sloops. More, too, than Fritz Höger's large expressionist constructions, the Reeperbahn, the Bach organ in St. Michael's Church, and the impressive dry docks of Blohm + Voss. Hamburg was also home to abandoned gravel pits, for example; to fishing ponds where thirteen-year-old boys went fishing without a license; to enormous, two-hundred-year-old, blue-glazed farmhouses stationed behind mighty elms; and to upper-crust ladies in green leather English boots gazing skyward. Up there, where three immaculate glider planes were circling beneath the cold blue sky as the next blindingly white craft swooped sharply upward, wingtips flashing bright silver every time a pilot made a sharp turn westward.

Padding forward, Manz quickly felt the breast pocket of his leather jacket. It was a quirk, of course he had his police ID on him.

He spoke first with one Dr. Andreesen, an insufferable blowhard, followed by Ina Schmidt (who actually bore a striking resemblance to Helmut Schmidt's wife Loki), a Mrs. Tönning, and a Mr. Reese, a big shot at Hamburg's Thalia Theater who smoked "original Cuban" cigarillos.

Nobody had observed anything related to the crime.

"If they're back among the living, you might try Mr. and Mrs. Maurer, they chair the board of the Boberg Glider Club," Reese suggested. "Although," he continued, lighting a new cigarillo and blowing white smoke up into the blue, "my guess is that the Maurers won't have seen or heard anything more than we have."

Whir, whir, whir behind them, a blinding flash, and then another glider climbed steeply up into the azure sky. The six women in the lawn chairs followed the ascent with their binoculars in perfect synchronization. Shortly after came the thump of the hook, leaving another dent in the sand.

It's worth noting as well that the women from the Boberg Glider Club regarded Manz with unfeigned interest. Three flicked their tongues much in the manner of the fearsome anaconda, a fourth bared a pair of lengthening canines, while a fifth downed glass after glass of champagne.

And why wouldn't they? Manz was young, lean, wore leather, and stood nearly six foot five. Add to that his heavy, almost lazy eyelids, and full, manly lips that would quickly burst open when bit. Lips, in other words, that stirred the fantasies of the women on the terrace of this barracks in western Hamburg. Then there was Manz's quiet, deep voice, and the chin of someone used to butting open locked doors. In brief, young Manz acted like a man who hadn't yet recognized his effect on women, much like an adolescent boy, as though he didn't possess any consciousness or will of his own. Beauty, pure and unaware. Donatello's bronze *David*.

On the other side of the looking glass was a high-born Hanseatic league of women, with necklaces fashioned from bones dyed turquoise; every last one looking as though she came from Cuba or Mexico or South America. How to explain? Hamburg had been a port town throughout the 1700s, the 1800s, the 1900s. Rigged, barnacle-encrusted, four-mast ships laden with barrels filled with saltpeter and human flesh, lukewarm swells off of Madagascar, gulls in a storm off of Cape Horn, and by night all cats were gray.

Manz ventured a final glance as he walked away, and there, set off against the barracks which was anything but a barracks, was a shed. Locked. Manz peered through the boards. He could make out beer and wine, but no barrels of caviar.

Investigations aren't complicated in and of themselves. Especially not when your witnesses have details and an eye for vehicles. Uwe and Till turned out to be right: the three men who would often pick up Nerine Böge in a red Ford Capri were construction workers. They lived in contractor housing in Mümmelmannsberg, where they worked on one of the sites and . . . one drove a red Ford Capri. Two antennas, one with a fox tail.

Their names were Stefan, Horst, and Miron. Miron

sounded Polish though he was German. Böll baffled Manz by deciding to interview them together. Nobody from the district attorney's office was present. And a defense lawyer? "We don't need one," Horst declared right away, "because we didn't do anything with her."

"Her?" Böll leapt in immediately.

"I mean the body in the lake. Nerine. It was there in the *Morning Post*."

"When did you see her last?"

"It was . . . I don't know." Glances, shrugging shoulders. "The last Friday in October. We were broke cuz," a hard cough, possibly a laugh, "we hadn't gotten paid yet."

"So Friday, October 27?" Böll asked.

"Could be. We went out with her. It was late, but . . ."

". . . that was all."

"That's right."

"Where did you go?"

"Not far from where she lives. Over by the fishing ponds."

"Be more precise," Böll said.

"Over that little bridge that crosses the Bille farther down on Billwerder Billdeich, then farther on to the narrow cove," Horst replied. The others nodded. "'The notch,' she called it. We thought she knew where she was."

"Did any of you have sexual relations with her?"

Miron and Horst looked at each other; Stefan snickered.

"What's so funny?"

"It's because the two of them . . . because they had something with her," Stefan said. The topic seemed embarrassing to the other two. "And that's why they were always arguing. With her too."

"There was a fight with Ms. Böge?"

Stefan hunched his shoulders. "It happens."

"Be a little more precise."

"Some women like it when two people want something from her."

"Frau Böge was a woman who liked to be with more than one man at a time? Is that what you're trying to say?"

"Mhm."

"She wasn't interested in you?"

"I didn't care. I wasn't really . . ." Stefan broke off.

"Finish your sentence," Böll said.

"I don't want to talk badly about her now that she's dead."

"How old are you?"

"They're both nineteen, I'm eighteen," Stefan answered.

Horst and Miron kept silent. They had been all smiles at the beginning, even laughing a little—now they seemed uneasy.

"What exactly happened that evening, Stefan? Start at the beginning."

"We went to the notch with her and were drinking."

"Alcohol?"

"Maybe too much. We got pretty plastered."

"So you had enough alcohol with you that you were all drunk?" Manz interjected for the first time. "I thought you hadn't gotten paid yet."

"Mhm."

"Were you drinking in the car?" Böll took back over.

"At first. It was cold. Then she got out. *What an idiot*, I thought. It was pitch-black out."

"Was Nerine drunk too?"

"More than we were. It's always like that with her. She drinks too fast. *Drank*."

"And why did she get out?"

"Because she was pissed, because Horst wanted to roll around in the sand with her."

"In the sand?"

"I already told you."

"She said no right away," Horst added. He was blushing, two veins stood out on his forehead. "She kept whining. The whole time."

"And then?"

"Then they both got out after her." Stefan seemed a little overwhelmed, and looked to his friends for help. They kept their silence, lowering their heads slightly.

"Should I send them out?" Böll asked.

"No," Stefan answered.

"Well?"

"I got out too. She kept nagging, insulting us."

"What did she say?"

"That we were limp-dicks!" Miron cut in loudly. "She was a slut, then she comes drinking with us, and that's that."

"What happened then?"

"That's all I'll say," Miron replied.

"Me too," Horst echoed.

"Stefan?"

"She went off with Horst and Miron."

"Shut up!" Horst snapped.

After that, Horst and Miron had to leave the room.

"So, Stefan, what did you mean when you said she went off with them?"

"I mean into the dark. I listened for a while to the three of them fighting and . . . I mean, when someone like Nerine just starts nagging at you like that. In her annoying voice. And won't stop. It can make you lose your mind. At some point I didn't hear anything anymore. Then I got back in the car—it was cold outside."

"Did you have the feeling that your friends might have done something to her?"

"I don't think so. And then both of them came back, like nothing happened."

"Did they say what happened?"

"Just that Nerine . . . had gotten on their nerves. Then we left."

"What? You just said it was pitch-black."

"And cold," added Manz, speaking for the second time.

"It was."

"And you simply leave a young woman behind in a deserted area?"

"That's what she wanted. Besides, we had to be back at our caravan by midnight, or one at the absolute latest, because everything shuts down. There's a lot of theft at construction sites, I guess you know . . . Plus, Nerine was from the area, she knew her way around. Anyway, we didn't kill her. That was someone else."

Commissioner Böll brought the other two young men back in. They must have conferred together outside, because Miron had hardly sat down before the words came out: "We want to confess."

"To what?"

"We stole. We only had four beers on us because . . . like your partner just said, we hadn't been paid yet."

"Stole? From where?"

"I went with Horst. We had flashlights."

"That was before we fought. We heard music so we went in that direction. We got to some kind of building. There was a party there, rich people."

Manz straightened up a little at Miron's words.

"One of them caught us in the act. He was smoking some

. . . I don't know. It looked like a cigarette but it wasn't. He got interested when we told him that it was for a girl, then he let us take some beer and wine from the shed. All he wanted to know was what kind of stuff we did with her and how old she was. There was something funny about how he spoke. Maybe he was drunk, or something like that. Do you think Nerine could have . . ."

"We'll see."

Böll broke the interrogation off. It was high time to bring in the DA and get on firm legal footing. They were all minors, one barely eighteen.

The next day Manz split off from Böll, who had his hands full with paperwork. "What happened to your lip?" Böll had wanted to know. Manz didn't respond.

The DA meanwhile had voiced concern about the age of the suspects. "You should have brought me in sooner," he kept repeating to Böll.

The room where the court proceedings eventually took place and the man and woman heard their sentences had wood paneling up to the ceiling. A judge with a reputation for being strict presided. The words *barbaric*, *flesh*, and *underage* may not have appeared in the sentencing statement, but it didn't turn out well.

Yet all that was still to come, nothing had been decided yet. Early that morning Manz had brought Christine to the train station, where she gave his lower lip a tender kiss. He would see her again in three weeks' time, when he would rent the same small room in Bergedorf that she liked so much, with the large bed, washbasin, mirror, and brocade wallpaper. They could listen to the trains clatter by.

That's how it would be. At the moment, though, Manz

was on the move. A pretty blue day. He walked across the sand, knees buckling slightly, then made his way through a small stand of birch resplendent with fall foliage. And behind the woods a familiar humming and . . . a flash of white . . . as another glider climbed into the sky.

The barracks was the same gray as before, dotted with colorful people.

And then Manz was standing before Mr. Reese as he spoke for a second time in place of the Maurers who were, as he explained, still "sick."

Reese's wife stood at his side. It seemed somehow necessary because . . . something about Mr. Reese today exuded nervousness; he kept looking over toward the sandy starting line where the heavy hook landed time after time.

Manz's thoughts and attention shifted. "So you're Mrs. Reese—"

"More questions? You already spoke with my husband the day before last," she cut in, staring at Manz's lower lip as she spoke.

"He's something like the chairman here, is that right?"

"He represents the Maurers. They're both ill."

"He explained to me that nothing special occurred those last days in October. Nothing out of the ordinary."

"Because that's how it was."

"Really? We've since found out there was a party here on October 27. With loud music. There was eating, drinking . . . a lot of drinking?"

Her eyelids dipped for a moment, then lifted again. "The members of the Boberg Glider Club are not all identical," she responded, speaking with the voice of her conservative Hanseatic forebears. "Some drink less, while others . . ."

"Now that you mention *identical*—is there some kind of dress code here?"

Her smile was grandiose. "We wouldn't dream of something like that."

"I may need a list of all those present at the party. Including staff. There was staff?"

"Two young men from Denmark."

Manz turned: "Mr. Reese, did you leave the party at some point?"

"No," his wife replied.

"Do you have any more questions for me?" the husband asked.

"I think I can clear everything up with your wife."

Mr. Reese took a couple of steps over toward a group of men.

"Did somebody bite you?" she said.

"Cut myself shaving."

"Ah! Shaving. I see."

Determining why the female members of the Boberg Glider Club were wearing high heels on sandy terrain and the men were wearing silk shirts on a fifty-degree day in November was not a part of the investigation. But there wasn't much else to investigate anyway, given what Manz had already established:

- The list of party guests
- The party
- The statement from three barely adult construction workers from Mümmelmannsberg that a lot of beer and wine was stored in a shed.
- The fact that blackthorn is prickly.

It was enough for Manz to put one and one together. There were only two people on the list who lived directly by the fishing ponds, and they were Mr. and Mrs. Maurer, who Mr. Reese had been speaking about for days now. The Maurers, like the parents of Uwe the pike fisher and Nerine Böge's mother, lived on Billwerder Billdeich.

A bungalow. A driveway of concrete slabs leading up to a double garage. The conversation took place in Mr. and Mrs. Maurer's bright, not exactly compact living room. A corner sofa with Swedish flair in good taste, beside it a lamp hung over a heavy table and a low sideboard table made of tropical dark-stained wood. On the sideboard there perched a large number of African souvenirs, women with spiraling eyes and exaggerated genitals set off in different colors. Thus far everything matched the taste du jour, which reflected an increased interest in the wider world and gave the impression of considerable openness and curiosity about the unfamiliar. It was the age of Willy Brandt, of agreements with the East, the age of détente between the two German states. On the walls, behind glass, hung work by the biologist, Darwinist, and eugenicist Ernst Haeckel. Microscopically exact reproductions of orchids, jellyfish, anura, human heads of different races, and the snow-white skeletal configurations of plankton and diatoms. Manz asked himself whether the selection and composition of all the works of art held some kind of meaning, but quickly brushed aside whatever thoughts followed. People like Manz didn't base their knowledge on psychological or sociological reports. Judges and defense attorneys might, but the only thing he needed had long since presented itself. Outside, clearly visible through the large panorama window, the forensics team was inspecting piles of blackthorn clippings that lay along a vigorously trimmed hedge. Blackthorn had been mentioned so many times now that it had become a household word for everyone present.

Manz asked about the Maurers' vehicle. They had two: a poorly maintained Mercedes 220D and a prehistoric Land Rover. Even if the branches were small, they had found them, clinging there in the luggage space of the Land Rover. And once again they were talking about blackthorn.

Still, it was hardly a surprise when forensics found the front of the freshly washed car even more interesting than the bits of blackthorn they'd found inside.

The Elbe stretches a good thousand kilometers, on certain days exhibiting a certain shade of turquoise. The river springs up in a country that in 1972 wasn't called the Czech Republic yet, wending its way toward Hamburg, where it twists and turns through the German harbor before flowing on in a more or less direct line. Finally it forms a sort of delta, spreading out into a German bay that often reflects a blackberry-red in the evening light.

Christmas is right around the corner, and Christine is back in Hamburg for a visit. She and Manz have just left the room with the brocade wallpaper arm in arm and now drive in his beige Ford, along a road that stretches out kilometer after kilometer. Leaving from Bergedorf, the road begins as the highway-like B5, changing names frequently. In the end it's all the same road, says Manz, incorrectly lumping all the lined-up street sections into something he calls the east-west corridor. Still, he's not entirely wrong; the Ford's route brings them directly to the heart of the city.

At the end of the east-west corridor, in a neighborhood where people know how to enjoy themselves, he and Christine have entered a dance hall where the floor is packed with hundreds of other couples. The dance hall is known for its gaping entrance, which at nearly sixty-five feet across resembles something like a garage door. The dance floor extends out to the edge of the dirty sidewalk.

The two twirl in the middle of the dance floor while the orchestra plays. Men appear in getups one sees only rarely today. Above them an enormous oval cavity; along its edge a balcony and tables set up with little lamps, where groups observe the couples spinning below them in little eddies.

There they are, in plain sight. Manz has brought his wife to her feet. Hundreds of dancing couples swirl about them. They share a long kiss, then Christine asks: "What ended up happening with your case?"

"A bender at a flying club. It was foggy that night, a couple left around one a.m. The wife drove, her husband was even drunker than she was. Three young guys had left a girl behind in the dark. She got on their nerves, they said. She was drunk herself. The guys were all tucked away in bed by one a.m., but she was still staggering about in the mist."

"God, how awful."

It isn't difficult to picture exactly how awful it must have been. As a night scene. The clean tar of the road along the edge of the cove they call the notch, lined by alders. The faces of the couple, blind drunk, lit from beneath by the glare of the dashboard lights. The woman's chin glued to the steering wheel of the Land Rover, her eyes bugging out like some form of Graves' disease. So she can see better. A fool's errand. Because in the diffuse glow of the headlights, wrongly set on bright, she can't see anything but a white wall. Alder branches jut through the frame to the left. Then a shadow comes flying into the pearl-white and . . . the impact.

Upon which the Maurers find themselves in stark disarray.

* * *

After the thud, Mrs. Maurer stopped the Land Rover. Eleven seconds of silence. Two faces. Shining. Greenish-yellow. Their eyes open much wider now, and with question marks looming. Still lit from below. "What was that?" she whispers to her husband.

"Something big. Don't you think?"

"It wasn't a person though. Right?"

"Wasn't there something off to the left?" His voice scarcely rises above a whisper.

"What could—"

"An animal?"

They grab the flashlight out of the tin crate behind the seat, both get out and . . . repeat the question . . .

"An animal?"

Then they see the body of the girl on the asphalt and . . . bending over . . . feeling cautiously . . .

"No pulse. Maybe her neck."

Time crawls by.

"Then something in us flipped," Mrs. Maurer had explained to Manz during his questioning. "We don't know what."

Apparently, no plan had been made; suddenly everything seemed to go automatically. Lifting the dead girl up by the shoulders together, dragging her over to the water . . . going back for the shoe . . .

"We took off all her clothes."

"Why'd you do that?" Manz had asked.

"We don't know."

Then into the water. Both of them. Up to their waists.

With the body still warm.

"The moon! Right?"

"Yes, dear. The moon. I had thought of that too."

"We knew the cove, we used to take the children there in the summer. It's where our two oldest learned to swim."

Into the water, then. They pushed the body of the girl under . . .

"It was really difficult because . . . because she kept coming back up."

. . . and pinned it beneath two pinkish alder branches that had cracked off in a storm and lay just beneath the surface of the water.

"Our boys always practiced their diving beneath the branches."

"Then we went home . . . I can't even remember who had the idea. You?"

"We had just had our blackthorn shrub trimmed, I don't know who thought of that. You?"

"We loaded up the Land Rover and went back, then laid the blackthorn over the spot."

"We kept going back again and again, and—"

"With more and more blackthorn."

"Why so much?" Manz asked.

"It's what my wife wanted."

"Did we mention the fog already?"

"We did, dear, just calm down. Should I bring you a schnapps?"

"Then, later," Mrs. Maurer seemed to have missed the offer of a drink, "when we had thought everything through again and were wondering why she'd jumped out in front of the car . . . we both had the feeling . . ."

"Like she had been running away from something, right?"

"No—like she must have seen our headlights!"

"We aren't sure, but after, when we felt her pulse . . ."

"You know that feeling?" Mrs. Maurer's chest heaved as though she was struggling for air. "When you sense that somebody is still there?"

"But who would have been there?" Manz asked.

"The moon!" she screamed. "The moon, the moon, the—"

"Dear, please! You're repeating yourself."

"Am I?" Her face had taken on a crumpled look, some parts covered in dark cross-hatchings.

"Yes, you're repeating yourself. He's taking notes. If anything's missing, he'll ask again. Isn't that right?"

Manz had nodded.

The rest of the questioning would reveal that psychologically speaking, Mrs. Maurer hadn't been entirely stable from the first load of blackthorn on. Even though she had eventually been the one to take charge of transporting and laying the cuttings.

"My wife, I don't know what to say either. We barely had the Land Rover filled with blackthorn . . . when she ran back into the house . . . to the phone . . . and when I asked who she was going to call, she said, 'The babysitter, who else?' That's how far gone she was already. For all my troubles, I broke my little toe that night, the big one too. I got caught on a doorframe two times."

"Were you naked?" Manz asked.

"Yes."

"Both of you? Even inside the house?"

"Of course!" she declared. "We had to go back into the water."

Again and again. Load after load. They had piled blackthorn over the body in a way that made no sense whatsoever. The question that presented itself was obvious: what could have gotten into the two of them?

An intricately carved color engraving of nude bodies and ghosts enmeshed in blackthorn lodged itself in Manz's mind.

At long last Manz looked up at Mr. and Mrs. Maurer. It seemed as though they were posing for him. Wrapping up his thoughts, he turned to Mrs. Maurer: "I ask because blackthorn has nasty, long prickers. And your face, your neck, your hands and your husband's . . ."

"If you knew what we looked like naked!"

So it had been like that. A lot of blood had been spilled—the Maurers'.

"We can't explain it except by . . . Should we get undressed?"

"Don't bother, dear. Maybe you do want a drink?"

"No, goddamnit!" Her throat extended, her hair seemed to grow in volume.

"But we weren't trying to hide her, isn't that right? Tell him, dear."

"It was awful because . . . she kept coming back up."

"Nerine, that was her name, she helped us in the garden sometimes. We're happy you're here because . . . our underarms, neck, chest, face . . ."

"We should get undressed."

"Please, dear. He doesn't want us to. He doesn't want to see us like that."

Later, the judge heard the following: "When the young man from the police came and saw us with our scratched-up faces, throats, and arms, and stood there in the living room looking out through the large picture window into the garden and the pile of blackthorn cuttings swimming there among the white cotton of the mist . . ."

"All he said was, 'From the beginning.' He already knew everything."

"We were grateful."

* * *

"How tragic," Christine said. She and Manz were still sur-rounded by the other couples swirling about them on the honey-colored parquet floor.

"The coroner doesn't think the victim died of injuries from the accident. He thinks she drowned."

"Under blackthorn."

"Technically they were blackthorn cuttings. Those planes were amazing. Gliders. Blinding white. They pull them up al-most vertical. Well? Got another in you?"

"Always."

She responded as he took hold of her. The orchestra be-gan its next number and he spun, spun, spun her, just the way she liked. Later, in the Ford, on a dark side street behind fogged-up windows, she suddenly grew larger. She leaned over and pressed him down in a seat made of artificial, En-glish green leather. It wasn't long before Manz had another burst lip.

PART II

Dream & Reality

ANGEL FRICASSEE

BY TIMO BLUNCK
Niendorf

Translated by Noah Harley

"Semisweet! Here boy, Semisweet!"
  "Your dog's name is Semisweet?"
  "That's right, like the chocolate. Mostly cacao."
The lab that came storming out of the water toward us was a deep brown, short coat shining like a Hershey's bar. He bounded up to his owner at an alarming rate, making no effort to slow down. At the last moment he corrected course, diving headlong into my thigh.

"No, no jumping!" I cried.

Too late. Semisweet was hard at work covering me in muddy paw prints. His owner grinned in embarrassment, but didn't intervene.

"I'm so sorry about that, chocolate labs are really difficult to train. Semisweet just does what he wants."

As if to prove her point, the rascal shook himself off, spreading more muck over my pants.

I lied: "No worries, these are my throwaway clothes anyway."

As if I even owned "throwaway" clothes. Fortunately, the mud bath hadn't covered my sky-blue suede jacket, which I might have thrown out otherwise. Ms. Semisweet seemed quite embarrassed by it all, she was even blushing slightly. Charming. She pointed to my fluffy companion.

"And what is this sweet little fur-nose called?"

"That's Knef, as in Hildegard."

"Hildegard Knef? The singer?"

"That's the one. I'm a fan."

"Hrm, Knef. It doesn't exactly roll off the tongue."

"You could say the same for Semisweet."

Touché. Her smile morphed from one of embarrassment to receptivity. She peered intently at me, seeing the man behind the dog for the first time. Evidently, she liked what she saw, instinctively folding her arms across her chest. A little body language 101: *Defensive posture, this guy could pose a threat.*

This was exactly the reason why I had gotten my mixed-breed Knef. Forget Tinder—the quickest path to an attractive woman's heart is via her four-legged friend. Whether at a café, restaurant, ice cream shop, a flea market, stoop sale, bus stop, or just out and about, dog owners all belonged to the same tribe, and immediately had something to talk about.

I had spent hours on end thinking up the perfect pickup line—it had to be original and fit the situation to sound spontaneous, not rote. More than anything, though, it couldn't be too pushy, even if the pairing of my charm and good looks allowed for some breathing room. Sometimes I had the best luck with a slightly overdone cliché—"I didn't know angels could fly so close to earth"—but timeworn classics like "I'll bet twenty dollars you won't give me your number" also worked, or something funny like "Do you believe in love at first sight? If not, I can go out and come back in again." Still, any phrase, no matter how masterly, paled in comparison to the question, "What kind of dog is that?" It couldn't be beat for its impersonal nature, but in the same breath it established an intimate connection, making it far and away the world's most seductive phrase. Only if you had a dog of your own on the leash, of course. And Knef was especially well-suited to the follow-up question that arrived with about 97 percent certainty: "And yours?" Knef wasn't a single breed, but four: a cocktail of sheepdog, keeshond, and a shot of Eurasier, topped off with a spritz of dachshund. How that had all worked technically might have remained shrouded in mystery to me, especially the last bit, but Knef unquestionably had the ears of a dachshund. What was more, she came from an animal shelter, giving me bonus points as a do-gooder. And just like that you were engaged in profound conversation about the nature of dogs in general, their superiority to cats, and why it's now impossible to imagine life without our rare specimen.

The best place for this sort of not-entirely-chance encounter was obviously the dog park, a quintessentially German institution that could be found in practically every park in the republic. These were the only areas where a person's canine companion was allowed off-leash, although their freedom was regulated with cutthroat regularity: the Hamburg police even had a dedicated commando unit. Dog parks weren't large, so you couldn't walk around them. Instead, a person stood there watching his or her animal play with others of their ilk. Anybody who couldn't get into a conversation here had probably taken themselves to prom. It was an ideal loitering spot for a fellow in his midthirties such as myself who was happy to connect, always in search of human inspiration, and not averse to physical proximity, however brief.

One of the largest dog parks in Hamburg was located in Niendorf—a vastly underrated neighborhood in the northwest of the city that the average pedestrian likely associated with the Niendorfer Gehege, a well-maintained nature park with a stand of old trees and a host of leisure activities. Still, the park was far too restrictive for the serious dog owner, even downright hostile. As it was, for real Niendorfers the park was situated in "old" Niendorf, in the area around the central square. The area was a sort of "Blankenese light" (for those not from Hamburg, Blankenese is the Hanseatic city's most exclusive neighborhood, reserved for the nobility); there were even a couple of celebrities living in art nouveau villas! "New" Niendorf—and the only true Niendorf for those in the know—was the "wild north," around the Ohmoor wildlife refuge and the area northwest of the Helmut Schmidt airport. The area was somewhat less elegant, dominated by joyless fortresses of poured concrete and what were probably Germany's narrowest row houses. But hey, it was home. When I was a younger man, I could hardly wait to move out—today, I was happy to set down roots. I ♥ Niendorf!

My neighborhood was also home to Rahweg, a "local recreation area," and Hasenheide Garden Colony Inc., both positioned idyllically alongside the Tarpenbek, one of the city's less-significant waterways. If you really thought about it, the area was a complete anomaly—a prime building site relatively close to the city center, reachable in twenty minutes with the U2 subway line. But as much as real estate speculators might have licked their lips, it was simply too close to the airport. Aside from the noise and the air pollution, there was also the fact that the area's softly rolling hills were actually the final remains of World War II. Up through the early fifties, the site was used to bury the rubble left behind by British bombs. This meant drainage in the area didn't work—the small garden homes were constantly flooded and the paths covered over by rainwater. As a native Niendorfer,

I knew the "local recreation area" when it was still called "Bagger Pond," an artificial pond complete with a small strip of sand. As a kid I could be found splashing about here most weekends throughout the summer; it was where I learned to swim and went fishing with my father. The pond had since suffered ecological collapse—unfortunately, decomposed algae had taken over the surface and it gave off a musty smell, with brown-green foam collecting around the embankment. It also likely explained why park administrators had set up the exercise area there—you could do that with dog owners.

Semisweet ran back into the clouded water. "Labradors are retrieving dogs, they're crazy about the water," my new doggy-acquaintance explained to me. "Their coats are so thick they don't get wet."

No shit! I thought, wiping the mud off my pants. "Might be something for the textile industry to look into."

She giggled. "I'm Josepha, by the way. And you?"

That was quick, no formalities here! "I'm Mar—"

A massive Airbus jet in landing position cut me off with an ear-deafening roar. Knef started to whimper and pressed up against my legs. I stroked her head. "Everything's okay, sweetie."

The plane passed.

"I'm Marius."

"Hi, Marius, nice to meet you."

I flashed my sunniest smile. "The pleasure is all mine."

Josepha was an eight-and-a-half, at least. Long legs and sporty, but with enough curves not to get any bruises when snuggling. She wore her blond hair up in a ponytail, blue eyes sparkling behind long eyelashes. A narrow nose and a delicate curve to her mouth completed the Hanseatic look, which was accentuated by a green Barbour jacket with a corduroy collar. She wore beige jeans and rubber boots made by Hunter. An outdoorsy type with a fashion sense—a woman after my own heart.

"Knef doesn't like the water. She only goes in up to her stomach, and only to drink."

As if on cue, my dog tiptoed into the pond, where she received a hero's welcome from Semisweet. Knef watched on in visible distress, then flashed me an annoyed look. Labradors are always so dramatic. And so awkward at the same time. Josepha made a circling motion with her right index finger.

"Clockwise?"

Had Christmas come early? Had an eight-and-a-half really just invited me for a stroll? And clockwise around the pond, to the right? Any true Rahweg recreational area connoisseur would know the route, which could be stretched out across the entire park.

"Fine by me, my right leg is a little bit shorter than my left."

Josepha gave me a perfect smile, her immaculate teeth rivaling the clarity of her eyes. "Hee-re, Semisweet, hee-re."

Her clumsy chocolate lab leaped back out of the pond, shaking itself off vigorously. Once bitten, twice shy: this time I kept a safe distance.

It was one of those glorious Saturday afternoons in October, the heat of the sun diminished, but still as bright as August. Fall was much more aesthetically pleasing than summer for that matter—the leaves glowed in shades of red and yellow, while the slant of the sun bathed the park in iridescent gold. It was the ideal weather for a promenade. Josepha and I thus blissfuly ignored the signs requiring dogs to be on-leash, much to the chagrin of all the fishermen who seemed to take the *No Fishing* signs posted everywhere just about as seriously as Porsche drivers took a speed limit. Knef was a street dog—you could let her out at the next bus stop and she would manage on her own. In the park it was always the garbage cans that piqued her interest the most, and she had no hang-ups about begging from total strangers or stealing breadcrumbs off people feeding ducks. She especially loved fishermen with bait in their bags, which Knef had no qualms about rifling through. As was the case today.

"Knef, no! Come back here!"

"You speak English with your dog?"

"I do, I want her to grow up bilingual."

Josepha laughed. "You really are a comedian. But why English?"

"I lived in London for a while, I just moved back to Niendorf last year."

"Ah. What do you do?"

"I'm—"

Another jet disrupted the conversation. Josepha covered her ears.

". . . an investment banker."

A lie, obviously, but in this context, "administrator in the credit wing of Commerz Bank" seemed a little mundane. Besides, I had actually worked in England for years, albeit not in the financial center of London but a Barclays branch in Putney, one of the city's suburbs.

Josepha peered at me intently, her eyebrows forming perfect arches. "How thrilling."

Was she flirting with me? It was getting warm in my suede jacket. Ms. Semisweet was definitely not the prototypical reserved Hanseatic lady that she appeared to be on the outside. And she kept going.

"Would you have any interest in a coffee together afterward?"

Now I was actually sweating. That was usually *my* line, and I would have tried it by the parking lot—at the earliest.

"Uhm . . . well, sure."

"What about the café at the mini-golf course? On Burgunder Strasse?"

What? She even knew about my culinary trump card, my favorite tip? The café was a surprise oasis in the gastronomical desert that is Niendorf. Damnit, I was almost getting a little annoyed. I wasn't used to relinquishing the initiative, I had to regain my footing now that I was outside of my usual mating dance. But I kept calm—as Hildegard Knef says, "You don't look a gift horse in the mouth."

Three hours later I was at Josepha's dining room table on Goten Strasse. Her chic apartment was in a recent construction built on the footprint of a single-family house. It wasn't an architectural masterpiece, but it was an efficient way of getting four living spaces out of one without ruining the block's overall character. This form of real estate speculation was increasingly visible in my neighborhood; there were already a couple of the same tin-can structures on my own block.

"This is absolutely delicious!" What had been intended as a compliment came out more like a moan of pleasure. Josepha was a divine cook. Immediately after the coffee, she had invited me over for a bite to eat.

"Espresso gives you an appetite, am I right?"

It was the opposite, really, but before I could answer she had continued: "I still have a little duck paté at home, some fresh bread, and a good Burgundy—might do the trick, right?"

She had pointed up to the street sign at the entrance to the mini-golf course. "Burgunder Strasse, ha ha!"

I guessed that was her sense of humor. Ms. Semisweet was definitely not run-of-the-mill, but I was quickly getting used to her directness. Her pace was breathtaking, but hey, go with the flow—it gave me a chance to play the wallflower. And just like that, she was serving me a third course in her well-appointed apartment.

"What do you call this dish?" I asked.

Josepha gave an impish grin. "That's my angel fricassee."

"Angel fricassee? Because it tastes so heavenly?"

"Something like that."

She went into the kitchen. I called after her: "What kind of meat is it anyway? It's so tender and juicy. Or is it some soy product, or seitan maybe? What's it called, Beyond Meat?"

She came back with another bottle of pinot blanc. "Wouldn't you like to know."

"I would, it really is heavenly. How did you season it? I've never eaten anything so delectable."

Josepha kept her silence. She made the same seductive motion with her eyebrows, cocking her head slightly to the side.

I persisted: "Oh come on, give me the recipe."

"Not a good idea. If I did tell you, I would have to kill you afterward, unfortunately."

She vanished back into the kitchen. I took my glass of wine and followed her in.

"Wow!"

I stood there, mouth open. "Kitchen"—there's no true synonym for the word, and it seemed vastly understated for this room. This was an artist studio, a gourmet temple, a culinary cathedral. Over the six-burner gas stove, a range of cast-iron and copper pots and pans hung from a silver rack. She didn't have one, but *two* extra-wide ovens. Behind a set of glass doors, cans and jars of spices, oils, and exotic ingredients stood in neat rows. Cartons and glasses filled with (to me) unfamiliar provisions and preserved fruit were stacked high in the open pantry. On the kitchen island stood an impressive wood knife block with an even more impressive collection of Japanese knives. I reached for the handle of one. She gave me a little slap on the back of the hand.

"Better leave it. They get dull just by looking at them." She grabbed a lighter off the shelf and lit a flame. "In the mood for dessert?"

We had another espresso. As could be expected, the crème brûlée was also to die for. Altogether the meal had sent me into a strange sort of trance state—the assault on my palate, coupled with the exceptional wine, had had its effect. I felt oddly light, not a trace of having overeaten. I was floating on a gourmet cloud and could have easily kept eating the whole night through.

Josepha was back on the subject of the dog park: "You know that it's not just rubble they buried along the Rahweg, right?"

"I did not."

"There are a bunch of bodies buried there as well, and not just soldiers either, but women and children too."

"Are you sure about that?"

"Absolutely. Marc-Dieter told me."

"Marc-Dieter?"

"My ex. He was a history professor."

I raised my hand. "Hold the phone—*was?*"

The grin she gave was slightly off, with a touch of the diabolical. "That's right, *was*. But that's beside the point." She brushed off an imaginary fly. "Nobody talks about it, of course, but after the bombings, the authorities didn't have time to identify all the bodies or give them a proper burial. So they just buried them along with all the other wreckage."

"That's hard to believe, it's so barbaric, so—"

"Oh come now, it's just practical. The bodies were on the street and were starting to stink. We'd do the same thing today."

I was a little shocked. Without warning, the conversation had taken an almost morbid turn, hardly postprandial small talk. But then, just as abruptly as she had steered the conversation down a dark alley, Josepha now seamlessly guided it back toward the light of day.

"Well, handsome, it looks like you enjoyed the meal." She patted my hand. "A full stomach suits you. I'm going to smoke." She pointed to the balcony.

"You smoke?"

She winked at me. "I do, but only before sex."

Afterward, I drifted off into an unquiet sleep. I dreamed I was standing at the edge of the dog park in Rahweg. It was early morning, mist still hovering over the wet grass. Before me were the rolling hills of the park. I breathed in deeply, savoring the fresh air and the stillness. Stillness? Without warning, a fighter jet flew in so low above me that I had to duck. I had barely righted myself when a second plane came, followed by another. Then another. It felt like an entire squadron was after me. The volume was infernal, and a high-pitched ringing started up in my ears. Thick black smoke blotted out the rising sun as the heavy scent of kerosene wafted into my nose. I hacked violently and shut my eyes. When I opened them again, the squadron had disappeared over the horizon with a slight echo. Slowly the cloud of smoke dissipated. But the hills in the background had lost any trace of charm. The ground was split open, as though someone had ripped it apart at the seams. Earth gushed out of the tear blood red; wrecked beams and other rubble jutted through the fog like broken teeth. The light had also changed—the tender light of dawn had given way to a cold neon-blue that backlit the scene eerily. I heard myself speak: "The only thing missing now are dissonant violins and we'll have a horror film."

But instead of a string orchestra, a single trombone sounded far off to my right. And as if that wasn't inappropriate enough of a soundtrack, a reggae beat with a subtle swing now started up on my left.

"Reggae? In a horror film? Don't make me laugh!"

I shouldn't have spoken. With a menacing hiss, a dark figure emerged out of the mist in front of me. Its long shadow fell over me; things grew jet-black, so that for a moment I thought I had gone blind. The darkness had barely passed when I became aware of other silhouettes, rising out of the gaping wound left behind by the fighter jets like creatures from the deep. Like predatory undersea creatures, they now bared their teeth, and began to hum and buzz in low tones. Their voices mixed in with the trombone and the reggae beat, providing passable bass accompaniment.

The first figure had drawn so near to me in the meantime that I could make out its facial features—surprised, I realized that it was Josepha. At least she looked similar enough to the woman who lay beside me in bed, but different at the same time, akin to a zombie version. Strips of skin hung down from her skull, revealing the white bone beneath. Her eyes rolled about in the middle of empty cavities, while yellow teeth dangled in a jaw with no gumline. Her hair hung in greasy strands over emaciated shoulders, which glimmered palely through her ripped Barbour jacket. In spite of her condition, she was swaying back and forth to the reggae rhythm. She lifted her arm and reached out a hand that was almost entirely bone.

I heard my own voice again—this time I was singing: "*What's the name, dear, of that impossibly tasty meal?*"

Zombie Josepha responded in a hoarse voice, her corroded vocal cords making a smokey whisper: "*Angel fricassee, angel fricassee.*"

I took her hand and drew her to me. She smelled like earth and moss, not so bad after all.

"*And the snack, dear, that the baker won't ever make?*"

"*Angel fricassee, angel fricassee.*"

We danced a couple of steps. I changed the melody, raising my voice to a higher register: "*These spices, dear, go so well together.*"

Josepha lifted what remained of her eyebrows. "*Angel fricassee, angel fricassee.*"

She fit like a glove in my arms, except, that is, for the spots where my hand reached into nothingness. There was nothing inside of her rib cage, and I grazed the inside of her ribs.

"*I taste cinnamon, dear, thyme, dill, and coriander.*"

Once again Josepha murmured her refrain, which was evidently going to be her only contribution to our song: "*Angel fricassee, angel fricassee.*"

As we spun around each other, I became aware that other zombies had formed a half circle around us, with the band set up behind. Next to the trombonist, a trumpeter stood at the ready, decomposing. The rest of the musicians were also living corpses, and now the whole gang chimed in, throats rasping:

Greetings from the kitchen, love melts on the tongue
A thousand scents, spirits and beers fail
Tea coats the belly.

They rubbed their sunken bellies, those at least who still had them.

Tea coats the belly.

I now realized that I must be in a waking dream. I was aware that I was dreaming, that this musical mockery had sprung entirely from my own fantasy, meaning I was also in control of what happened next. I decided to finally shed some light on the mystery meat on my plate.

"*What's in it, dear, it's not from the hill here, is it?*"

Even without lips, Josepha managed a smile. "*Angel fricassee, angel fricassee.*"

Yeah, yeah, but . . . "*Dear, where is the meat from? Is it lamb, cow, chicken?*"

But all I heard was . . . "*Angel fricassee, angel fricassee.*"

I was growing impatient, but the zombie chorus started up again:

Greetings from the kitchen, love melts on the tongue
A thousand scents, spirits and beers fail
Tea coats the belly.

The living corpses had now started to move in sync with each other, performing a simple dance routine.

Tea coats the belly.

They drew closer and closer, first forming a closed circle out of the half circle, then a tighter and tighter ring around me. I stood shoulder to shoulder with them; their numbers seemed to be growing exponentially. I stood up on my tiptoes; skulls as far as the eye could see gleaming in the neon light, musty bodies pressing toward me. The humming was no longer harmonic but had morphed into a dangerous, slavering sort of noise, while the scent in the air had also ceased being pleasant, replaced by a noxious rot. I looked for Josepha, but my zombie girlfriend had vanished in the crowd.

"Ow!"

One of the corpses had bit me on the back of the neck.

"Get off me!"

Another zombie sank its teeth into my calf muscle and wouldn't let go.

"What are you doing? Stop it!"

I felt teeth all over my body as they nibbled from every direction. More and more zombies pressed forward, climbing over each other, threatening to crush me.

"Don't, that hurts!"

It must have been too much of a good thing; whoever was in fact in control of deciding that I had had enough to dream now woke me up with a particularly painful bite on my shoulder.

"Oh, Marius, you're so hot I could just eat you up!"

I was back in reality, though to my horror I realized that even on this side of reality the biting wouldn't stop. The first rays of dawn found Ms. Semisweet naked on all fours. She crouched over me, doubled up in an odd position—and bit! I lay on my back, scarcely able to believe my eyes. Again and again her head shot toward me and snapped at my skin. And where were my T-shirt and boxers? I was totally exposed. My chest, stomach, legs, arms—she kept tearing and tugging.

"What do you think you're doing? Have you gone totally crazy?"

She had obviously been at it awhile—I had lobster-red bite marks all over my body.

"Ah, it's just a nibble. Do you have any idea how good you taste? You've got me all hot!"

Mmhh . . . the unexpected compliment got a rise despite the even more unexpected situation. In spite (or maybe because) of her odd position, my bedmate was also an exceptionally stimulating vision. I grew even more excited, immediately bringing Josepha's attention to the most visible sign.

"No, no, not my—" I cried out in despair, but it was too late.

"Knef, sweetie, it's all right, I'm up!"

Knef licked my ear, pressing her damp nose up against my cheek. I looked down at my phone—eleven fifteen already! I must have fallen back asleep. I glanced over to see Josepha still snoring lightly. I made a spirited effort to get up, but a searing pain directly above my right eye forced me back onto the pillow. So I had drunk a little too much Burgundy last night after all. I tried again more slowly, steadying myself against the bed frame. This time it worked. A little dizzy, I pulled on my boxer shorts and lurched into the kitchen. Semisweet and Knef both followed me in, tails wagging in anticipation of breakfast. The hangover was brutal, my headache a vengeful boa constrictor that had wrapped itself around the right lobe of my brain, mercilessly increasing the pressure. A single thought formed inside my tormented mind: ICE! I tore open the refrigerator, but the freezer drawer didn't have any ice cubes. There was only a neatly stacked assortment of frozen meat packets wrapped in plastic. So be it. I grabbed one of the packets and held it up to my forehead with both hands. Ah, better already! I closed the refrigerator and sat down on one of the barstools at the kitchen island, propping myself up by the elbows and leaning into the frozen meat as it slowly began to thaw against my body heat. Ice water dripped onto my wrist, running down my underarm and collecting on the marble counter.

When I finally set the meat off to the side, planning to get a new bundle from the freezer, I became aware of a small piece of paper stuck to my forehead. I pulled it off to inspect. It was one of those self-adhesive freezer tags for writing the contents and date. Although it was completely soaked through by now, the writing was still clearly legible—in neatly curving letters, somebody had written, *Thomas, 9/17/21*. Thomas? I went back to the refrigerator and opened up the freezer drawer. I took out another packet—*Sven, 1/5/22*. I set it aside and kept looking. I found an *Angelo, 6/7/22*, a *Klaus, 10/15/20*, and another Thomas, *9/17/21*. Beneath that lay three packages marked, *Marc-Dieter, 5/13/21*. Marc-Dieter? An alarm softly began to sound in my head. Hadn't that been the name of Josepha's ex-boyfriend, the history professor? The alarm began to flash.

"What are you doing in my fridge?"

Josepha was barefoot and wearing a silk bathrobe with a cherry blossom pattern, a stunning fit. She looked enchanting. Until she started to scream, that is.

"What are you doing? You're going through my things, you fucking stalker?"

I turned to face her, gripping a packet of Marc-Dieter in each hand. "Of course I'm not. I just went looking for ice for my headache. But then . . ." I held Marc-Dieter up, and asked, voice trembling: "Angel fricassee?"

In a single savage leap Josepha was on the kitchen island, where she grabbed one of the Japanese knives out of the woodblock. "Bingo!" she hissed. "The contestant gets a hundred points. But I warned you."

I let the packets fall. "Warned me? About what?"

"That I would have to kill you if I gave away the recipe. What exactly didn't you understand about that?"

She pounced like a big cat. In a flash she let the blade fly forward, landing on her hands and feet. At first I thought she had missed me, until I felt a stinging pain on my forehead and my field of vision turned red. Josepha emerged from behind the bloody curtain, watching me curiously, her eyes drawn wide. She waved the knife back and forth in front of my nose, chuckling hoarsely.

"This is my *Yanagi ba*, that's *willow-leaf blade* in English." Smacking her lips, she licked the bloody blade, then whispered: "Angel fricassee is human flesh."

With a practiced flick of the wrist, she sliced my throat. The knife was so sharp that I felt no pain at first, though I could hear my blood splattering on the kitchen floor. Then I felt nauseous, cold sweat dripping down my back. My body collapsed—my knees gave out, and I slipped down into a pool of my own blood. I tried to grab hold of the pot rack as I did, ripping the shelf from the wall. Undeterred, I lashed out around me, bringing pots and pans to the floor with a thunderous clatter. Knef was instantly at my side. My strength ebbing, I stroked my loyal companion.

"Well, this probably didn't turn out the way we imagined, did it?" I gurgled.

But Knef was showing little interest in my final words,

sniffing instead at the blood that was still pouring from my wound. Curious, she began to lap it up. Semisweet joined her, and both dogs licked my lifeblood off the parquet floor with growing enthusiasm. I closed my eyes. Quietly, off to the left, a reggae beat started up; a lone trombone began to play to my right.

Somewhere above me I could hear Josepha singing: "Angel fricassee, angel fricassee . . ."

WHO'LL LOOK AFTER OUR WOMEN IF *WE* DON'T?

BY BELA B FELSENHEIMER

St. Pauli

Translated by Noah Harley

"For God's sake, not Rocken Roll! That really would be too stupid for words."

Markus shakes his head, reading back over the names by the door. Two Schmitts, each with two *t*'s, probably related, one Herdehügel, Pančević, Ibrahim, Sacks, and Amara.

And Rocken Roll.

He had found two keys in his daughter's bag. Jennifer's friend had given him the address to the shared flat; a little unwillingly, maybe, but Markus could be very convincing.

The first key lets him into the apartment building. The stairwell is quiet.

He heads straight up, starting his search from the top. Markus inspects the shoe scrapers, the nameplates by the doorbells, anything for a sign of Jennifer. Nothing.

One of the doors on the third floor is plastered with stickers—skateboard brands, band logos, the St. Pauli football club. He already has an idea about what the nameplate will read.

You have to start somewhere, Markus thinks to himself with a sigh, and rings the bell.

When there's no sound from inside, he knocks.

No response.

Markus grips the second key, hoping against hope that it won't fit.

The lock turns with a click.

Rocken Roll?

Markus still understands the neighborhood's appeal more or less, the affordable rent and the Reeperbahn right around the corner, but a pseudonym like Rocken Roll? It just doesn't fit his Jennifer.

Jennifer, first in her graduating class.

Jennifer, who until recently had also been among the top students at her law school. They had already had a place for her at Oliver's firm.

It wasn't long ago that he rented her her first apartment, within reach of his own house in Wellingsbüttel. He held on to a spare key out of precaution; he had to keep at least one eye out for her, his Jennifer.

Then she had started with all the therapy nonsense. He had suggested a year abroad with business friends instead. She responded by withdrawing entirely.

Even that hadn't been so bad; Markus was young once too. He too had rebelled, played bass in a hardcore band, gone straight edge. They were wild times, but he hadn't missed a single lecture because of them either. Jennifer had missed more and more, as he found out. By that time she had cut off all contact with her father and moved out of the apartment.

For a while he was still able to trace her whereabouts through her cell phone. But then she changed her number and plan, and that was that.

His only child had slipped out of reach.

Until, that is, he had seen her earlier that day, at the university hospital. Sedated, thinner than before, hair disheveled, fingernails chewed down. She had collapsed from an overdose, a cocktail of fentanyl and cocaine. A popular and lethal combination, the doctor told him.

It was so unlike Jennifer. From now on, though, he would be back in charge, and this time he would get everything right.

Markus draws a deep breath and balls his right hand into a fist, the key digging into it. He pushes lightly on the door.

"Hello?"

He feels around for a light switch and finds it.

A number of leather and college jackets hang off hooks directly in front of him. Beside them is Jennifer's designer poncho.

Markus has come to bring some things to the hospital, and has with him a backpack and a couple of large plastic bags from a Swedish furniture company. Ultimately, all of his daughter's other possessions will be going in those plastic bags.

His daughter won't be coming back here. Not after what happened.

The walls are papered with concert posters that swallow whatever light is cast by the dismal lamp overhead.

"Is anybody home?"

Markus pauses to listen a few seconds, then cautiously draws the door closed behind him, takes the poncho off the hook, and drops it in the bag. He moves into the first room. The windows are darkened by blinds; instead of opening them, Markus flips on the ceiling light. This one at least gives some proper light. The mess takes his breath away.

This is how she's been living?

A sofa with a stained sheet draped over it. An oversized television sits next to game consoles and a stereo system framed by obscenely large speakers. Video game and DVD cases strewn everywhere, with articles of clothing scattered throughout. A low table covered in dirty glasses and plates, two full ashtrays, and a glass bong in the middle. Markus retreats into the hallway and finds the bathroom next to the kitchen, where he spots Jennifer's toiletry kit and drops it into the backpack. He sees her electric toothbrush on his way out and grabs that too. The final door in the hallway leads to a bedroom.

Inside it is even more chaotic. Pile after pile of dirty clothing—filthy even—rise up from the floor: T-shirts, men's underwear, a threadbare summer dress that he recognizes . . . is that Jennifer's? The bed is a total mess, also covered in stains. At least there aren't any food scraps lying around. And aside from a glass with clouded water, he doesn't spy any dishes.

It takes him a moment, but then it all becomes clear.

This isn't a shared apartment at all.

Jennifer is living here with a man.

A man who calls himself Rocken Roll.

His eye falls on a lace thong lying on the floor, it's practically see-through. His heart skips a beat. Is this the sort of thing his daughter wears now?

Markus jumps at the sound of a key turning in the entrance lock. He steps back into the hallway to see a man enter. The man doesn't seem bothered by the glow of the ceiling lamp. He does, however, seem bothered by Markus.

"What you doing in my apartment, bro?"

A flood of thoughts rushes through Markus's mind. He stares at the man, unable to respond. He keeps staring even as the man grabs a baseball bat from a recess in the hallway. It's only when the man is ready to strike that Markus holds his hands up in self-defense, forgetting the electric toothbrush he's holding in his right hand, which accidentally turns on. The whirring sound it makes is monstrously loud. For a moment time stands still.

Markus fumbles to turn off Jennifer's toothbrush.

"That's cute," the man says, his voice flat.

The guy is bigger than Markus but weedy, dressed in a yellowing band T-shirt and a lined jean jacket. His pants look as battered as he does. A baseball cap covers his straggly hair. Even with his eyes set far apart and an unkempt five o'clock shadow, he has a sort of charisma, he's even handsome in his own way.

"You're going to leave, bro, or you're getting beat. I'm only calling the cops after. You hear me, grandpa?"

Grandpa? Markus may not have all his hair anymore, really just a fringe at this point, but the guy standing in front of him can't be more than ten years younger.

"Listen, I can explain my presence here."

"YOU'RE NOT *EXPLAINING* ANYTHING, BRO! YOU CAN LEAVE THE EASY WAY OR THE HARD WAY, YOU CHOOSE! Hey, wait a second . . ." Rocken Roll, if that's who it is, frowns and squints. "I know you. Before, didn't you . . ."

Markus's breath has caught in his throat. What next?

". . . play in Hardsome? Bass, right? Of course, dude! What's up? I knew you even with the bald patch! I must have seen you guys a thousand times." He lowers the bat to his side with a smile, takes Markus by the arm, and drags him into the living room.

"Man, you guys were the shit . . ." His tone changes, grows dismissive. "When I was still into hardcore, I mean. It's not even my thing anymore. But it's probably not your thing either, by the looks of it, bro."

The ex–hardcore fan lets the bat fall on the couch and plops down next to it, smacking the open seat next to him. Markus remains standing, relieved.

This joker and Jennifer—it's inconceivable.

"Nice threads, bro, you changed lanes, huh? Shit, I can't think of your name. What are you doing here anyway?" He eyes Markus suspiciously. "How'd you even get the key, bro?"

"I'm Jennifer's father. And you?"

The man gulps but quickly recovers. "I'm, uh, Felix, but most people call me Johnny."

Markus can't make out a connection between the two names, not that it matters anyway.

"Jenny didn't say anything about me? Really? Aw, you guys aren't so close after all, huh?"

Markus feels a wave of anger wash over him. He laid the world at his daughter's feet, gave her every opportunity, a future. And what does she do? Trades it all away to live with Rocken Roll Johnny here. That smug smile of his, all the bastard's teeth flashing—what Markus really wants is to bash it off his face.

"I have Jennifer's key. She needs her things, she was taken to the hospital today."

Johnny's smirk doesn't change. "What's the matter? Everything was fine this morning. Accident?"

"You might call it that."

Markus manages to keep calm.

"She collapsed after ingesting drugs. Maybe you know something about that? It's lucky they found her in time."

Johnny doesn't seem to pick up on the innuendo. "Fine, take your time and get her stuff, I've got some stuff to do."

With that, the matter seems settled for Johnny. Markus looks around, his nerves wearing thin. Is he supposed to take

Jennifer's dirty laundry with him just like that? He would only burn it out back in the garden at home anyway. His gaze falls on a flimsy set of shelves with a couple of books. He recognizes one.

"*The Gulag Archipelago*, Solzhenitsyn. Is that your book?"

Johnny pushes himself up off the sofa. "READ, BRO? YOU THINK I'M A HOMO?" He grabs the heavy book and flips it open. "Sorry, dude, I'm not gay. Just ask your daughter, she can attest, if you get what I mean, bro. Ha ha."

Markus understands all too well, and stares silently at Johnny, stunned. Heat courses through him. His hands clench into fists.

"Aw, look at that, there's even a message. *For my*, what does it say? *For my parti* . . . Man, this handwriting sucks."

"*For my partisan*—I wrote that," Markus sputters through clenched teeth. "That was something private between us. She wanted—"

"Aw, what a sweetie." Johnny tosses the book on the table. "Ha ha, Jenny, she's a little grabby, you get me? It's not my fault what happened. I told her she should watch out with the stuff. But she's hardheaded, you know that yourself, right, bro?"

By now everything is completely clear to Markus. It was Johnny who got his daughter drugs. He's a dealer. She's living with a drug dealer who goes by Rocken Roll.

Markus's lower lip begins to tremble visibly. Unmoved, Johnny takes a cigarette between his teeth and holds out the pack to Markus. Markus shakes his head.

"But she'll be back, right?! I mean, otherwise she wouldn't need her toothbrush. Tell me something, bro: Jenny just borrowed a hundred euros from me. You wouldn't have a little cash on you by any chance? I've got a couple things to pay coming up."

Johnny's already lying on the floor before Markus realizes that he's punched the guy. His heart is a drum. His mind flashes. Then, just like that, he has the bat in his hands.

POK

A muffled sound as he makes contact with Johnny's skull. In Markus's head, it sounds like a clock ticking.

POK
POK

Breathing heavily, he comes to himself and looks down at Johnny, who lies there motionless. "Hey, everything all right?" He nudges the guy's leg with his foot, waiting on a sudden attack.

Not a sound from between the blood-smeared lips.

Markus kneels down and holds two fingers to Johnny's neck, just like he's seen them do so often on American TV. There's no pulse. He lays a hand on Johnny's chest. There's no movement. He pounds his fist against Johnny's rib cage, but the dealer just lies there. The shock makes his stomach churn.

Rocken Roll is dead.

Markus flies out of the apartment, down the stairs, and out into the open, where he's met by the cool air of the coming spring. He walks toward his car as calmly as possible, when suddenly he remembers Jennifer's things.

He forgot the bags.

There's a whistling sound in his ears as panic grips. He takes a deep breath and turns around. He looks at the front door and takes the key out of his jacket pocket. He hesitates briefly, then makes his way back up to the apartment.

* * *

Manuelle Herdehügel is just letting her wire-haired dachshund Waxie off the leash when her phone rings. It's her mother.

"Hi, Mom, how goes it? Manuelle, with *elle* at the end, not *ela*, how often do I have to . . . Why? Just get used to it, okay? What? No you're not bothering me, I was just taking Waxie out for a walk."

Her mother launches into one of her tirades, as Manuelle only half listens.

"Yes, Mom, I'm fine. Huh? Yes, I know you're supposed to say, 'Excuse me.' I'm sorry. How are you? What did the doctor say?"

Obviously it hadn't been cancer—it wasn't some malignant lump, just an ingrown hair. Like always. Not that it would assuage her mother's fears in the least. That much Manuelle knew already. As she listens, she turns to watch a man in a dapper camel-hair coat opening the door to her apartment house. Isn't he the same one who just came storming out? She doesn't recognize him. He disappears through the entrance.

And right after him, tail wagging like a whip, her dog darts through the closing door into the hallway.

"Waxie, here! Come here, please!"

It's too late.

"Mom, I'll call you right back, I have to go get the dog. Huh? Sorry, I mean 'excuse me.' I'll call you right back, okay?"

Manuelle hangs up to hurry after the dachshund. With a soft click the door closes right in her face.

"Ah shit!" Manuelle fishes a key out of her handbag and opens the door. "Waxie?" she calls out into the stairwell, tentatively at first, then with greater force: "Come to Mommy!"

Nothing.

With a sigh, she starts climbing the stairs. "Waxie, come here now!"

All the doors on the second floor are closed. Maybe Waxie is already waiting outside her apartment? They had only just left . . .

"Waxie where are you? Bad dog, you're a BAD DOG!"

Manuelle is a little taken aback by the volume of her own voice, when she hears a yapping. Halfway up the stairs she can already see the open door. As if things could get any worse. Out of all people, her dachshund ran off to the sketchy hardcore guy's place?

She hears words being hissed from the apartment: "Out, dog. Get away from there. Scat! Scat!"

The voice doesn't belong to the actual tenant, whose hoarse croaking she knows all too well. The tenant's voice is sleep-deprived, always a little too loud, and always using the same arrogant tone, which obviously changes the minute the police show up. It happens often enough that she has suspected the louse of dealing drugs for a while now. Then there's his girlfriend, who's way too young for him.

At least she still says hi when Manuelle sees her on the stairs, unlike the other visitors to the apartment. Vague figures usually just as run-down as the tenant himself. The man in the camel-hair jacket is of a different caliber. A relative? Maybe the would-be rock star is sick? It would serve him right, what with all the times he ignored the COVID regulations.

"Waxie? Hello?" She stays standing out in front of the door. "Hello? Sorry, I'm sorry about that . . ." Why is she always apologizing? "Waxie, come out of there now!" She pushes the door farther open with two fingers and takes a step over the threshold.

"WAIT OUTSIDE, PLEASE, WOULD YOU?" The voice comes from the living room. "Get out of here, damnit, out!"

Manuelle is wondering whether to put up with what she's hearing when Waxie comes running out to her, tail wagging. She scoops the dog up in relief. "Never do something like that again! Mommy is very mad at you." She glances up in the direction of the voice, and for a second glimpses the face of the man, who immediately disappears back into the room. "Sorry," she calls out, then hurries back downstairs with Waxie. She doesn't let the dog down until they're back outside the building.

The stranger definitely didn't fit in with Rocken Roll. He was too well-groomed, too well-shaven, the thinning hair styled too carefully. And a camel-hair coat?

Mulling it over still, she looks down at Waxie and only notices now that he's holding something in his teeth. White, pink, and . . .

Ecchh! Is that blood? She feels nauseous. It must be something nasty out of the dealer's garbage. She reaches into her purse for a poop bag, crouches down, and removes the object from the dog's mouth, her fingers sheathed in plastic. The thing is harder than she expected.

She tosses the bag into the bushes in disgust and stands back up. Her phone rings. Her mother. She had completely forgotten.

"Hi, Mom, I'm sorry, it took a little while longer. *Elle*, Mom, I already . . . I never really thought Manuela was . . . NO! Manu is even worse, but it's also . . . Huh? Sorry. 'Excuse me'? No, I do care about you . . ."

In the meantime, Waxie has gone off into the bushes, in search of his prize.

* * *

Roger already has some liquid courage in him, though there's plenty of room for improvement.

He's at the Ritze, probably the neighborhood's best known bar, with an even better known boxing ring in the basement. Directly behind the Pink Palace sex house, the place has served as both a training ground for future world champions and a spot for movie stars to sip beer. Countless photos on the walls attest to its popularity, one of the few authentic spots left from a St. Pauli that has long since vanished.

Before he became a regular along Grosse Freiheit, Roger had gone by Rudi. But early on in the job, before they stuck him with some nasty nickname, he had preferred to take the name of his favorite comic book hero from childhood, Buck Rogers.

His glory days might be behind him, but he still commands respect among many of the old-timers for continuing such back-breaking work at seventy-two, even if it's part-time. Today his powers of persuasion mostly serve him to wring a couple of drinks out of people visiting the neighborhood at night. Roger isn't doing so well anymore; times have changed.

"You're a dinosaur, Roger! You're a bully and a racist. It isn't being manly, what you do, much less charming, so get it together or find yourself another job!" That was the choice his Iranian boss had put before him, and Roger had acquiesced, gritting his teeth.

Even so, he keeps losing shifts, and is spending more time in the bars than before. It's the end of his career in the neighborhood. Not that he's looking to moan about it, that was never his style. One way or another, at some point he'll wind up in a pool of 100 percent schnapps at the Elbschlosskeller, or at the Goldener Handschuh around the corner. Tonight, though, he's still a welcome guest at St. Pauli's most legendary club.

It's a Tuesday, not much is happening.

"Good God, just now over on Tal Strasse I saw the most horrible thing, Kitty . . ."

Kitty, whose real name is Gitte, stands behind the bar.

"They're just kids, Kitty, and they're already going around like zombies." Roger's voice lowers at a glance from her. "These friggin' dealers, they're selling drugs cut with who knows what to minors and everyone just watches. Someone should tear them a new one, know what I mean?"

"Roger that, Roger. Change the channel. Another beer and a shot?"

He taps his pants pocket and feels some loose change jingle in reply. "Yup, I can do one more."

He peers over at the elegantly dressed man in a camel-hair coat, who's been sitting at the other end of the bar for a while now. He looks as though he might be good for a couple rounds. He's no tourist, the man wants to drink, maybe forget the world for a bit—Roger has a nose for the type.

Kitty sets down the beer and a shot of liquor and takes his coaster to make a note of it.

Roger stops her. "This one's on him. Friend of mine." He winks at Kitty. "Brand-new friend."

Brows furrowed, Kitty follows Roger's glance and studies the man quietly staring into his beer glass. "Hey, hon, more of the same?" she calls over. "If you can't stay on the level, neither of us have anything to do."

Markus snaps to and clears his throat. "Sure, why not?" His speech is already a little heavy from the drink.

"Do you agree that the world's going to hell, mister?"

Roger has taken the next stool over from Markus and gives him an encouraging look.

Markus is at a total loss.

"Jeez, these cheap drugs are ruining the entire country. What kind of life is it for young people when all they want to do is shoot up and then . . ." Rolling his eyes and letting his tongue hang out of the corner of his mouth, Roger launches into his tried-and-true junkie routine. "'Yu-yu-yu-you got some change, m-m-man. I c-c-c-can't find any wuh-wuh-work.' Hahaha." With a wink, he raises his shot glass to Markus. "Who'll look after our kids if we don't?"

Kitty arrives with a shot and a beer and sets the glasses down in front of Markus. "You'd better get a move on, sugar, your buddy here got a jump start on you."

Roger smirks. "Mmh, a good Pschorr, you only get that here. Hey, I hope it's all right if you cover this round—I'm a little short at the moment."

Markus nods and takes a sip of the booze.

"What's that? Down the hatch, like they say—you have to *take* a shot, you can't just sip it." As if to underscore the point, Roger downs his own.

Markus waves him away with his hand. "I ha—I haven't eaten anything since breakfast."

"Oh! Well, Kitty can help you out there. Kitty, why aren't there any pretzel sticks today?"

Somewhat reluctantly, Kitty sets a rounded glass of pretzel sticks out on the bar. Markus reaches for a couple, then takes more.

"Ey, mister, can I guess where you're coming from? I'm guessing the north, Poppenbüttel, maybe around Sasel. Am I right?"

Markus takes a sip of beer before answering. "Close. Wellingsbüttel." He clears his throat again. "Cheers."

"So I was right? I knew it the minute I saw you sitting here . . . I don't mean to say you're stuck up, just some kind of fancy SOB. I mean that with respect though, right?" Roger's glass knocks against Markus's shot glass. Kitty raises an eyebrow from the bar. "Cheers! I'm Roger—and you?"

All the unsolicited camaraderie immediately reminds Markus of Rocken Roll Johnny, the only difference being that Roger doesn't bug him as much. That might be due to the alcohol. Or maybe the fact that the company is welcome.

As the full scope of his actions dawned on him leaving the apartment for the second time, Markus had been overcome by a desperate need for a drink. It had taken everything in his power to stick Jennifer's possessions in the trunk of his car. Not long after, he had ended up at the Ritze.

"Andreas."

After everything that's happened, Markus isn't drunk enough yet to give his real name. "Roger" must have been given a different name by his mother, too.

He raises his glass and drinks, then turns to the bartender. "Can we get some more pretzels?"

Kitty swaps the empty glass with a full one. "That's the last of them. Everybody share nicely, we're not a buffet."

Roger rolls his eyes and grins at Markus, silently mimicking Kitty. "It's no surprise kids today don't just get good and drunk anymore and want to shoot up instead. It's the rotten bar staff . . . OWHA!"

A wet rag catches Roger right in the face.

For the first time that day, Markus can't help but smile.

Over the next hour, Roger regales Markus with all the glorious and not-so-glorious times he's had in the neighborhood, at the Ritze especially. Back in the day, when all the TVs were still showing pornos, like basketball games at sports bars. Parties and raids that got out of hand, the legendary boxer and pimp Stefan Hentschel's surprise suicide, the first time Vitali and Wladimir Klitschko showed up. And he'd drank with all of them at least once—Maske, Michalczewski, Horst Frank, Elke Sommer, Udo Lindenberg of course.

All of a sudden Roger falls serious. "So wha's the matter with you anyway? You didn't look so happy before."

Five beers and just as many shots have done quite a number on Markus. The question gets to him more than he would have wished. "Muh-my daughter's in the hospital," he manages. "Drug overdose. It's a mess, I don't feel like shellebrating."

"An overdose? Really. Gohhhhd . . . I'm sorry. I'm telling you, these dealers are ruining this beautiful world. 'NOTHER ROUND!"

"Not for me . . ."

"NONSHENSE, what you need now is a pick-me-up."

Kitty fills the shot glasses and takes Roger's empty beer glass, then fixes an eye on Markus's nearly untouched glass. He grabs it and downs half of it, then hands it to her.

"There you go."

"I-I'll take another fresh one."

"Your daughter, huh? So how old'shee?" Roger asks.

"Sh-she's twenty-three."

"Disgusting. If I got my hands on one of those bastards, I'd give him his own dope then chain him to a radiator, take a beer, and just watch as h-he croaked on the shit. I'd do it, believe me. And you know what? The cops, they wouldn't give a rat'sh ass. They'd be happy about it. I'm telling you. Less work and a bleshing for everyone."

Roger's big talk suddenly leaves Markus thinking clearly. He had pushed all notions of the police out of his mind. How could he be so stupid? He looks over at Roger doubtfully. "But dealers are dangerous," he says slowly. "Don't they have guns and stuff like that?"

"Nonshense," Roger waves him away. "What are they going to have? A kitchen knife? Gas pistols? Maybe a baseball bat? You can take those away, no problem. Think they're all big gangsters and then they stand there holding a chair leg? No, not when Roger's there, I'm telling you."

Markus is barely listening. His mind is whirling about like a carousel. What would someone like Roger have to lose anyway? But Markus—his entire life, a daughter, his Jennifer. Through the fog of the alcohol, the outlines of a plan begin to emerge. "What would you say," he asks, "if I had taken one of them out?"

Roger's forehead scrunches up. "You *what*, mister?"

"The guy who gave my daughter the stuff—I killed him. A little over an hour ago."

Roger motions for Markus to speak more quietly, lowering his own voice. "You offed a dealer? You? You in your fancy-schmancy getup, you axed one of those bastards? Is that what you're telling me?"

"It was easy."

"You're not kidding, are you?"

"Not if that's what I'm telling you." Markus suddenly gets annoyed with Roger's questions. It's time to act. "You want to see him? We can go there right now. I still have the key. It's around the corner."

"You bet I want to see that. We can just settle up and then you'll show me the dead roach. *That* I would like to see. KITTY, THE MAN HERE WANTS TO PAY!"

Markus and Roger have been standing behind a tree for ten

minutes now, about fifty yards away from the door to the apartment building where Rocken Roll made his final entrance. Roger pees while Markus watches the windows. He's waiting for the lights to go out. He has to be sure nobody sees them. That woman with the dachshund was quite enough.

Each has a bottle of Astra that they bought at the St. Pauli kiosk, along with a couple of chocolate bars. Roger's idea. They hadn't drawn any notice among the crowd of youngsters hanging around near the shop. With the chocolate bars, Markus's situation has become somewhat clearer to him, and doubts have crept in. Should he really return to the scene of the crime? How well can that really turn out? With some drunk he barely knows?

But it's too late. Roger's excitement and a little hip flask of Stroh rum are standing in the way of any change in plan.

"Let's go, my dick's growing icicles. Or were you shitting me?"

"Enough!" Markus barks.

"Then let's go!"

"Almost looks like he's taking a snooze." Roger stares at Johnny's body, transfixed.

All of a sudden, Markus has a splitting headache.

Roger crouches down. "Man, just a regular guy—why would someone like him deal? I don't get it. It checks out if the darkies or Chinese or whoever else sell their stuff here. They don't know any better, it's in their blood. They hate our country. But a German—he shouldn't be doing shit like this. I really don't get it. Do you?"

Markus takes a deep breath. "My daughter is lying in the hospital because of this creep. Does it even matter what color his skin is?"

"Hey, mister, take it easy, you can see the ass-clown had it coming. He wen' after your daughter and now he's lying here. Who'll look after our women if *we* don't?" Roger's face lights up. "You mind if I take a selfie, Andreas?"

Markus is disgusted. With Roger. With Rocken Roll. With the entire situation. And maybe most of all with himself. What has he ever really done for his daughter? It makes it all the more important not to mess this up now. He has to be there entirely for his Jennifer. It's his responsibility.

Who'll look after our women if *we* don't?

Roger's right.

Markus eyes the baseball bat, still lying next to the body.

"Hey, a photo? It's all right, right?"

Markus nods. His anger has passed, and he's completely calm now. Cold.

"Awesome!"

Thrilled by the prospect of taking a photo with a dead body, Roger cheers and goes at it, then inspects the picture on his phone before immediately taking several more.

"Ewwww! The retard doesn't have any front teeth in his trap, you saw that? Your daughter kissed this guy? Man is this place a dump."

POK

The blow meets its target with surprising accuracy.

POK

The second falls just as squarely on the back of Roger's head. Unable to speak, a questioning look scrawled across his face, the guy collapses to the floor.

Markus studies the situation with fascination. Who would have though it would be so easy? He wipes the handle of the bat clean with a T-shirt off the floor, then takes Roger's phone and places the bat in his victim's hands. The camera app is still open. Roger's breath is rising and falling. Blood seeps out of the back of his head, but he's still alive. *Unconscious*, Markus thinks, *that's enough. It's even better that way.*

He looks through the photos, erasing the two where he's partially visible, considers for a second, then erases the rest. He sticks the phone into the back pocket of Roger's jeans.

Then he searches Johnny's pants and finds his phone. The home screen has a picture of Jennifer. With Johnny.

Jenny and Johnny. The alliteration is almost enough to make him laugh. Instantly, the pounding in his temples returns.

The telephone has a touch ID set up. Markus opens it with the help of Johnny's middle finger. Of course it's his middle finger. Pathetic.

He looks through the photos.

Roger moans softly. Markus waits. The moan dies off. Quiet again.

He keeps scrolling, and finds a couple dozen with Jennifer. He deletes those and opens the phone's message app. He finds the thread between Johnny and his daughter, which he also deletes without reading.

"Filthy piece of shit," he mumbles to himself, and dials the number for the police. As he's listening to it ring, he spies a speck of blood on one of his pant cuffs. By now his entire head is one constant throbbing.

"*You have reached the emergency number for the Hamburg Police*—" The recorded message cuts off, and the voice of the officer on duty comes through: "Police. What is the reason for your call?"

Markus gulps, but keeps his voice calm. "Hello, please come quickly, there's a man here threatening me."

"Give me your address and name."

Markus doesn't know the name, and definitely doesn't want to say "Rocken Roll." With the call still going, he throws the phone onto an armchair and knocks the furniture about, simulating a struggle. As he's doing so, he realizes that he's never been in a real fight before. He take his Astra bottle and smashes it over Roger's head with all his might.

"Hello? Hello?" the voice calls out through the phone.

It won't take long for the police to figure out the address. When they do arrive, they'll find two men: one wounded, one dead. After he comes to, Roger won't have anything except a dubious yarn about Andreas from the Ritze. He had said it himself: the police won't spend much time investigating the case.

Better you than me, pal, Markus thinks to himself. *Any way you look at it, everyone got what they deserved.*

He leans over Johnny again; the guy's mouth does actually look somewhat slack. Rocken Roll really is missing his front teeth. Had Markus hit him that hard?

He squints, surveying the room, then hears the sound of police sirens approaching in the distance. High time to get going.

He opens the door and recoils.

Three police officers stand in the doorway, next to the dog owner from that afternoon.

"Is this the man?" asks the lead officer.

"Yes," the woman replies.

A second officer clasps Markus's left arm and places a handcuff on him.

The third pushes past into the apartment. "Holy shit!"

she calls out. "We've got two males, one is 107. The other I'm not sure."

The second handcuff closes around Markus's right wrist.

"We've got *what?*" the officer before him asks.

A noise from below. Markus lowers his gaze. The dachshund pants at him inquisitively. Markus stares down at the dog, then up at the officer, who is holding a clear plastic bag in her hand.

In the bag is a set of dentures covered in blood.

Four incisors.

Markus looks back down at the dog, then at the dog owner, and finally at the officer, who nervously reaches for her gun.

Out of nowhere, a thought occurs. "Do you think he would take those out before he slept with my daughter?" he asks, and starts to laugh.

"NICE CHOMPERS YOU'VE GOT THERE!" Waxie barks at the laughing man. "GIVE THEM TO ME!"

CRAZY ANGELS

BY JASMIN RAMADAN
Eimsbüttel

Translated by Noah Harley

It was Nour's first time in Europe, her first time ever out of the country for that matter, all the way north on a new continent. Her mother's only words of advice on parting had been to be respectful, and to honor those who take you in.

For her own part, Nour had learned that what really mattered most in life was not to act falsely, and not to disappoint anyone.

She had felt a pang of guilt on the way to the landing strip. Yet as the plane doors closed, her perception began to shift the colors, and as the flight progressed they even sparkled slightly—a trick of the eye, but still there.

The man who was going to put a roof over her head had spent all of December on an island called Sylt, not far from the city.

While he was gone, he'd made his apartment available to a foundation supporting female artists who suffered political persecution. That's what it said in the email that had arrived just a few days before.

Nour would be able to stay in the apartment until the water damage to the foundation's housing had been repaired.

She hadn't told her mother the reason why she'd received the stipend, because her mother didn't know that Nour was a political target. Nour's mother already considered her daughter's painting an unbecoming occupation for a woman. But a little supervised self-expression might make a more satisfied wife out of Nour yet. Her mother had no idea about the large-scale images of naked, faceless men and women in chains with which Nour had applied for the stipend. She didn't know either that it was Nour herself who was the reason for *everything*. The trip was nothing less than a way of preparing to leave home forever.

She had landed in Hamburg on Sunday afternoon; a man holding a large sign with her name on it picked her up at the terminal.

The air felt cold, though in a pleasant sort of way, and the light was murky, hanging there limply under already illuminated streetlamps that stretched the entire course of the ride. As they drove on, the thrill of travel gave way to a light fatigue, the melancholy cityscape outside the window gently reflecting her own mental state.

Nour could feel the distance from home in her bones, even as it dawned on her with a flutter of happiness that she had now arrived in a European harbor. As a teenager, she had often dreamed of living in a place where morality was something flexible, where at any moment you could climb aboard a ship, stow yourself in a corner, and steal away to some unknown destination decided by fate.

Now she was being driven across a city as though she were someone whose longings mattered. Nour raised herself in her seat to ask the driver if they could head along the harbor and through the forbidden part of town. He laughed out loud, replying that nothing here was really forbidden, and that it would be a lovely detour toward St. Pauli. She definitely didn't want to take another detour, she replied without thinking.

The driver asked where Nour came from; his English was halting, but after a six-month intensive in Khartoum, Nour's German was solidly intermediate.

The driver happily recounted his own arrival in Hamburg twenty years earlier. Like her, he had arrived from Istanbul, though it hadn't been a stopover but his point of departure. He explained to her that her name was Aynour in Turkish and meant *moonlight*. He was sorry that he didn't know the equivalent in German.

When they reached the apartment building, Nour climbed out of the car, limbs aching, while the driver lugged her father's old leather suitcase over to the door. He wished her all the best, and they parted with a firm handshake.

Nour took a long stretch as he drove off. An exotic sort of silence descended, giving her a cold shiver as the milky fog seemed to soak up the coming darkness. With a feeling of fear that she didn't shy away from, and without understanding the meaning behind it, Nour realized suddenly that there was a reason for being exactly where she was.

She searched out the name *Cranz* on the nameplate by the light of her phone. As she pressed the button and the buzzer sounded, an uneasy feeling passed through her, a first wave of homesickness and love for her mother, father, her siblings, even her annoying cousin. Then came the familiar sense of numbness that she had experienced the first time she'd read about the year-long stipend on the Internet. She had pushed the feeling away each time it surfaced over the past few months, and did the same now.

Ms. Cranz seemed to live all by herself on the ground floor. Wearing a blue wool dress and mother-of-pearl lipstick, she gave Nour the key with a trembling hand. Then, signaling upward with her index finger, she tried a couple times before managing a faint "Welcome, young lady," with a smile.

Three floors farther up into the unknown building, Nour leaned against the wall in exhaustion. The light switch just inside the apartment entrance was broken. Soon the stairwell light reaching in through the milky-glass panels on the tall, old wooden door went out too, leaving her in total darkness.

It took Nour several minutes feeling her way around the dark hall before she finally got hold of a standing lamp, and located the switch halfway down the cable.

She only half remembered what part of town the apartment was in, Büddel or something like that. The driver had repeated the name of the neighborhood when she showed him the iPhone screenshot of the email with the address.

"It's easy to get lost in a big city in a foreign country without anyone noticing, even yourself," her brother had insisted loudly after driving her to the airport. Then he had grabbed her phone and taken a series of screenshots of the address in Büddel and sent one to the entire family. She was already missing her brother, even his overbearing concern.

Originally it was Ms. Klausen from the foundation who was supposed to pick up Nour from the airport and take care of everything, a fact that had helped to calm Nour's mother's nerves a little. At thirty-one, Nour was still living at home, as was common in Sudan as long as one didn't have a family of one's own. Now, standing under the floor lamp in the long hallway of an apartment in Büddel, it was as if a spotlight were being cast on her own shame.

At the gate in Istanbul, Nour had learned that a severe case of type-B influenza would prevent Ms. Klausen from picking up Nour and looking after her. Nour hadn't mentioned that to her mother in the endless stream of texts, nor that it meant there wouldn't be anybody on call, as it were, during the upcoming holiday season, and that she would be left to her own devices for the time being.

Ever since Nour had turned on the light, the apartment had taken on an oddly strong smell of licorice. Cork bulletin boards lined the hallway, covered in photos and postcards stuck up haphazardly with pins and thumbtacks. Every last picture showed the same two people, a man and a woman. They were older in some, maybe mid- to late fifties, younger in others, in some even younger—those were largely faded and perforated with small holes, as though they had been taken down and put back up repeatedly.

Three large, unwieldy sets of drawers further crowded the hall; lamps and cables sprouted out from everywhere. The bureaus held colored bowls filled with costume jewelry, marbles, all manner of little objects, and were surrounded by small figures made of glass, ceramic, and plastic, mostly owls and penguins. Written notes covered what little free space remained.

Out of respect and a vague sense of fear, Nour didn't read any of the notes, but continued hunting for lamps throughout the other rooms instead, to orient herself and get a sense of where she had landed.

Unlike every room back at home, there wasn't a single overhead lamp in the apartment. All she could find was indirect lighting, including strings of little bulbs scattered throughout nearly every corner of the house. When Nour turned on the final light source, she found herself back amid the jumbled life of a couple, mountains of memories stacked up in the form of unnecessary furniture and other junk. Even so, the chaos—which held no relation to Nour's image of an average German apartment, and which her mother would have whirled through, dervish-like, to clean instantly—had an ambience to it, and the sense of coziness calmed her. She was in a home. Nour fell asleep almost instantly, still in her clothes, on top of a mustard corduroy bedspread covering the large double bed.

She woke up in the middle of the night, the smell of licorice penetrating her consciousness more strongly than before. Shuffling into the kitchen still half-asleep, she found the giant electric kettle next to the sink hissing with boiling water, the licorice smell blending with calcium carbonate and overheated plastic. She quickly yanked the plug. Like everything else in the apartment, the kettle looked old, though not old-fashioned. The automatic shut-off no longer worked, and the temperature gauge hadn't registered.

She pushed open a yellow-tinged balcony door and stepped outside, took a deep breath in, and let it out. A coarse woven mat hung over the small balcony, which had a net stretching out over it that she couldn't find any explanation for. Pressing her face against the net, she looked down onto the lonely street, where a traffic light kept switching to green though no one crossed. Below was a small square with four streets branching out; one was covered in cobblestones so that a car rumbling past would mercifully drown out the absence of people.

The light had turned green for a fifth time as Nour slowly sank into a meditative state, when a phone rang in the depths of the apartment, its shrill, piercing sound like in one of the old films she had watched in a script seminar at the Goethe Institute in Khartoum.

The landline stood on one of the sets of drawers; she had

noticed it before but taken it for decoration. It was an orange rotary phone attached to a cable that shuttered every time it rang. She lifted the heavy earpiece up off the receiver; it felt as though it were covered in a layer of wax.

"Hallo," she whispered.

"Nour?"

"Yes."

"Jens Dierks. It's my apartment you're in."

"Good evening, Mr. Dierks."

"Did I startle you?"

"Yes."

"The list is with my luggage."

"The list?"

"All the notes are there."

"Notes for what?"

"Everything you need to know."

"Can you send a photo of the list?"

"No, I don't have that kind of phone, the sort of . . . thing where everything is."

"I'm surprised to hear that. Why not?"

"Out of principle, Nour. Just because something is new doesn't mean it's good."

"That's what my mother is always saying."

"Your mother is an intelligent woman."

"What do I have to know?"

"What do you *want* to know?"

"Why does it smell like licorice, and why does the kettle turn on by itself?"

"My wife Luzia, she liked drinking tea with licorice in it, happiness tea, women's-liberation tea, she liked that sort of thing. She's been gone over a year now, disappeared on St. Nicholas Eve. The police say she left me."

"Did she?"

"She got more beautiful as she got older, while I only got older, and then she wanted to visit other continents, be free, be herself. She read one book after the other, wanted to open up our relationship, that kind of thing."

"Is she dead?"

"The smell is everywhere, of her tea I mean—she's still heating up her water, her spirit has some strange power."

"Lovers never say goodbye forever," replied Nour.

She listened as he cried, then fell silent and finally said: "Do you have any more questions, Nour? My grief saps all my energy."

"Where is everybody?"

"You'll find a few at Crazy Angels."

"Crazy Angels?"

"Luzia's *Kneipe*. She had a sympathetic audience there."

"*Kneipe*? Is that like a bar?"

"Sort of. People are always there, talking about everything and nothing."

"It sounds like being at home with family. Where is it?"

"If you go out on the balcony, look around the corner to your left and you'll see a red light shining down below."

"I can't, there's a sort of net there."

"Just take it down and throw it out."

"Why was it put there?"

"For our cat Wiebke, so she wouldn't jump down. She's long gone, but I didn't want to take the net down, I couldn't."

"Why not?"

"I'm hanging up now, Nour, I need to sleep. Look after yourself."

Nour walked through the kitchen and pushed the door open to the small balcony, where a surprisingly warm wind enveloped her. The balcony had a little plastic table with a crystal ashtray; there were no chairs or any trace of ashes. Nour rolled herself a cigarette and set it down in the ashtray. She carefully undid the net from the hooks on the wall and folded it as her mother would have, then stored it away in her shoulder bag in the bedroom.

Back on the balcony, she lit the cigarette and peered around the corner. There was the light, a red and violet glow pulsing out of the corner windows. Above one, a brightly lit sign flashed *Crazy Angels* in blue and red lettering.

Nour could make out laughter, German music, heard the words *Liebe* and *Schmerz*, love and pain, repeated over and over again. It was the same everywhere—people differed only in how well they bore pain and how well they sorted through it.

That's what Nour's father was always saying, you have to sort through your pain and it would lose its dread; you could make the pain your own if you only sorted through it in the right way.

Nour thought about Luzia, saw her perched upright on the barstool, forever with the same drink and twelve cigarette stubs in the ashtray, each lit twenty minutes after the last, night after night, instead of leaving Jens; saw how at the exact moment when it had again become bearable for the great love of her life to be ending, she went home, poured herself one of those teas with the auspicious names, and drank it out on the balcony while smoking her thirteenth and final cigarette of the day before crushing it out in the crystal ashtray. Then she'd lie down beside Jens and, if he woke up, dissuade him with the same two words as always: *Not now.*

Nour sensed a longing that wasn't her own and saw the face of a plump, orange cat with a steady, trusting gaze, heard its low purr. She had seen the picture of the cat Wiebke in the corridor, framed by golden tendrils. But the longing, the longing was real—and it was unfamiliar. It didn't belong to her own life, at least not yet, though maybe it belonged here.

Nour showered; the water didn't heat up properly and the pressure was low, water leaked from a hole in the shower cable, weakening the jet, and it smelled metallic. Yet the shower gel, Luzia's, still smelled of vanilla and bergamot.

It was Luzia's longing that drove Nour out into the night, into a bar of drunken people. Things blurred more and more in Nour's mind or heart, or in the whirring in between them that linked everything, paired with a strong desire to drink, even though Nour hadn't so much as tried a single sip of alcohol before.

Nour searched herself for Luzia's love for Jens but found only a tired memory, that and the image of a tube of dark-red lipstick, which was in fact lying in the bathroom cupboard. She inspected the worn surface, closed her eyes, and felt Luzia's lips as she brought the makeup to her own.

In the bedroom, another splintery bureau held a drawer full of nylon stockings. Nour slipped a pair of Luzia's fishnet tights under her own army pants, then put on her black lace-ups.

Right as Nour started to cross at the green light, a taxi shot out of nowhere, hitting her like a speeding bullet. But it kept going, passing straight through her as though she were a ghost herself. The taxi seemed to pixelate, then burst apart as she watched. The commotion left a hissing sound in the air, and Nour heard women's laughter from all around. For a few moments the cool night air shimmered bloodred. Then it was as still as before, not a soul so much as cracking a window or stepping onto one of the balconies of the surrounding art nouveau houses.

Trembling, Nour ran to the pub as fast as her weak knees

could carry her. A large sign stood blinking in the window: *A cozy smoker's bar in Eimsbüttel.*

"Moin!" a large platinum-blonde called out from behind the bar. Nour froze in the doorway, watching everyone's eyes turn toward her.

"And where are *you* from?" asked an older man as the tall bartender turned the music down.

"You can't ask that kind of question anymore, Modesto!" said the woman next to him.

"Why's that, Ebba? I'm not from here myself originally."

"Ah, come off it!"

"I lived in Andalusia for three months."

"Good evening," Nour said. "I'm from Sudan. I arrived today."

"Welcome to Eimsbüttel!" the woman behind the bar answered. "I'm Rixa, that's Ebba and Modesto, and that one there, the quiet guy, that's Helmut. What'cha drinking?" She turned the music back up.

Nour sat down at the bar. "I'll drink what Luzia drank."

"Where do you know Luzia from?"

"I didn't know her, but I'm living at her place."

"Luzia," Modesto mumbled, seemingly lost in a memory. "For the fascination of wickedness obscures what is good—"

"Shut your trap," Ebba cut him off. "Nobody knows whether she just up and left. Nobody knows anything!"

"You're living with Jens?" Rixa asked.

"No, Jens is away, he opened up his apartment. I'm here on a stipend."

"Luzia always took a shot and a beer, a blond wheat beer and a Kümmel."

"Then I'll take the same," said Nour.

"What kind of a stipend is it?" asked Ebba.

"A stipend for female artists experiencing political persecution."

"And why?"

"Because I don't want to marry a man."

"They put you in jail there if you don't want to get married?"

"No, but they do if you'd rather marry a woman."

"I'd like to give Sean Connery a kiss one of these days," Modesto said.

"He's dead!"

"Even so."

Rixa served Nour the drinks. "*Prost.*"

Nour drank the Kümmel first, which was sweet and goopy, and tasted a little like herbs that she knew from home. She took a sip of her beer, then drank up half of it and asked, "Where's the bathroom?"

"'Round the corner and down the stairs, but don't use the one on the left, something's been wrong with it for a while now."

Nour stood in the small, dimly lit antechamber facing two stalls, trying to remember whether Rixa had said left or right.

The alcohol had gone to her head, and a sense of well-being stole over her. The unfamiliar rush was welcome, like dancing on a tightrope above an abyss and by some miracle not falling off, unlike in the recurring dream she had been having for the past couple years.

Needing to go so badly that she could hardly think, she simply chose one of the two stalls. At first glance things seemed normal.

But when Nour opened the door back up, the small room was bathed in greenish-yellow light and the air was so humid it felt almost tropical. It smelled of moss and mold, but also of bergamot, or orange zest.

Nour moved quickly through the damp air to get back to the bar. Everybody was gone, but there at the counter, as transparent as a holograph, sat Luzia, watching Nour with a sad smile. The room was overgrown with huge plants that Nour didn't recognize. Crooked branches drooped down low, as though wilted, yet enchantingly beautiful.

"Where am I?" asked Nour, then quickly corrected herself: "Where are we?"

Luzia took a drag of her cigarette, and as Nour watched the smoke slip down through her shimmering transparent image, she replied: "In between."

"What kind of trees are those?"

"They're weighed down with grief, they always have been, though we were happy among them." Luzia exhaled and a bird emerged out of the smoke, a duck that shook its feathers and waddled across the bar before dissolving, leaving only a few large drops of moisture behind.

"What happened?" Nour asked.

"He wanted to take me out dancing."

"Jens?"

Luzia shook her head. "I never wanted to stop dancing. If you're always sad, you don't dance—dancing makes everything stronger, just like drinking."

"Did you go out dancing last year on St. Nicholas Eve?"

"I didn't—I'm married to Jens after all. I went with Jens, like always. But then . . . I wanted to go, to be alone, for me. All Stefan did was remind me of who I was *before*, who I still might be. You do understand that I wanted to leave?"

"Yes, very well."

Tears streamed from Luzia's eyes, more and more until they filled the room and her figure melted away. A torrent sprang up and Nour was swept back toward the bathrooms.

She kicked and fought her way out of the current, barely managing to reach a door and close it behind her before the water could slam it shut. Inside, she continued to struggle against the water, but soon the roar softened, then fell silent. A moment later the music from the bar returned, a man warbling, "*The devil he made booze for us so we would go to rot / You can hear the devil laugh when we take a shot.*"

When she heard Ebba's hoarse laugh, she opened the door and went back into the bar. Everything was as it had been, just more crowded.

Exhausted, Nour plopped herself down on the last free barstool. "I had a vision," she announced. "I was here, everyone else was gone except for Luzia—she was sitting right here where I am."

Ebba approached. "Luzia? Did she mention three men?"

"No, just one."

"There were three of those idiots, definitely from Eppendorf! We always get that type at the end of the year; they have their Christmas parties in some fancy place then come here and drink till the lights come on. They stare at us the whole time like we're animals at the zoo and think we don't notice. We're zombies for them, sloppy, drunk zombies."

"Ah, come off it, Ebba, they tipped well," Rixa said.

"Luzia went with them!" Modesto interjected.

Helmut, silent up to this point, suddenly rose and drew up to Nour: "She told me about him once, about Stefan."

Rixa folded her arms. "What'd she tell you?"

"I've kept myself out of everything since 1999. That's why I've spent every single day here—I don't want to have anything to do with anything, everything can just stay the way it is and that'll be fine, I thought, but now Luzia is gone and nothing is how it was."

Ebba shook her head. "Ach, Luzia took a turn for the worse. She thought she was better than all that and went along with them."

Helmut searched for words. "Dull, it was a dull, overcast night, but it was dry, warm for December. And that's when she met back up with Stefan—he'd made something of himself."

Nour said, "There were these trees with low-hanging branches everywhere, they were beautiful."

"Weeping willows," Ebba responded, taking a deep drag off her cigarette.

Nour put the two words into her phone. "Yes, that's exactly what they looked like. Where are they?"

"Down the street, right by here."

"Is there a lake there too?"

"Well, there's the pond—the willow trees are all around it."

"We have to go there, you have to help me, you have to come with me. I think her body is there somewhere."

Everyone winced. "But we never leave," Helmut said. "We don't go past the PENNY store up the street."

"We don't even go to the doctor when we have to," Ebba agreed.

"We're always here," Modesto chimed in. "Whatever happens, it only happens *here*!"

Rixa set up a row of shot glasses and filled them with Kümmel. "There aren't any bodies in the pond; nothing will sink there, it's not even six feet deep, and it's not like you could bury anything there either—it would stick out like a sore thumb. It's all neat and tidy and the neighbors fuss over it, they know every last patch of grass. Families go there with their kids, the same dogs are always running around, some harmless teens from the neighborhood might smoke weed at night—but no one's being murdered around the pond, or drowned or buried."

"So why then?" Nour asked.

Helmut spoke up: "The pond meant something to Luzia—you have to listen for what things mean to people in order to understand."

"Jens knew everything about her."

"Not everything," Helmut said.

"I have to go!" Nour suddenly declared.

"I'll hold onto your tab," Rixa said.

Nour ran out, crossing at the red light, and raced up the stairs into the apartment.

She had left all the lights on, and knowing all she did now, her gaze fell on the second of the heavy chests standing in the long corridor. The smell of licorice assaulted her even more strongly than before, as her attention lingered on something that had already struck her as strange, but she hadn't inspected very closely.

A cable led out of the chest, ending in a plug at the socket. Nour felt her heart pounding as she approached the chest and the licorice smell grew more intense. She paused for a moment in front of the long corkboard, and her eyes fell on a photo hanging directly in the middle: There were the trees, the weeping willows, and beneath them stood Luzia, young and beaming. She was holding her hand up to the camera, and a ring sparkled on one of her fingers.

The phone rang and Nour picked up. "You proposed to her at the pond."

"Yes," said Jens.

"I'm going to open up the chest now."

"Yes," said Jens.

Nour set the receiver aside and slowly lifted the lid to the old wooden chest. Inside, she found another chest, an electric one, like the kind her mother used to keep ice cream for the neighborhood kids. She lifted the second lid and found nothing but empty tea bags. Jens had opened them all and scattered them over Luzia. Nour closed the electric chest and then the wooden lid, went back to the phone, and picked up the receiver.

"Is that how it is?" she asked. "Do you have to die if you want to leave?"

THE OUTER FACADE

Winterhude

Translated by Noah Harley

H e stood at the crib, watching his son. The baby lay sleeping, eyes closed, little hands balled up into fists. He seemed to be sleeping soundly now, after what had been a horrible night. His wife lay on her side of the bed by the window, legs drawn up against her body. She was exhausted and snoring lightly. Hoping she would get a moment's rest from the little one, he went to pee. He washed and dressed in a hurry, then filled the coffee machine and flipped it on. There on the kitchen table was the shopping list his wife had written before going to bed. He glanced over it and tucked it away. He lit a first cigarette at the open window, sipping at black, unsweetened coffee. Outside it was gradually growing bright. A noisy chorus streamed in from Wandsbeker Chausee, a central artery that was pure hell 24/7. Hotshots and gridlock, frenzied honking, and always an accident right outside their doorstep. A two-bedroom apartment with a kitchen and bath, married life with an eight-month-old in a little over four hundred square feet—it wasn't exactly fun, but it was what it was. They were there for the long haul—last stop.

Work was starting an hour earlier than usual that morning; his company had been hired to set up scaffolding outside an old apartment building in an inner courtyard in Winterhude. They wanted to fix up the outer facade of the building and repaint it. They were working on something there— everything was done up all nice and clean with greenery in the windows. The masons and painters were hoping to get going before lunch. He was one of four setting up the structure; his team had worked together for a long time and got along.

He was there on time and went around with handshakes and slaps on the back, putting on a smile though he felt like hell from the night before. The scream, the child's scream piercing through again and again, the stamina, the force of it was unbelievable. And on top of that his wife's sharp nagging—the whole thing was a horror show. The company truck rumbled up and they unloaded quickly, navigating the steel rods through the low, narrow corridors of the basement to the house on Fleming Strasse and out into the courtyard.

She was woken up by the work noises coming from beneath her window. It was hardly eight—an imposition, if you asked her. Her husband didn't stir. He lay on his belly half-naked with only his wristwatch visible, a fortune just for show. She got up, grabbed her smartphone, and pulled on her bathrobe. In the kitchen she started up the espresso machine and poured herself a glass of orange juice, then sat down in their eating nook and scrolled through her messages. One she replied to: *See you later*. That was enough. Another half hour passed before her husband came in and joined her at the breakfast table, set by now, his hands raised in a gesture of appeasement.

"I heard, I heard, we don't have to talk about it. It's happening."

"We have to make a decision, decide together."

"Just not at breakfast, please." He sliced into a warm roll, scattering crumbs. "I have an appointment in Nordheide today, renovations to that old barn. The people are really nice—they might invite me to eat with them afterward."

"You're back when you're back," she said.

He sighed. "Listen, there's nothing pressing to worry about with the apartment, not a thing. But we'll obviously think something up. Haven't I been saying that this whole time?"

"Do you want a cappuccino?"

"Jesus!" He dropped the roll, slammed the knife down, and fished a pack of cigarettes out of his shirt pocket.

She rose and went over to the window, opening it wide.

Workers calling to each other, the clank of metal on metal, and heavy footsteps grew audible.

He got up too, tucking his cigarettes away, and left the kitchen without a word. Leaning against the windowsill, she tilted her head back and took a deep breath.

A woman on the third floor waved to him and asked whether she could bring him anything, maybe a lemonade, it was so hot out already. He went over to a spot below her window and thanked her, motioning the others to hold up for a second. The woman handed him glasses and told him how long she had been living in the building, continuing to even after her husband died and the apartment had grown too large for her. Four, actually it was five rooms—she would have liked to take in some refugees, a mother and child ideally. Other people in the building were against it, though, they had made that clear enough, and she didn't have the strength to fight it anymore. They shook their heads. There were people out there who just made you want to punch them. They nodded grimly, but that was all—there was still work to do.

It came as he was going over their work, the moment landing like a blow. From the corner of his eye he caught something moving behind a set of balcony doors on the fifth floor, a bright flash and then a woman's body, naked except for her panties. Her back was to him, arms lifted, hands tousling her thick, curly hair—then she turned around, and he froze.

She was gorgeous.

She was unspeakably gorgeous.

He had never seen a woman that beautiful, not even in a movie.

She seemed to come from a different planet.

He stood at the window, as if in a trance.

Later, with the crew getting ready to leave, his gaze darted back up to the fifth floor. Venetian blinds had been lowered, gleaming silver. Somewhere behind it the woman lay, hidden.

Panting, they broke off from one another, stretching out and wiping their sweaty bodies off with the sheets. It was early afternoon and the temperature had climbed into the mideighties. The older man smiled. They lay next to each other for a while in silence.

"It's nice with you," he said finally, "it's always something new." He felt for her hand. She gave it to him and he pressed it to his lips. She closed her eyes at first, but then sat up, running her hand through her hair and reaching for her cigarettes.

"I've got a problem," she said.

"Oh?"

"Our building is being renovated and they want to convert it to owner-occupied units. Work started today. They offered to let us buy the apartment—it's a reasonable price and I'm convinced we can do it with the bank's help, but I don't think Jorg wants to. He keeps putting it off, anyway."

The man pulled himself up too and grabbed his rimless glasses from a side table. "Reason being?"

"I think he's looking for something out in the country. I can't stand the thought—never."

"You *think* he is?"

"Actually, I'm sure of it. Then he'll want to divorce me."

"Okay, okay," the man wagged his head slightly, "easy now, honey. Why would he want a divorce?"

"So he can live out his country fantasy unfettered and crawl into bed with some other chick. He's probably doing it already." The words burst out of her. "I hate him, I could kill him."

The older man laid his hand on her shoulder. "Kathrin, that's nonsense, don't get yourself all riled up."

He didn't realize he had forgotten the shopping until he was opening the door to his building. *Damnit*, he said to himself, heading back out. The supermarket aisles were choked with people and there was only one register open, with two kids messing around behind him in line. He was tempted to give one a smack. He was furious with himself.

His wife was busy with the kid when he got back. He kissed her on the cheek and wiggled his index finger at his son, brightening for a second at the gurgling laughter. At least there was that. He put the groceries away, stuck the beer in the freezer, and made for the bathroom. In the shower he went back and forth between hot and cold until he was out of breath, then shaved for the first time in days. He hadn't really lost any of his youthful drive, he thought to himself, leaning in closer to the mirror and seeing the woman, the gorgeous woman from the fifth floor in the old apartment building, her delicately carved face, those wide, blue-gray eyes full of desire as she beckoned him in, handing him a tall fluted glass, a cold drink—lemonade—it was hot, too hot, the city lay under a fiery blanket of heat as they sat down next to each other on a bright corduroy couch, everything in the room bright, gleaming so whitely that it hurt and he had to lower his head, burying his face in her lap between her thighs, which were bare and cooled him; he heard a distant humming sound, someone singing quietly. It was his wife's voice coming from the kitchen. He heard dishes clattering and she called out, asking what was taking him so long in the bathroom. She had made chicken salad and the news was already on.

Later on they sat in front of the TV, he with legs splayed, beer in hand, staring out blankly in front of him. She sat legs propped up, flipping through a magazine, looking up from time to time at the screen to comment about the German expats who spoke about their life in Mallorca or wherever else, that they didn't have it all that easy, either. The sky grew dark; the beams from passing cars flooded the room with light, the screech of their brakes piercing his ears like hot irons. An evening like any other. The kid lay in his crib. For now. Sleeping for now. Not screaming for now. He yawned and downed the rest of his beer.

"I nearly locked you out," Jorg said as she came in and slipped off her shoes. "I already had the door locked, there was no light on."

"The neighbors could have helped me."

"The neighbors." He snorted dismissively and leaned back on the couch cushions. They were decorated with heavy woven fabric in an Asian design. They made Jorg want to throw up. "The key wouldn't have done anything by itself, darling. The door would have been locked from the inside—no chance there."

"Well, I'll have to call myself lucky that you noticed." She walked over and lifted his glass. "Whiskey?" She took a sip.

"Where were you?"

"Right, where was I, where was I—let me think . . ."

"Kathrin," he said, "please."

"Just a minute." She rubbed her forehead, closing her eyes. "We were . . . that's right, we were . . . I can't remember now."

"We . . . ?"

"It did me some good, it was really . . . very exciting, so intense."

"This . . . this isn't exactly pleasant for me to hear."

"Of course it isn't." She gave a slightly drunken laugh. "How could it be? Ach, you're . . . you're such a darling man."

She tried to hug him. He pushed her away.

"Go to bed!" he snapped at her. "We'll talk later."

He slept poorly that night. He kept waking up—the last time at two thirty a.m. He listened for his wife's breathing to make sure it was even; their son was quiet too. He remembered his wife giving him something. He tiptoed into the kitchen, took a beer out of the fridge, and cracked the window to smoke.

There had been a time when he'd get home well past midnight to his spot by the city fish market, eight-hour shifts or longer serving at his uncle's restaurant, on his feet the whole time, dog-tired. That had been his mode, since always and forever: dog-tired. He had still been single then, sleeping in late and hoping that he still might go to sea one day, visit far-off countries, a foreign world. It lingered as a hope, a dream. He looked out into the starry sky. Was she looking out the window too? Looking for him? Longing for him?

Then her voice broke through sharply: "Can you hear me? Are you deaf?! The kid!"

He forced his eyes open and came tumbling off the chair.

"What . . . what's the matter?"

His wife held their screaming child in her arms as she fiddled with the bottle. "Don't just stand there, help me! What's wrong with you, you've got all your clothes on!"

"I have to go."

"At three? In the middle of the night?"

He rubbed his face, his eyes. "It's three?"

"Three, three thirty, what's the difference?"

He didn't respond. He helped her with the baby—the kitchen clock read a quarter past three. He couldn't believe it. He had just been wide awake, he had drunk a beer and smoked. But the kitchen table was empty—no can, no ashes. He felt in his overall pockets for the cigarettes. They weren't there. He kicked a chair away without thinking. It fell over with a crash. His wife stared at him speechless, eyes open wide.

"Maybe a half hour, not much more, just gone, completely erased," he confided later that morning to an older coworker. They sat high up on some office scaffolding in Altona looking down at the train station. Below them was a throng of traffic: busses, tractor trailers, bicycles. He took no notice of the sounds.

"Blackout," his workmate said. "It happened to me once, too."

"I wasn't even plastered, it was . . . I don't know, I don't get it."

His workmate laughed, choked down his sandwich, and coughed. "Don't sweat it if nothin' else happens. Or is it something with your sweetheart?"

"What d'you mean?"

"A mother that young can get annoying—you reach your limits pretty fast."

"No," he said, shaking his head vigorously. "It's nothing like that." That definitely couldn't be it. It was . . . it had to be the heat, it hadn't cooled off at all that night, that must have been it. What else could it be?

She feigned sleep as he set the cup of tea down by the bed and kissed her lightly on the cheek. He did that whenever they'd had a bad night, when they had fought. She kept her position, opening her eyes only as he was leaving the apartment. Heard his steps on the stairs, heard him greet somebody and make small talk, friendly as shit probably. Really, he couldn't give a rat's ass about the other tenants. She stretched out and went through the day's to-do list. A mani-pedi at the Urban Spa on Marktplatz, grocery shopping, then the fish store. And the bank. She looked at the clock—almost ten already. She picked up her phone and stepped out onto the balcony to set up an appointment with the bank people. Nobody was working on the facade.

He had announced at home that he would be getting back late after work, they were taking a new crew member out. No problem for his wife, she wanted to go over to her sister's to discuss their father's birthday. So after work he took the 25 to Winterhude, sitting all the way in the back row, observing mothers trying to wrestle their strollers on and off the bus. Nobody helped. He didn't like that, but he didn't do anything about it either. For some reason he felt like he shouldn't draw any attention to himself, traveling a route that he had never taken. Crazy, but that's how it was. There was no other way. Damnit, all he wanted was to see that woman, just one more time, anything more than a second, enjoy the sight of her, soak it up, nothing wrong with that.

Time dragged. He circled the block several times, five- or six-story apartment buildings, all turn of the century or earlier. Narrow front gardens along Dorotheen Strasse, hedges and shrubs, a patch of grass, a couple of stairs leading up to the door. Balconies with flower boxes looking out onto the opposite side of the street: a Korean restaurant, an Italian spot, an ice cream shop, wine bar, and a Spanish place. Tables were arranged outside under large umbrellas, all full. Life in all its color, full of human warmth. It was Winterhude after all, the heart of the city, right by the large park, its green lung. A strawberry stand out in front of an organic grocery. A bus stop. Two men with a guitar and an accordion got out and started to play.

Gryphius Strasse was lined with tall trees. He strolled on, keeping an eye out for a way to reach the inner courtyard. Dusk was falling when he saw a bicyclist emerge from the basement of an apartment building on Sierich Strasse. He waited a minute, then headed down the stairs. His lucky day—a gentle push and the door gave way. The corridor housed a number of garbage cans, among them two large yellow bins for plastic and the like. He quickly found his way to the courtyard. Just like that he was out in the open, where he paused to get his bearings before slowly making his way through the thick foliage back to the house where he and his team had set up the scaffolding the day before.

He looked up to the fifth floor.

The balcony door was open.

He held out under the protection of the overgrowth. There were people sitting out on the balcony drinking and chatting, laughing. Somewhere, somebody had a grill going. It wasn't dark enough yet. He slowly relaxed, allowing images to rise before him—a body with delicate contours, her beautiful, sad eyes.

It was past eleven by the time he began to scale the scaffolding, pausing and listening at each floor. When he reached the top, he inched forward toward the balcony door, back against the wall.

". . . fear," he heard. It was a woman's voice—it had to be hers.

"So you just go ahead and look through my finances?"

There she was, facing a thin man with a shaved head. He wore dark pants and a white shirt with the sleeves rolled up.

"That's *our* money."

"No it isn't, Kathrin! Those are *my* savings, *my* income! Not like they didn't warn me. *Such blinding beauty, but behind it . . .*"

"That's not true!"

The man raised his hand and he watched as the woman—Kathrin, such a beautiful and fragile woman—raised her own arm in self-defense, and a glass fell to the floor.

"I'm warning you!" the man said, bending down. "You'll see soon enough . . ."

The glass rolled across the parquet floor and out toward the balcony door, toward him. He jumped up and swung himself over the crossbar and back down the scaffolding. The man appeared above him, yelling something, and he thought he caught the guy's face, twisted in rage. He didn't listen. He let himself drop.

What he had heard and seen wouldn't let go of him. He lay awake for hours that night, his body a solid mass of pain. Even so, at the first signs of his son whimpering he was up on his feet and at his wife's side, on automatic, probably babbling to himself.

"What? What do you want to know?" she asked.

"Did . . . did I say something?"

"You definitely did. I didn't understand it though."

"Sorry."

"Well?"

He sat down on the edge of the bed, noticing the sweat that was beading on his chest. Tired, he was dog-tired. It was unspeakably humid in the room; outside was just as oppressive. "Tomorrow, tomorrow afternoon," he said. "Wasn't there something with . . . with your father?"

"Tomorrow is Friday. His birthday is Saturday, and we've been invited to grill with them. I already . . . No, I didn't tell you that yet. God, you can really drive someone crazy."

Her phone call to the building manager brought nothing. She was politely but firmly informed that covering the scaffolding wouldn't be necessary. The renovations would be finished by early the next week, midweek at the latest, after which the structure would be taken down immediately. The manager suggested keeping her curtains closed, and alerting the police in the event of an emergency.

"My everlasting thanks," Kathrin said, hoping that her sarcasm came through, before hanging up.

At twelve on the dot, she stepped into the neurologist's office on Kümmel Strasse, where she worked two afternoon shifts a week. The last treatments were generally at seven or eight, and she could made it back to the house before Jorg.

If there weren't any emergencies. Her colleague handed her the file for the next patient, commenting on it, and noted in passing that "il doctore" was in an exceptionally good mood, even if it left her feeling somewhat uneasy. Kathrin laughed just as a somewhat older man dressed in a white lab coat appeared; he raised his glasses and winked hello at Kathrin. "See you later," he said on the way to his office, as cooly as he could muster. His words had come at just the right time—she needed his advice.

He felt sick all day; several rounds after work didn't help. That night was even worse. He was hounded by feverish, vanishing dreams of pale faces; a tender vision of the gorgeous woman, followed by a hideous mug hurtling toward him, spitting fire. No mysteries there—the man in her apartment was a monster, a thug. He had threatened her, *You'll see soon enough, you'll see soon enough . . .*

He felt the ground slipping out from under his feet, as though he were plunging head over heels into the darkness. He felt his son urinating on him and was about to slap him before he shrank back in horror, feeling for his wife, who pushed him away, mumbling something. Dawn found him broken, dog-tired once again. Death warmed over.

His sister-in-law arrived later than they had agreed on, face flushed. She had forgotten the child seat. The sisters traded accusations. He took the child from his wife and had her crawl into the backseat of the Opel, then handed the kid to her and plopped down in front. His sister-in-law hitched up her thin skirt provocatively, flashing some leg. They were pretty, slender. He didn't react, though his pulse quickened at his temples. His eyelids grew heavy as they drove through the city, and he started to drift off.

"The sun," he muttered when his wife nudged him, "it's that . . . it's this damn heat."

"Just get out already!" she said.

His sister-in-law had parked on the shoulder directly in front of the Hagenbeck garden colony. With everything in tow—child, cooler, salad spoons—they made their way to the father's plot. He stood there at the gate, the picture of health, just turned fifty-eight. He pressed them into a round of schnapps—no use refusing, it was his day. They toasted to his health and made small talk, there was nothing new to report. Pork belly and sausages from the discount section sizzled on the grill. The sisters arranged the folding chairs and distributed plastic cutlery.

"Olaf will be here later," his sister-in-law announced suddenly, to the surprise of both father and sister.

"Olaf? Who's Olaf?"

"You don't know him."

"But I—" the older man began.

"You don't. We just got together."

"You mean in the sack," his wife said.

"You bet—we fuck hand over fist."

His wife and her sister laughed in a way he had never heard before. The child started to scream. He turned away, his entire body trembling. The pounding in his skull became unbearable. His hands clenched into fists.

The child screamed and screamed, and kept screaming.

His wife did what she could, cradling the infant and speaking to it in soothing tones. But it just kept screaming, pushing the pacifier away, kicking and wriggling in his wife's arms, screaming, screaming, screaming.

His eyes narrowed.

In a single motion he was up at his wife and child.

He was bellowing now.

"You shit! You miserable piece of shit! Leave her alone! Leave your paws off her, get off her! You'll see, I'll get you, I'm going to *kill* you!"

The child fell silent.

He caught himself. All nearby sound ceased. He saw his wife's face. She was staring at him, mouth agape. He turned to his sister-in-law and their father. They were also staring at him.

He didn't wait for them to react, whether with words or anything else. He took off running.

He ran and ran, through the neighborhood by the zoo, on through Eimsbüttel, out past the ring road, ran until he couldn't run anymore, till he was completely spent. He leaned against the wall of a house for support, chest heaving, looking around for a street sign, any sort of sign. He didn't know what was wrong with him, what could have set him off like that. He couldn't think clearly. He felt dizzy, his eyes burned. He gasped for air. His legs buckled.

"I ended it," Kathrin said.

"Ended it? What?"

"You know what," she replied. "It was nothing special."

She kept hearing the words of "il doctore": *Calm him down, show remorse.*

Jorg arched his eyebrows skeptically. Kathrin poured them more wine. Jorg reached for the remote and muted the television. He cleared his throat.

The sky outside grew dark.

Night flooded in.

* * *

He stalked his way forward step by step, expressionless, speaking out loud to himself: "I want . . . I'll show him, you can count on . . . He won't do anything else to you . . . Are you kidding me? . . . Shut up, you piece of shit, I'll . . . I'll shut you up . . . Hands off her . . . I'll kill you . . ."

Passersby steered clear of him; it was a familiar sight in the neighborhood, a patient from the nearby hospital complex in Alsterdorf, the psych ward for the severely disturbed.

A low rumble sounded off in the distance.

There was a storm gathering.

"Kathrin," Jorg said, "it would be so nice if you . . . if we weren't always fighting about this apartment . . ."

"I think so too," she said. "You're right."

"But that's not the point. It's not about me being right. I—"

She got up and slipped the straps of her dress off her shoulders. It fell to the floor. She stood there, naked except for her panties. She brought her finger to his lips . . .

He arrived at a house on Gryphius Strasse, pressing at random on one of the top bells. The buzzer sounded and he stepped into a carpeted hallway. Marbled tile on the walls, bronze railings. The basement door was unlocked. He quickly passed through into the inner courtyard and glanced up at the scaffolding on the building's facade.

Lightning tore across the sky.

Kathrin clasped her husband, collapsing onto the wide couch with him, the piece with the Asian patterns Jorg couldn't stand the sight of.

She kissed him, fumbling for his belt buckle.

* * *

He had just climbed onto the scaffolding when it thundered again and the first raindrops began to fall. He ascended quickly, launching back into his litany: "Don't lay a finger on her . . . You'll see, you won't do anything to her . . . I'm only going to say this once . . ."

Kathrin parted her legs and guided him—he began to move rhythmically, more forcefully now, faster and faster as first sighs and moans, then a scream emerged from her lips.

He could hear her.

Gusts of wind rattled the half-open blinds amid the pouring rain.

With a violent motion he burst into the room and saw her, face contorted, covered by the man lying on top of her; he grabbed the guy and ripped him off. The asshole staggered to his feet and clung to him, the smell of alcohol on his breath as he screamed—the man was screaming something, as was the woman, he could hear her, like she was calling to him; with all his might, he drew back from the man then leaped at him wildly, crashing into him, and the two tumbled out onto the balcony grasping each other, and he didn't notice that the waist-high scaffolding had broken out of the mounting support, and he . . .

When Kathrin stepped out onto the scaffolding, she looked down to see the intertwined bodies of the two men lying lifeless on the tiled terrace five stories below. Head raised, her face reflecting neither joy nor grief, she closed her eyes and let the rain run down her bare body.

THE ASSIGNMENT

BY KATRIN SEDDIG

Altona

Translated by Noah Harley

I moved through the city because I had to. I wasn't just moving about of my own free will, I was moving for hire. I'll get back to that. It was that hour of the day when everyone went home. I watched them do all sorts of things, saw their longing for home, for warmth and a meal. Saw them flip on the light over the kitchen table, set out the cutlery, eating together, talking to one another. I sank down into their lives, filling with nostalgia.

It was night and I could hear the neighbor. He was always talking to himself, especially after dark—he sang, he laughed, he swore, he was his own best friend and worst enemy. I pulled the blanket up over my ears but I couldn't sleep, he was everywhere.

He didn't come across as someone who would talk to himself by light of day. He looked completely normal out riding his bicycle, not the type to make clicking, trilling noises the whole night through, laughing long and loud enough for it to escalate into a cackle, bird sounds, animal sounds, before receding and fading off into a long, drawn-out sigh, when at last he pulled himself together and sang "Enjoy the Silence," his favorite. He never got tired. He never had to sleep. But then, at some point, he would get on his bicycle and ride off down the street, without giving the slightest impression of being the person who was cackling next door at night.

The phone rang, and it seemed like he was the one talking to me, in a female voice—he had so many voices.

"We have an interesting assignment for you."

Who's *we*? (How did "they" purport to know what I might find interesting? I couldn't help but take such speculation about me as presumptuous.)

"It's very straightforward."

"I see!" (I wanted this to sound derisive but it didn't, I couldn't control my voice, I felt unstable.)

"You'll be appropriately compensated."

That was something—I had to consider for a minute.

"You go on a couple of walks and describe the essence to us."

I hung up. It was the middle of the night. It was disingenuous. It was all sorts of things.

Still, I was tempted. I was a writer, though not a very successful one. I wrote novels and short stories, even sold some, but it just didn't bring in much. Money was tight, and that thing about appropriate compensation had a pleasant ring to it.

A few days later I woke up knowing that if "they" did call again, I would ask some questions. I lay in bed and thought it through. What figure would have to be on the slip that would let me sign on the dotted line? There was no slip, or dotted line for that matter. But I couldn't imagine it any other way than them sliding a piece of paper toward me, keeping it covered under their hand of course, under their joint hand; a small pizzeria in Eimsbüttel, Italian pop music on, garlic and olives, and I'd take the slip as if it were nothing, glance at it, and be amazed. *What a sum!* I would think to myself, such a pretty round number.

"Yes," I said out loud in bed. "Yes!"

I began to sweet-talk myself. Describe something. Describe the *essence*? It was an assignment built for a writer. I set the fee I would do it for.

But if they did offer me that amount, they must have something in mind—something not all that kosher—to drag me out of bed just like that, early morning, still warm and innocent under the blankets.

I wouldn't do it, not under any circumstances! Not even for such a colossal amount.

Two days later they did actually call again, offering me much less money than had been printed on the imaginary slip of paper. I searched inside myself and didn't find any resistance. Nothing shady—it wasn't like I was going to shadow somebody.

That I wouldn't have done. *Unless . . .* I thought, leaving the door open just a crack. What if it were something really important, something not at all morally dubious, which I and I alone were in a position to do? But what could that possibly be? A professional operation that was worth anything would go to detectives, because those were the kind of people who specialized in tracking people unnoticed, *by the books*. I didn't know the books, I, a not especially conspicuous-looking woman, though not entirely inconspicuous, either. I still wore ocher sneakers and an ocher coat after all—in the right light I could glow like a warm lamp. Plus I wore red lipstick—it just seemed wrong to walk about pale and nondescript. Except if I were a detective and pale lips made up an essential part of my professional costume, an indispensable form of invisibility; except maybe if whatever environment I was monitoring was suddenly red-lipped and conspicuous, in which case pale lips and being inconspicuous obviously became conspicuous.

I had already become ensnared in thoughts that let the door to the surveillance assignment open a little wider.

But I wasn't supposed to surveil anybody. I was supposed to leave my dwelling on Schnell Strasse, walk along Harkort Strasse, cross the intersection at Kaltenkircher Square, turn onto Plöner Strasse, walk past the post office tower, the subway, the postal distribution site, and the Diebsteich station, cross the bridge that not too long ago still led over brackish, brown-green water but now went over an excavation site, and keep going. I found the instructions in my mailbox; the money came in the form of a bill, same envelope. There were no other traces of who'd sent it, just the envelope without a return address and the bill. My instructions had been set in Helvetica; I often used Helvetica, though I also liked Arial or Times New Roman depending on my mood. In the past I had been involved with a passionate typographer. (As you can see, it *is* possible to combine these two words in one sentence.)

As I proceeded according to my instructions, I glanced down at the new ocher sneakers that I knew to be housing well-formed, dependable feet. My feet always looked cute, and never gave me problems. My *sweet, darling feet!* I thought. It was important to love yourself. My feet made it easy to love them—a different story than my teeth. My shoes—that was about all that I saw of myself, aside from dark-blue jeans and my shadow of course, rising and falling beneath the street-lights. It was evening—right on time, I was doing everything they wanted me to, I was someone you could rely on.

I dictated into my phone: "Gericht Strasse, rosy lady with a leg brace / Haubach school, plastic child / Outside the Holsten brewery—man photographing demolition / Harkort Strasse, man transporting white foam material with a bike cart / Woman with a Drillings baby carriage, babies asleep / Drizzling rain (relevant?) / Cardboard box under the train bridge, there's a yellow pillow, five mini-bottles of Jäger / Kaltenkircher Square intersection, heavy traffic . . ."

I had to dictate all this after the fact, because I had to wait for people to be far away enough not to hear me describing them. In the meantime, other people came whose features I had to commit to memory so I could describe them, while I had already forgotten the features of the first group, and so on. It wasn't an easy task, and it left me flustered. I had no idea how I was supposed to describe people without my language demeaning them. It was all the same to the city. But I didn't want to demean the city either. This was *my* city after all, the city I lived in. The features I mentioned weren't relevant. I was supposed to focus on the essence. But how, if it was only in passing, if I saw everything in a brief flash, or not at all?

I had the feeling I was being manipulated.

Four days later I was walking down Plöner Strasse behind a man, he was tall and strongly built and he stunk. *God, this guy stinks!* I thought to myself, then immediately wondered whether you were allowed to think that about other people. Wouldn't it be better for me to think, *He doesn't smell good?* God, he *didn't* smell good! He didn't smell good to such a degree that I held my breath. But then I had to draw a breath, a big greedy gulp of air, meaning the smell asserted itself all the more forcefully. It was possible that this experience came closer to what my assignment had described as the *essence* than anything else I had reported on in such drab fashion. But was that what I wanted? Wasn't this essence corrosive, penetrating me without any means to counteract it? Was that the difficulty, the danger of the assignment?

I couldn't help it—I had to tail the man. What kind of a person was he anyway? I could see his bare legs flashing through tattered pants, even his underwear was torn and I caught sight—not that I wanted to—of his rear end. A radio blasting opera dangled from one hand; he was scratching his head with the other. From time to time he would pause and look around fiercely. That's how it seemed to me anyway— maybe he didn't have the least bit of ferocity in him, maybe it was just nerves. He seemed exceptionally strong. How could a man who seemed entirely foreign to any sort of personal care or hygiene still look so strong? Shouldn't he be weak and gaunt? He looked like someone surviving in the wilderness, where the outer shell went neglected while internally his muscles grew more and more supple, unlike mine, which tightened up the second I even thought of stretching.

Whenever he stopped to look around fiercely, or maybe just nervously, I also stopped. I didn't want to get any closer to him, least of all become the object of his gaze. I would have overtaken him if I were able, but he was moving too quickly. I slowed my steps to increase the distance between us, but then he stopped again, almost as if he knew I was trailing him, and that his smell had already penetrated me to the core, that I was breathing it in nonstop. That's what people do with each other, I thought bitterly, they get close and infiltrate you with their words, their gestures, their looks, their smells.

The post office fence was to our left, to our right the street, and behind it the embankment leading up to the train tracks that crossed over Stresemann Strasse on iron bridge posts. There was no other route; I had to follow this man, breathe him in, see him and hear the arias coming from the radio that dangled comically from his hand.

I wouldn't want to gloss over the fact that these considerations—whether or not they were more essential, by standards more objective than my own—now caused me to neglect any other observations I might have made. This was the only person I was capable of delving into, perceiving, speculating about.

I quickened my pace as we approached Stresemann Strasse and came closer. He turned around and peered at me intently, almost as if he had known that I was following him this entire time. His face was savage, dirty; he squinted at me pointedly, staring into my inner depths as though in recognition.

It's him, I thought, *my neighbor*—there was no doubt about it. He looked different than usual, he had grown a beard and needed a bath, and it occurred that I hadn't heard anything from him in quite awhile. It had been silent from behind the wall at night, though I couldn't say for sure, because I had been sleeping quite soundly, the effect of spending more of my days wandering the city. Was this bearded, unkempt figure really my neighbor?

The assignment I had been carrying around with me the entire time, which kept me occupied and was already beginning to torture me, now overlapped with the shock that ran through me at his piercing look, merging into a single thought: if there was something to find, something to describe, something that made any sense—it was him.

"Yah!" he screamed. "What do you think this is?" He spit on the ground; he hated me.

"Nothing, I don't think anything."

"Stop lying!" he hollered again. "You liar!"

I bolted. "Liar," I muttered furiously to myself. I crossed the intersection at Kaltenkircher Square and stopped under the train bridge on Harkort Strasse and spoke into my phone: "Large man, totally unkempt, ripped clothes, penetrating gaze, smells unpleasant, listens to opera on his radio."

That night I got up and put my ear against the wall. Silence. That calmed me. So I wasn't crazy, it *had* been him. He was homeless now and things had quickly gone downhill. For a moment I even felt some sympathy for him. The song, his laughter. *Enjoy the Silence.* The night was completely still.

". . . / Streseman Strasse is the dirtiest street in Hamburg, it's so gray. So gray. The squat businesses on either side are completely covered in the filth, acting like a shell and a preservative. The rent is affordable, there in the belly of an inferno of noise and exhaust fumes and particulate matter survive the things that nobody is interested in except the poor, the financially destitute, who aren't bothered by the surroundings. That's also why I like walking here, observing the random, ramshackle architecture, the old set against the new, which itself is already old, like a bored, listless kid lining up building blocks in a row only to kick them all over and then smack his little brother. A barred basement window peeps out at street level by my orange-colored feet, behind the dirty pane an open bottle of wine stands next to a bouquet of dusty silk flowers, and behind both a person with a heart and a sense of taste, sitting there in the darkness of his apartment, where he lights a candle and enjoys a couple of mealy potatoes while somebody is getting shot on TV and outside, where I'm standing now, an ambulance siren wails, while inside the wine runs down his dusty throat—that's Streseman Strasse, where every day a bicyclist gets run over and a pigeon bleeds to death / . . ."

I noticed that I was adding things that seemed true to

me and that seemed to belong more to the realm of the essential than anything I could actually see. They came to mind and seemed true and essential, and that calmed me. I had found a flow. I walked and dictated and was more or less content. I couldn't go home now, even if I had already taken my designated route. I walked on, giving them what they wanted. That's how good I was. I emailed what I had written to renate47@gmx.com. I never got an answer back, and imagined Renate47 knowing nothing about what I was sending.

I met the child at the Mitte Altona Quartierspark. If "mid-Altona" was actually supposed to be in the middle of something, it would fall roughly between Alster and the A7. It had been built on top of the former switchyard for the Altona train station, and was chock-full of new five-story apartment buildings filled with young people on sensible career paths, each with one to two children who played with each other in the Quartierspark while their parents sat outside the Blaue Blume in the old work-uniform store on Harkort Strasse drinking Aperol Spritzes. That was during the summer. Now they meandered through the dead fields with their dogs or kicked a soccer ball to their kids.

It was already dark, and lights were burning in the Blaue Blume as one of the pretty blue Hungarian trains slowly screeched along the elevated rail at the far edge of the park. It had been my daily routine during summer to sit on the stairs along the lawn watching families and drinking beer—it all seemed far in the past.

Suddenly there was a child standing in front of me, dressed in a snowsuit. "So there you are," it said, finger pointed at me.

I was certain the child was confusing me with somebody else, but it smiled at me as if we knew each other well.

"You've got the wrong person," I said.

It shook its head.

"I don't know you," I told the child.

"I know *you!*" they replied.

"From where?"

"Where do you think?"

"I don't know," I answered, starting to grow unsure of myself.

"*I don't know,*" it mimicked. There was something unpleasant about the kid and I found myself feeling real aversion. It stood there, crammed into a light-blue snowsuit. Its face was round, the cheeks were round, it had round eyes, it was a kid, a kid like any other, fresh out of the oven. Nothing wrinkled or flaked or slowly breaking off. Everything was still taut and brand new. The longer I looked at the face, the more it seemed to me that the kid looked like every other kid, as though there were no differences at all between kids.

"What's your name?" I asked.

"What's your name?" the kid asked.

I furrowed my brow, sensing a growing ill will, and kept walking, leaving the kid just standing there. When I turned around after a few steps, it had gone. Normally something like that wouldn't have unnerved me. Children are quick and mystifying, it's in their nature. But I established a connection, slowly I established a connection. It couldn't be coincidence—coincidences didn't really exist, not in written pieces, which this was. In the meantime, everything had become something written, text—that much was clear to me. "Kid in a snowsuit," I dictated into my phone. It seemed so significant that I ran home and wrote down all sorts of things about the kid. It was a child of this city, a very important child, an essential child.

* * *

The faceless man showed up not long after Radio Man, before the kid in the snowsuit in fact, though it took me longer to process him. I ran into him in early November at the Diebsteich cemetery, which I had been assigned to visit for just fifty euros—that's how low my going rate was. The Diebsteich cemetery was right next to the overground commuter rail, though it was no longer in service. They were building a new long-distance station meant to replace the one in Altona; anything old, boggy, moldy, rusted, or overgrown that remained would disappear and make way for the new, shiny, clean, futuristic. Even as I was writing about it, a lot had changed, and much was gone. The cemetery was still there, though, and it was worth visiting. I would have visited for free, I liked it so much.

I was making my rounds at twilight between the gravestones and crypts of the Sinti and Roma, freshly decorated for All Saints' Day, when out he scurried before vanishing just as quickly. I had been full of pleasant thoughts at the time, about what a warm, pretty fall we were having—the leaves rustling above, the ground a colorful tapestry underfoot, all of it lifting my spirits, bringing me courage and filling me with an odd sense of pride in the cemetery, the city, and myself. It was precisely at this moment, when I was feeling such a sense of well-being, that he scurried out from behind a bush. Like anybody except the shiest among us, I was in the habit of directing my gaze first at a person's face, but he didn't have one, so my gaze simply slid down to the short dark-blue jacket he was wearing, quite elegant, though closer observation wasn't possible because he had already scurried past me by that point—he was a first-rate scurrier. I spun around after him, but from behind he didn't make a faceless impression; he had hair. The back of his head was there. And just like that, he had vanished among the trees.

I was obviously scared stiff; both my heartbeat and breathing had quickened and I kept glancing around to see if he was lurking somewhere in the half light. But would he even be capable of lurking in his state? Plus, doubts had started to creep into the picture—people have faces, without them we couldn't walk around just like that, how would we get our bearings? He *had* to have a face in other words, one I had somehow managed to overlook. But what did that say about me, as an observer, if I overlooked such basic details?

I should have followed directly behind him, overtaken him, and gotten another look at him from the front. Then I would have seen that he did have a face.

"Man in a short dark-blue jacket, didn't have a face."

At home I tried to bring him to mind. I boiled tea, listened to the silence at the wall, which was more silent than ever, and wrote a sentence about myself: *I'm losing my grip on reality. I'm constructing my own. The madness on the other side of the wall is gone. The madness is now mine.*

I laughed out loud. I tried cackling. It didn't work.

"3:27 p.m. / Präsident Krahn Strasse / three women in / beige-colored quilted coats / dyed-blond hair / Altona train station / man aflutter / soaring with the crows / dotting the sky / with bitter croaking / Neue Grosse Berg Strasse / three small dogs / hearts and kisses / to them / man outside TK Maxx / 'Für Elise' / on the guitar / painful / that the people / that they flee / that nobody / Neue Grosse Berg Strasse / yellow leaves / sticking / flat / crumbling / squishing / on the street / on the skin / in the stores / the open / warm / pumpkins / it's always / Halloween again / pumpkins / plaster and iron / plastic and rubber / Altona balcony / HSV / train of fans / 'No, it'll be something again' / says the woman / it'll be something again /

that's why they're marching / for our / while the / ships below on the Elbe / containers / while the sky / indifferent / pale / the sky / blind . . ."

It was too much, too many people on balconies in Altona watching Hamburger SV fans march before the big match, all these excited people that I couldn't take in as such, just as a single thing, a solid mass, like a dough of skin and blood.

I bought some headphones. I had to detach.

I had to capture the essence of it in a single sentence, the man standing outside the TK Maxx plucking "Für Elise" on the guitar—what was I supposed to say about him other than the fact that he was playing "Für Elise" on the guitar, a song everyone and their mother plays on piano. People walked past him like he wasn't even there, and the essential thing about him was that he was invisible, that he wasn't there at all.

I was drained, but I kept walking. I couldn't stop anymore, I knew I was getting close, I was getting there with the man at the TK Maxx, I only had to walk a little bit longer, extend my route a little, finish recording, I just had to keep at it. The faceless man didn't have a face, that was obviously essential; the man with the radio was *not* the man who lived next door to me, that was the essential thing about him; and the kid in the snowsuit didn't have any idea who I was, nor was the child one I knew. I realized that the essential thing about these people was what they *weren't*.

I felt exhausted, uncertain, ill. I realized the city was nothing to me except the people there, and what was essential about them was what they weren't. I heard myself laughing out loud. The city was overwhelming me, it was killing me. It was too much. Its essence was lethal.

I'd calmed down, and sat in the armchair listening to music with my new headphones: "Ascenseur pour l'échafaud." The soundtrack to the film *Elevator to the Gallows*, composed by Miles Davis in 1958. Miles Davis didn't have any trouble finishing an assignment. It hadn't bothered him. Or maybe it had bothered him, but it hadn't stopped him. I couldn't do it. I wasn't Miles Davis. The world wasn't a film noir, the world was gloomy and foolish, it had no beauty. That was the difficulty: to track down the beauty in it all. Wasn't that the essence? Everything always looked like something else to me—that, or I was left searching for it, something that I already knew and hoped to find in what I was seeing.

"You aren't doing your job properly!" one of the voices said through the telephone.

"What's that supposed to mean?"

"That thing about the faceless man, it's not true."

"How would you know?"

"We know."

"Well, he was there."

"We think that you aren't reliable."

"I won't say the opposite is the case."

"That wouldn't make any sense anyway."

"I quit."

The person on the other end stayed silent. It wasn't a pregnant silence, just an empty one. I hung up, got undressed, and slipped into the shower. In the shower I remembered that I hadn't mentioned the kid. I didn't care. Something out of all this had to belong to me.

When I emerged from the shower, dripping and warm, the phone was ringing.

"Okay," I said. "Fine . . . okay."

My street was full of brown oak leaves; the acorns themselves were yellow and brown, mostly yellow though. At night the acorns came hurtling down on car hoods and roofs, as though bent on murder. At Millerntor Stadium, St. Pauli was duking it out with HSV. HSV would win, they didn't belong in the second league, not after St. Pauli. Who belonged in St. Pauli? A bunch of people washing dishes in old apartment buildings.

I couldn't stop.

I walked past the Holsten Brewery. It was just ruins now, a heap of rubble and iron beams bent at bizarre angles. Everything got covered in dust when the bulldozer sank its teeth into the walls and ripped out large chunks, once the wrecking ball had knocked it all down. Clouds of dust rose over the area; we courageously breathed them in and watched as the old fellow collapsed in on himself, gulped twice, burped, screamed, then fell flat on his face and died.

The smell was gone by now—yeast, hops, malt. The rats that used to march up and down Harkort Strasse, proud little beer-y soldiers—had their retinue decamped to Harburg, bundles tied to sticks? Had every last one of these splendid, well-fed brewery rats gone to Harburg or Hausbruch, where the beer was brewed these days—the same old beer as always?

Apartments were supposed to go up here, even more housing, a pretty residential area for pretty people with pretty children. They had it depicted on banners set up along the tall fences of the site—it would all be just darling!

I stared through the fence on Harkort Strasse. I was doing it for seventy euros, I had let myself get talked into it, and why not? I found it fascinating: broken things, wreckage, collapse, emptiness—it gave me a rise, a cool sort of elation. Did I wish for destruction? *If at some point not so far off in the future everything old is gone, we won't have to be afraid of loss anymore,*

I reasoned out my feelings. I wondered why I had used *we*, as though I didn't want to think such a weak thought all by myself.

I went back to the cemetery. It felt so good there. The Buena Vista Café by the underpass to the Diebsteich station was closed now, forever. The neighborhood no longer sat outside here with their dogs to drink beer and eat chili. At some point right here, this narrow, shady spot, everything would be wide open and clean. New stores, spacious, bright shops with Scandinavian designs, filled with young people, large illuminated letters, women skaters and coffee-sippers, banks and bicycles, the future.

Workers were raking up leaves in the cemetery. Single leaves drifted down; a dim glow infused the damp air. A headless angel poised at the headstone of Elisabeth Görsch, née Lüddemann. A thin, sullen youth ravaged by acne walked his dog. An old woman, white hair tousled by the wind, came up to me with a green watering can and greeted me. But not as if she knew me, just because.

I had regained my hold on things. Everything was as it seemed. The people, the city, they were exactly as they seemed. I recognized myself in them. I knew the routes, knew who I had to avoid and why. I was home.

The woman with the windswept hair, that was me. Not now, but at some other point. On some future day I would be the one using this green watering can, the trees in the cemetery rustling like the sea, to water the plants at the grave of someone I loved. I felt melancholy but wasn't unhappy. I found myself struggling to grasp hold of the essence of things. Of course I knew the faceless man, he was such a scurrier that you forgot what was essential about him the minute you laid eyes on him. I also knew the man with the radio, he slept on a bench between graves, he was a man of nature, loved opera, and maybe sometimes Depeche Mode. I knew the kid in the light-blue snowsuit, and it knew me too obviously, because it was me. I didn't need to lie, I just had to write it all down.

When the phone rang and I heard the voice, it was a completely foreign voice that belonged to anyone who might have sat in this Italian restaurant in Eimsbüttel at this table, while slipping me a note with a sum on it under their hand, though they hadn't done that. "Never call this number again!" I said quickly.

Then I hung up. Or rather I didn't hang up, because they hadn't called to begin with. It didn't matter anyway. There were the streets and squares, the houses, the people, the cars, and the writing.

There was the writing.

There was my neighbor, the kid in the snowsuit, the man with the radio, and maybe even Renate47.

I shouldn't forget to mention in my text that HSV lost 0–3 to St. Pauli. I still had a little bit of money in my account and climate change would come, it was already here, but to-day the apartment co-op was planting new trees inside our courtyard in Altona, Hamburg. At night I heard my neighbor again. I couldn't understand him but he sounded relaxed, and I felt relieved when he started to sing: "*Words like violence / Break the silence / Come crashing in / Into my little world.*"

REEPERBAHN 29 REVISITED

BY TINA UEBEL

Reeperbahn

Translated by Paul David Young

I f I were religious, I would think Reinhard is an angel. I'm not. I'm an atheist, and us northern Germans are all lightly Christianized heathens. Reinhard lives—and here "lives" is a euphemism—below me, and he cares for Rommel so lovingly that Mother Teresa herself could learn a thing or two.

Of late, Rommel is as thin as a skeleton, and he can't make it down the two flights of stairs to Clochard anymore. Reinhard does the shopping for him, at Penny, where else, and somewhere or other he dug up a wheelchair for Rommel, which Rommel doesn't use, although Reinhard presumably would carry it down the stairs.

Reinhard is a fat creature; Rommel was always on the small side. For almost twenty years I have lived up top at Reeperbahn 29, an unloved, decaying postwar building whose top floor nobody sees when they're running around below in the noisy neon jungle. The bordello lounge, the tiny fuck rooms upstairs, an elevator from the fifties that used to lead directly to sexual gratification. The elevator hasn't run for a long time. The cabin stopped decades ago in what is to-day my bedroom and simply quit running. Now it's my closet.

I'm a good kid from the suburbs who was about to suffo-cate out there on the periphery and began to gravitate toward

St. Pauli, since St. Pauli is the only place where we belong, us, the ones who don't belong anywhere. During my youth, I spent long nights in Clochard, perhaps not the heart of St. Pauli, but its kidney or liver or pancreas, one of the under-rated organs that keep the shop going. Clochard is open 24/7, except once a year when for two hours the exterminator acts like he can do something about the man-size cockroaches. Earlier, when I was a kid from the 'burbs and got drunk there and hung out, the Berbers slept on the benches—the Berbers of St. Pauli call themselves Berbers with great pride and com-plain about the bums in St. George, whom they call bums and asocial fucks. On the jukebox, there was pure garbage with three exceptions: "Hey Joe," "In the Ghetto," and, of course, "Midnight in the Reeperbahn." When I had money, I teed up those three as often as possible, just to prevent worse things from playing. When I moved into the fifth floor about five or seven years later, the owner had long ago changed. The Berbers had to sleep somewhere else. After that, there was heavy metal on the jukebox. What stayed the same was the bread with lard, which had always been there but which, as far as I knew, no one had ever eaten. Even the Berbers weren't that crazy. I hadn't been back for years when I arrived to look at the apartment, three floors up from Clochard, and had no intention of living there. Who in their right mind would do that? Certainly none of the two hundred people who showed up and stood in line. About half turned around and left as soon as they got to the stairway, since our stairway doesn't smell good, and the others retreated once they saw what was being called an apartment. Nobody would want to live here, me neither, but okay, I thought, I'll do it. Later I can talk about how for a couple of years in my youth I lived right on the Reeperbahn. Then I stayed for twenty.

Next to the Hesburg Sausage and Fast Food, our entrance, which always smells like piss, leads up past two landings, whose unevenness is hidden under steel treads, to the first floor, where Clochard, 24/7, without a break, thumps, lives, sweats, and smokes. Here there's always music, here there's always bass, here it is always night, here we all always talk with each other when we can still understand each other over the bass, here we understand each other even if we can't understand each other because of the bass. Here the beer is cheap and the bread with lard free. One morning I came home, or one afternoon, or whenever it was, and a gangly suburban kid fell into my arms and cried on my shoulder because Bukowski was dead. St. Bukowski, the patron saint of misfits.

Across from the entrance to Clochard is the steel security door leading upstairs. We don't have any doorbells. When people visit me, they have to call, and from the balcony I throw the key down, wrapped in a dish towel. Behind the door is the staircase, painted in fecal colors up to waist height in standard stool, above that in light diarrhea. On the next three floors, social services pays five or six hundred deutsche marks, later euros, for the lost people, so the ex-crazies can have a place to live instead of under the bridge. I was told that in the eighties some yuppies set up a party space on the fifth floor, fifty-five square meters with an uninsulated wooden exterior to the south and single-glazed windows which are pure sky, six meters high, in all the north German shades of gray. Below me, the Reeperbahn thumps on the weekend, at dawn seagulls rip apart the heavens with their claws, and I lie on my bed, a mattress on a shipping pallet, and watch the seagulls and know that I've never belonged anywhere so much as here.

Rommel is called Rommel because back in his youth, when he wasn't a starved ghost, he bopped around North Africa with wild deals and opaque jobs. What he did exactly isn't known, but anyway he's a devoted reader. I bring him books which we chat about. I loan him money which we both know he'll never repay. His room is constantly overheated because Rommel was always thin, and the skinnier he got, the more he froze. I invited him to my poetry slams, which I staged directly across the street at Molotow, but he never came. He said he stopped at the cable fencing of the traffic divider in the middle of the street. I've known Rommel a long time, and he told me himself, because Rommel is smart and honest: he's ashamed of himself. I talked to him for an hour to convince him to come over to the slam, assured him that he was on the guest list, but he said he was ashamed of himself, he was a mess. I don't think so, I said, because I like him and can't see anything for him to be ashamed about, but he wouldn't listen to me. Later, he didn't listen to Reinhard either, the one who shopped for him and found a wheelchair for him and offered to carry him down the stairs to Clochard, everything, even as Rommel decided to die in his little room because he thought he was no longer acceptable to the world at large. My Rommel, with his shaggy, red-blond pirate beard, his tart humor, his crooked glasses and emaciated Jesus body.

Reinhard, Archangel Reinhard, fought for Rommel with tooth and claw. Reinhard fought for himself too. The two of them drank moderately, and only beer. Both lost.

I'm coming home one morning after a party, or rather, I wasn't coming home because the Reeperbahn was closed off. Our Repeerbahn 29 had caught on fire. In the empty Clochard stood Horst, white as a sheet under his Ibiza tan, in shock, the blond-tinted strands of hair standing on end over his head. I had to see it, he says, I must see it: the first floor is completely burned up—crazy, but nobody's dead. Horst, boss at Clochard at the time, tells me what happened: a junkie was cooking his stuff over an open candle on the first floor; he shot up, then he tipped over, hitting the candle, woke up as the mattress caught on fire, had the presence of mind to toss the mattress out the window, upon which the eaves of the neighboring building started to burn. While the first floor lit up with fire, he popped into Clochard below, half his body burned, on his left side hair, beard, clothes gone, and he sat at the bar and lit a cigarette, pondering, and finally said, Horst, dude, you won't believe it, but right now, I'm telling you—man, my place is on fire. Hey, you know, old man, I need a beer something awful right now.

I am at home the second time it burns. I had bought a few smoke alarms after the first fire, which didn't work, I awake nonetheless because I am about to die and I crawl on all fours to the balcony, where my seagulls have beaten a retreat. Below, the Reeperbahn is blocked off by fire department vehicles. I cough my lungs out. The fire department speaks to me through a megaphone: I should go back in my apartment. I say, without a megaphone, that the place is on fire and they better have a look around. I have shared my thoughts as they seem amenable to persuasion. Big red vehicles, their big red vehicles, hey, hey, ho ho, maybe that's why they were in fact there because the place was on fire. I have shared my thoughts, as this seem amenable to persuasion. Eventually I will be saved by a rescue ladder, which is so cool. A friend from Sweden sends me a YouTube video of the event the next day.

When the criminal investigators are in the building, I am epically tired. I have just come back on a long flight from overseas, have only slept two confused hours before I have to go to the meeting. I run up to the first landing in *CSI: St. Pauli*: three men in white overalls with evidence bags and shoe coverings. Whether yesterday or the day before yesterday I heard anything suspicious and where I had been. Thank goodness, I have an alibi, and no, I didn't know the victim and didn't know who or why someone would want to kill him. He had dispatched himself somehow.

Rommel was dead already, and Reinhard not yet. Rommel gave up, but Reinhard kept fighting. Reinhard had always worked, even one-euro jobs, sometimes for nothing. The main thing was the work. Reinhard is good with computers, and when he asks me for money, then it's for Rommel. I give him the money and try to make it so that Reinhard also gets some of it, but he's too proud for that. Of course, he never gets regular employment, because his gums are all gone, and as much as I love him with every fiber of my being, I can't look him in the face. It gives me nightmares. His teeth hang on to his jawbone only out of habit. When Reinhard laughs or smiles, which he does often, thank goodness, because he is smart, loving, and big-hearted, every innocent bystander feels ill: not suitable for customer contact. In the ten years of our quasi friendship—since I keep a certain distance here, otherwise I'd lose it—I've thought a thousand times about how much money the state could have saved, if it hadn't settled him in at Reeperbahn 29 but instead had simply paid to have his mouth attended to. I am sure that Reinhard could have fended for himself. He took care of Rommel until the end.

I was in Shanghai with a grant, and the best thing about Reeperbahn 29 was that there wasn't any conceit, not from me, not toward me, even as I was occasionally featured in the newspaper with a certain well-known person in the sausage industry, and the state didn't pay my rent, and I traveled to Shanghai, while Rommel couldn't make it across the street. I was in Shanghai when Reinhard called me and told me that Rommel was dead. And there hadn't been any kind of funeral or burial, although he, Reinhard, had stalked the people in the office and explained that he was practically a family member; still, they hadn't told him anything about the burial. We never found out where Rommel is buried. I would have brought flowers and beer to Rommel's grave if he had one.

Reinhard had a stroke in the Penny Market. He had the good fortune that someone called an ambulance. That's not always the case here, in St. Pauli, where eight drunks fall down every five minutes. The ambulance came right away. Reinhard got treatment immediately. He didn't have any lasting damage. Horst, however, had died gone long ago, also a stroke. His Ibiza tan and blond-tinted tresses didn't prevent him from getting old. We kept up with each other for a few months, but the news became sparse and depressing. Then I moved out, although I always thought I couldn't, that it would break my heart, and that it did, but two days before I was to turn over the keys, the Esso Houses were cleared because of the danger of collapse, the gas station closed, the one whose crew I had congratulated twenty years ago on the birth of their children and then recently with high fives for their good test scores on graduation and their admissions to university. Molotow closed, and the Western store. I turned over the keys and for several months I took a detour to the subway because I didn't want to see the concrete tomb where decades of my life were buried.

I looked for a person to take over the lease of my won-

186 // Hamburg Noir

derful, nutty fifty-five square meters, one room in the front and a chipboard exterior wall on which, one fucking cold winter during which my landlord reliably turned the heat and hot water off at ten p.m., I glued Styrofoam which I lovingly covered with lacquered wood. In a small room at the back, I wrote with fingerless gloves in the winter. I had the elevator whose cabin was my clothes closet. I had a refrigerator hanging over my mini-pantry; kitchen and bath were not necessarily provided in a bordello. I had the best neighbors in the world, the biggest cockroaches in the northern hemisphere, the loudest basses one could hope for. Saturday night the cockroaches would vibrate on the floor, as the bass shook my six-meter-tall, south-facing windows. I had those six meters of windows toward the south, looking across the steps of the Reeperbahn's big plaza, the Spielbudenplatz, and, behind them, a balcony, on which we sat with three or four friends on a Saturday evening, a case of beer nearby, watching the Reeperbahn like Waldorf and Statler observing *The Muppet Show*. I was at home there, where for the first time in my life and then for twenty years I belonged, because in St. Pauli we don't care what you own, what counts is who you are. I had the sky full of seagulls that screeched at the dawn and sneered at the remains of the night. I still have "Hey Joe" in my ear. I didn't find anybody to take over the lease.

I had already moved out when by chance I saw Reinhard for the last time, at the Hesburg Sausage place downstairs. His teeth had given up and left the sinking ship. The worst part was: he smelled awful. Reinhard had never let himself go, and even if the five floors with their cramped rooms had only one shower, Reinhard was always clean as a peeled egg. Pride and self-worth, it sounds abstract, but they're obviously olfactory qualities. When we embraced, I had to hold my breath. I was late to learn that he had died. A neighbor who was no longer a neighbor told me, since I didn't live there anymore. I don't know how and why Reinhard died, or where he's buried, or *if* he's buried. If I knew, I would hope that he's lying next to Rommel, and I would visit them both, and bring along seagulls, and beer, and bass. We kept a respectful distance from each other. We were family of sorts then at Reeperbahn 29, above Clochard, which didn't survive the first COVID-19 lockdown.

PART III

Power & Oblivion

ABREAST SCHWARZTONNENSAND

BY ZOË BECK

Blankenese

Translated by Noah Harley

Dramatis Personae

Kai-Uwe: CEO of a storied family business in Hamburg
Bernd: Kai-Uwe's lawyer
Jens: Kai-Uwe's head of PR
Sören: Expert witness
Gerald: State prosecutor and golfing partner of Kai-Uwe
Cordula: Wife of the victim
2 Policemen
Waiter
Head chef
Bartender

I

A Hamburg marina on the Elbe, a warm weekend in early summer. Most of the berths are occupied, sailing boats and motorized yachts float side by side. One yacht stands out among the long piers, the Bull Shark, *somewhat longer and taller than the others, and shining bright as a new penny. Next to the yacht stands Kai-Uwe (57), the CEO and sole heir to a top family business in Hamburg, and a favorite topic in the tabloids. He's dressed in yachting shoes, red chinos, and a yellow polo shirt with the collar flipped up. He is on the phone but mostly listens intently, making affirmative noises. Jens (54), Kai-Uwe's head of PR, stands at a discrete distance, dressed much the same as his boss and typing on his smartphone as Bernd (60) rides up the pier on a rickety bicycle, the front basket holding an Aldi bag stuffed to the brim. Bernd sports the same style as the others, albeit in more muted tones.*

Jens: Are you crazy? You can't just take your fucking bike on—

Bernd: Hey, thanks for getting here so quickly, Bernd! So nice of you to jump right up when we call, Bernd! You're the best, Bernd! [*He gets off the bike.*] Morning to you too, asshole.

Jens: Right, right, sorry. But you can't just take your bike—

Bernd: [*Waving to Kai-Uwe, who paces back and forth, still on the phone.*] Why don't you just tell me why I'm here instead.

Jens: We had an accident. With the *Bull Shark.*

Bernd: Shit, did you hit another boat?

Jens: A solo yacht.

Bernd: And he wants to file a complaint?

Jens: Right now he doesn't want anything, he got stuck in the ship's propeller. I don't know how much is left of him. Kai-Uwe is finding out.

Bernd: You're shitting me. Dead?

Jens: No . . .

Bernd: Was he the one in the ambulance that almost ran me over?

Jens: No, that was for Anita. Did you see the helicopter? He was in there.

Bernd: And what the hell happened to Anita?

Jens: There was this dull thud, we stopped right away. His little boat was floating there in the Elbe, all scrap metal, he was lying facedown in the water. We fished him out, what was left of him anyway. It was Anita who fished him out, actually, I can't stand the sight of blood. She couldn't get hold of the left arm . . .

Bernd: Goddamnit!

Jens: Maybe half a right foot . . .

Bernd: Goddamnit!

Jens: Anyway, she got him up on the swimming deck. It was a total mess, he was bleeding everywhere, and I can't stand the sight—

Bernd: What a nightmare.

Jens: We hightailed it here full throttle and all hell broke loose, the rescue helicopter and whatnot.

Bernd: And Anita?

Jens: Kai-Uwe thought she should go to the hospital in case she was in shock—she was throwing up the whole time after we docked. It must be because of the foot, it was hanging on by a tendon, she said.

Bernd: Goddamnit!

Jens: I know. I didn't look, I can't stand the sight—

Bernd: And the guy's still alive?

Jens: So far . . .

Both look over to Kai-Uwe, who waves and walks toward them.

Kai-Uwe [*into the phone*]: Yeah, no, it drives perfectly, and you can't see anything from the outside. [*He claps Bernd on the shoulder in greeting, then wanders off.*]

Bernd: Who's he talking to?

Jens: The guy who maintains his yacht.

Bernd walks over to Kai-Uwe and grabs the phone out of his hand.

Bernd [*into the phone*]: Howdy, we'll call you back, thanks!

Kai-Uwe: What are you doing?

Bernd: Talk to me first before you say anything to *anybody*!

Kai-Uwe: But he has to know what happened! And clean it up!

Jens: I hope he can stand the sight of blood.

Kai-Uwe [*dismissively*]: I've taken Sergei hunting a couple of times; he can eviscerate a deer in record time.

Jens gulps softly.

Bernd: So Jens already told me about your fishing trip. Who was driving?

Kai-Uwe: I was.

Bernd: How did the accident happen?

Kai-Uwe: No idea, there he was all of a sudden. *Thunk!* And it had happened.

Bernd: Mmm . . . where?

Kai-Uwe: A little farther down the Elbe, out by Schwarzton-nensand.

Bernd: Mmm-hmm . . . . Was he allowed to be sailing there?

Kai-Uwe: They just dredged a new shipping channel there, I think so.

Bernd: How is it possible that you didn't see him?

Kai-Uwe: You're my lawyer, you tell me!

Bernd: Kai-Uwe, I can't work like this!

Kai-Uwe: He was just there.

Jens: We might have been going a touch too fast.

Bernd: Had you been drinking?

Jens: What do you think?

Bernd: But not you.

Kai-Uwe: Of course not! You know me.

Bernd: So yes, in that case. Have the police already been here?

Jens: No, they should be here any minute now. [*Looks down at his Rolex.*] I don't know where they are.

Bernd: Kai-Uwe, listen, please go get a bottle of booze this instant and take a shot here in front of us.

Kai-Uwe: Why do you . . . [*Pauses.*] Aaaahhhh . . . clever! Be right back. [*He disappears into the* Bull Shark.]

Bernd: Good, let's get that cleared up. You swear that when you were out on the boat he—

Jens: Not a single drop! Never! He's strict about that.

Bernd: We'll still have to practice a little. You can't lay it on so thick for them.

Jens: Right, of course, I see.

Bernd: Weather conditions?

Jens: Spotless. We were just out there. You can see for yourself.

Bernd: Hm. Hmmmm . . . Wind?

Jens: Not too strong, I guess.

Bernd: So the sailor might have been stuck?

Jens: I was up on the sundeck with Anita. I have no idea.

Bernd: We need Sören.

Jens: Who's—

Bernd: He's an expert for exactly this sort of thing. Where are the police?

Kai-Uwe returns with a bottle of anise in one hand and three stacked glasses in the other.

Kai-Uwe: Bottoms up, gentlemen.

Jens: Yeah, not for me, I still don't feel well.

Kai-Uwe: Now, of all times!

Jens: All right. [*Takes a glass and has a shot poured, then hands it to Bernd.*]

Bernd: No, one of us has to be sober here . . .

Jens knocks back the shot and hands his glass out to Kai-Uwe for another.

Kai-Uwe: I'm always out golfing with Gerald.

Bernd: The DA, Mr. Langenbeck?

Kai-Uwe: The one and only. He said the police were talking about jurisdiction; we still have a couple of minutes. [*He takes a double shot of the anise.*]

Bernd: Excellent. Then I'll write to Sören that he should come. And Anita should keep an ear out in the hospital for how the other one is doing.

Kai-Uwe: Would it be better for me if he made it, or better if he *didn't* make it?

Bernd [*focused on typing a message on his smartphone*]: That depends on what he says if he does make it. And how believable it is.

Kai-Uwe: But what if I *did* run him over?

Bernd: Accidents happen. But you have Anita and Jens as

witnesses, and he doesn't have any. And if he is dead, there's nobody to testify against you.

The pier begins to fill with a well-dressed crowd, many with sweaters draped over their shoulders and polo shirts. They greet the three men courteously, keeping a respectful distance. The other piers fill suddenly as well. Two policemen in uniform and Gerald (47) are among the crowd.

Bernd: What is it now?

Kai-Uwe: *Queen Mary 2.*

Bernd: Ah, that's right, that's today.

The luxury cruise ship Queen Mary 2 *sails past. The three men position themselves with their backs to the Elbe, arms around each others' shoulders, grinning for Kai-Uwe's smartphone. Jens snaps another selfie of the three of them, followed finally by Bernd, who tries to get in a shot before the ship sails past. The crowd waves to the* Queen Mary 2, *snapping photos like crazy. Bernd, Kai-Uwe, and Jens all post the selfies to social media. The ship passes, the people leave, and the three men continue as if nothing had happened.*

Bernd: DA Langenbeck! [*He motions to Gerald, who is walking along the pier with two policemen.*]

Gerald: Gentlemen!

Kai-Uwe: Hey, Geral . . . Mr. Langenbeck, Dr. Langenbeck, sir, good morning.

Gerald: What a horrible turn of events. You're the owner of the *Bull Shark*? [*He signals to the uniformed police officers that they should take notes.*]

Kai-Uwe [*playing along*]: That's correct.

Bernd: I'm his lawyer. Unfortunately, I wasn't able to prevent him from permitting himself a small nip due to his shock.

Gerald: Understandable, understandable. We'll still have to take a Breathalyzer test. And you're a witness?

Jens: It's awful, yes, I'm still in total shock. All of us. A tremendous shock.

Kai-Uwe: I don't think I'm even depositional . . . Bernd, what's it called?

Bernd: Eligible for questioning. He's not really in a condition to speak right now. He's on his way to the doctor.

Gerald: Of course. But can you contact us right after? You'll have to go on record about how it all happened.

Kai-Uwe: Naturally, Dr. Langenbeck. It's just right now, my nerves . . .

Gerald: Of course, of course, anybody can see that.

Jens: How's it looking with the . . .

Gerald: It isn't looking good. But the doctors are doing what they can.

Jens, Bernd, and Kai-Uwe all make long faces and nod gravely.

Bernd: I'll show you the *Bull Shark* then, so you can get a picture, and my client really does have to go to the doctor now, otherwise he'll collapse on us.

Gerald: You know what? We can just have your doctor take a blood sample.

Policeman 1: Dr. Langenbeck, sir, wouldn't it be better to do the test here?

Policeman 2 holds the Breathalyzer at the ready.

Gerald: Very well, but hurry, the man is in need of medical attention.

Kai-Uwe [*making an effort to look weak and out of sorts*]: Thanks, Dr. Langenbeck, sir. [*Breathes into the machine.*]

Policeman 2: Yikes. [*Shows Gerald the result.*]

Gerald: Yes, yes, but he just drank something because of his shock.

Policeman 1 takes notes.

Gerald [*turning to Bernd*]: Well then, let's take a closer look, shall we?

Bernd [*to Kai-Uwe, boarding the ship with Gerald*]: Can I leave my bike parked here?

Kai-Uwe: You're not really supposed to.

Jens [*putting on a show for the police*]: Kai-Uwe, let's get you to the doctor, you can barely walk on your own the way you're shaking! [*Leaves with Kai-Uwe.*]

The two policemen stay behind on the pier, staring at the old bicycle with the Aldi bag.

II

One week later. A luxury hotel terrace on the Elbchaussee in the Nienstedten district directly overlooking the river. It's on the "butter" side of the street with a view of the Elbe; the north side of the street is called the "margarine" side. The terrace of the famous hotel gives out onto Finkenwerder, a former island in the Elbe connected to the mainland by dykes since the 1960s; today it is mostly the factory site for a European airplane manufacturer.

Kai-Uwe sits by Bernd and Jens at a table laid out with oysters and other delicacies; two champagne bottles chill in ice-filled silver buckets. Kai-Uwe and Jens are both dressed in brightly colored golf clothes, sunglasses, and hats, Bernd is dressed a little more quietly as usual, the same Aldi bag lying on the ground next to his chair. To their side sits Sören (32) in a suit and tie, trying not to let on how much he is sweating.

Sören: And you didn't even see him?

Bernd: Just a minute! [*Whispers with Kai-Uwe.*] He couldn't see him because he didn't have his sail up.

Jens: Aahhh, that sounds good.

Sören: Hmm . . . [*typing on his iPad.*] But at some point you must have seen him, at least for a second, otherwise it sounds like you weren't paying attention.

Kai-Uwe: Maybe when we passed him earlier.

Bernd: Slowly and at a proper distance.

Kai-Uwe: Passed him slowly and at a proper distance.

Sören: Right. You could say for instance that he pulled into the channel on purpose, maybe to get hold of the yacht, because his sail was down. For whatever reason.

Kai-Uwe: Excellent idea.

Jens: Suggest that he got himself into this shit of his own accord.

Sören: Precisely. How fast were you going?

Bernd: Just a minute. [*Leans over and whispers to Kai-Uwe.*] He was observing the prescribed speed for yachts along this stretch of the Elbe. Find out how fast that is.

Sören [*typing on his iPad*]: Noted. Well, I don't see any issues at all where my report is concerned. [*He reaches for his champagne glass to top it up.*]

Kai-Uwe [*patting him on the shoulder*]: Excellent work, my friend. Excellent work. Then have a good rest of your day and I'll expect it tomorrow, right?

Empty glass in one hand, full bottle in the other, Sören looks at Kai-Uwe in confusion for a moment before understanding his marching orders.

Sören [*setting the glass back on the table and the bottle back in the bucket and standing up*]: Ah, right, of course. I wish you each a pleasant rest of your day as well.

Jens: Thanks, and say hi to your father!

Sören: Gladly, thanks very much. I should have sent you his regards, I completely forgot, sorry about that.

Kai-Uwe: It's no trouble at all, young man. How is your mother by the way?

Sören: Very well, thanks, I mean considering the circumstances . . . To be honest, she's not so well at the moment. But she has her ups and downs, and she—

Kai-Uwe: Your father should call if he needs anything. Private care like that is expensive.

Sören: That's very generous of you, thank you.

Kai-Uwe: Young man, you can't look at it like that. It's just the bonds of human friendship. It has nothing at all to do with your work.

Sören: Thanks, that's—

Kai-Uwe: Give them my regards, you're the best. And you'll email me the report?

Sören [*about to bow, but instead shakes hands with everyone and begins his retreat*]: And thanks for the champagne and—

Bernd: Take care, Sören, thanks!

Jens: We'll see you later!

Kai-Uwe [*waits in silence until Sören has left*]: Dear lord, there goes a hopeless case.

Bernd: We can't give him too much, it will draw attention.

Kai-Uwe: I thought I might pay the costs for his mother's care for a while.

Bernd: It'll draw attention. Make a donation to the care facility.

Jens: That's good. We can do a press release: *A generous donation from the Hamburg businessman in the amount of a half million to the private care facility* . . .

Bernd: No press release, it'll draw attention!

Jens: So I can't do anything with anything!?

Bernd: You already posted the picture with the *QM2*, that was already pushing it.

Jens: Oh come on, it's my job!

Bernd: And it's *my* job to keep you out of jail. The evening paper had both stories side by side. "Lone Yachter Critically Injured in Boating Accident" next to "QM2 Visits Hamburg, Famous Businessman There to Greet the Luxury Liner with Friends." All someone has to do is connect the dots and start asking questions.

Kai-Uwe: What kind of questions?

Bernd: Why you're standing there waving at the fucking *Queen Mary* but haven't wasted a single breath about heroically saving a sailor, for starters?

Kai-Uwe: Pure altruism—you don't have to shout everything from the rooft—

Bernd: It smells like a cover-up. Jens, think something up.

Jens: First you say not a word, now you tell me to think something up.

Bernd: Nobody could have guessed that he'd survive. How do things look, by the way?

Kai-Uwe: Anita got me his hospital file.

Bernd: Do I want to know how she managed that?

Kai-Uwe: Ole and I play tennis together. He's the lead doctor.

Bernd: Okay, so I don't want to know. We never saw the hospital files. Let me see.

Kai-Uwe [*slides him the iPad*]: Right arm missing, left leg amputated, a major blood infusion, four operations to date, more scheduled, currently in an induced coma . . . it's all there.

Bernd: But he's going to wake back up?

Kai-Uwe: Seems like a tough cookie.

Bernd: It would be simpler if he weren't.

Kai-Uwe: What am I supposed to do? I guess I could just go there myself and yank the tubes.

Jens: Or shut off the machines.

Kai-Uwe: Or ask someone to.

Bernd [*thoughtful*]: No, I think we're good as is. You have Anita and Jens as witnesses. He has zero. That should be enough. Then we have the report . . . Yes, that'll be enough.

Jens: So I draft a press release then?

Kai-Uwe: About saving him?

Bernd [*still pondering*]: No, no, it's too late for that. What we really need is a medical certificate for Anita. Do we have one? Severe trauma, yadda yadda yadda.

Kai-Uwe: I'll write Ole.

Bernd: Nothing in writing! Call him and set up a time for tennis.

Kai-Uwe: But I can just as easily write him.

Bernd: Just call him, for the love of god!

Kai-Uwe takes out his phone, gets up, and walks over to one side to call his tennis partner.

Kai-Uwe: Hellooo, my friend, and how are we doing? Tomorrow already? All right then, Tuesday. Excellent! Looking forward!

Jens: If it does come out, do we say that we held back out of concern for Anita's condition?

Bernd: I still have to think about it. DA Langenbeck said it was highly unlikely that any charges would be brought, and that the investigation will be over soon. All that's missing is his testimony, but that might be awhile yet.

Jens: How he managed to survive . . .

Bernd: Normally you're chop suey if you wind up in a ship propeller.

Jens: Tough cookie.

Bernd: An extremely tough cookie.

Kai-Uwe [*sitting back down*]: What do we actually know about him?

Bernd: Teacher.

Jens: But he's tougher than that.

Bernd: Gym teacher.

Jens: Maybe that's why.

Kai-Uwe: Where?

Bernd: Mümmelmannsberg.

Kai-Uwe: And he can afford a solo yacht?

Jens: They cost nothing.

Kai-Uwe: Ah. Well then. What do they cost?

Jens: Under ten.

Kai-Uwe: That isn't anything.

Jens: Like I said.

Bernd: Married, no kids.

Kai-Uwe: Good, a couple people less who might get a notion to sniff around.

Bernd: The kids wouldn't be old enough to sniff around, he's thirty-six.

Kai-Uwe: What about the wife?

Bernd: Physical therapist in the same neck of the woods. They have a small house there. All very modest.

Kai-Uwe: And his wife hasn't rung any alarm bells yet?

Bernd: DA says no, she's still in shock and at the hospital every day with her husband.

Kai-Uwe: But sooner or later she'll start to point the finger somewhere.

Bernd: We'll have to wait it out.

Kai-Uwe: Will we? Or maybe we should prepare ourselves, don't you think?

Bernd: You mean dig something up on him?

Kai-Uwe: Or her. Just for safety's sake.

Bernd: They're so modest you would look right through them if they were standing there in front of you.

Kai-Uwe: Sometimes those are the worst. Then they'll start

moaning about how the rich are to blame for everything, the press gets involved . . . I don't need it. We have to be certain that we won't catch anything from their end.

Bernd: Fine then, I'll take care of it.

Jens: What do you think about a weekend Instagram story about—

Kai-Uwe: Nothing with yachts! Or ships!

Jens: No, I thought here on the terrace—we get some more oysters, a little food porn, get the head chef in for a picture . . .

Kai-Uwe: Let's go for it.

Jens gets up to track down a waiter.

Bernd: You know what else would be good?

Kai-Uwe: Shoot.

Bernd: Swing by the police office that's working on this and offer your help. No, better—thank them for their hard work. A small donation for the police sports league. That's good.

Kai-Uwe: I have to go there myself?

Bernd: It's always better. Your time is valuable, you're not supposed to take a half hour for yourself really—but for friends, you'll make the time.

Kai-Uwe [*tapping on his iPad*]: Where am I supposed to fit that in? . . . I could skip out on the sauna, I guess . . .

Bernd: With this weather you don't really need a sauna.

Kai-Uwe: You still don't get the idea. You should come sometime.

Bernd [*reaches for his Aldi bag and stands up*]: You aren't the only one with things to do. I bid my adieu. [*On his way out, he says goodbye to Jens, who is just returning.*]

Jens [*sitting down next to Kai-Uwe*]: The head chef will be right out.

Waiter [*bringing fresh oysters and refilling their champagne*]: Anything else here for the gentlemen?

Kai-Uwe: We need anything else for decoration?

Jens: No, I think that'll be enough.

Waiter: The *Queen Mary 2* is just leaving Hamburg and will be passing by within the next half hour. For a short while the terrace might get somewhat crowded, I hope you won't be disturbed.

Jens: I completely forgot. No, that's great! Oysters, champagne, head chef, AND the QM2. That's a good story.

Kai-Uwe: Do people really care about this sort of thing?

Jens: If you don't want the tabloids up your ass then you have to take care of your own content. Then it gets boring for them and they can't sell anything, because your whole life is already online. How many times do we have to go over this?

Kai-Uwe [*sighs*]: Fine then.

The head chef of the restaurant comes out dressed in full attire and greets Kai-Uwe and Jens warmly. The terrace fills with people. The Queen Mary 2 glides by in the background, this time downstream. People take selfies and wave to the ship. The waiter shoots photos of Jens and Kai-Uwe with the head chef as they stand behind the sumptuous table grinning, the luxury liner in the background.

III

Three months later. A small but exclusive club just outside Blankenese, situated on the Elbchaussee in a pretty park along the banks of the river. To the side a couple of tennis courts, empty today in the pouring rain. The club itself is practically empty as well, all except for Kai-Uwe, Jens, and Bernd. They are dressed in white tennis shoes, light pants, and brightly colored but tasteful, pricey polo shirts; only Bernd wears a classic white tennis sweater with the telltale V-cut. Next to him is an Aldi bag. The waitstaff are cleaning up behind the bar.

Jens: . . . so then we can do a big fundraiser for the police dog squad next week. That seems good to me.

Kai-Uwe: Great, very good. But the dogs, I won't have to . . . ?

Jens: Well, for the photos it might be nice if you at least pretend you aren't afraid of them.

Kai-Uwe: But do I really have to? I mean, what if one of them bites?

Bernd: They're trained to only bite criminals.

Kai-Uwe: I see. But can't we do a photo montage or something like that?

Cordula, a pretty woman in her late thirties, storms into the club dressed in jeans, running shoes, and a simple blouse soaked from the rain. She walks straight up to the table where the three men are sitting.

Cordula: I'm the wife.

Jens: Uh . . . this is a private club.

Kai-Uwe: The wife of . . . .

Cordula: The man you chopped up into small bits. I thought that at some point you might have the decency to contact me yourself.

Kai-Uwe: Oh, so you're—

Bernd: Pardon me, I'm his lawyer. I discouraged him from contacting you before police investigations had been concluded. You have to understand.

Cordula: No, I *don't* have to understand. A normal person

would have asked how my husband was doing. A normal person would have wanted to know how *I* was doing. And whether they could do anything for us.

Kai-Uwe: Do anything for you . . . ? Excuse me, what?

Bernd: We inquired regularly about the state of your husband. Regularly. Continuously.

Jens [*muttering*]: Nightmare . . .

Kai-Uwe: But he's doing better now, isn't he? He's back at home, right?

Cordula: Since yesterday.

Kai-Uwe: I'm glad to hear it.

Cordula: Minus an arm, a leg, and a couple other nonessential organs. His spleen, a kidney, then there's—

Kai-Uwe: But he's alive. It's still good news!

Cordula: You are a complete asshole.

Bernd: Excuse me? You're insulting my client with witnesses present—you should be aware of that!

Cordula [*ignoring Bernd*]: A huge asshole. I only knew you from the media before, and I thought you might be one of the good ones. But what you did to my husband, to us . . .

Jens: He saved your husband's life! I was there!

Cordula: He drove over him because he was going too fast and didn't look properly!

Bernd: That's an assumption. Unsustainable.

Cordula: My husband told me everything.

Jens: But I was there! Anita was too!

Kai-Uwe: I wasn't going too fast at all. I mean, what is that supposed to mean, *too fast*? In a boat?

Cordula: You know I've had to get my entire house renovated? The bathroom, kitchen, multiple stair lifts. My husband can't drive a car anymore, even though he has to if he wants to keep working. Or if he wants even the least bit of independence or normalcy, if that's even possible. So now he needs a custom-built handicapped model.

Kai-Uwe: Don't you have insurance?

Cordula: Not enough. Insurance only covers a part.

Kai-Uwe: So you want money from me?

Cordula: At first all I wanted was an apology. An explanation. Just a conversation about what happened. But now—yes, you're right, I do want money. It's only fair that you absorb some of the costs—ultimately you're the one responsible.

Kai-Uwe: How much are we talking about?

Bernd [*laying his hand on Kai-Uwe's arm, whispering*]: Don't get involved!

Cordula: Altogether, I mean in total . . . we're short thirty thousand. Everything else I can do on credit, and I've borrowed money from relatives. My brother did a crowdfunding campaign. The thirty thousand I would need for the car.

Bernd: Excuse us for a minute.

Bernd stands up, takes Kai-Uwe by the arm, and drags him over to a corner.

Bernd [*whispering*]: It's an admission of guilt if you do that— you might as well go to the police station with her. With that sort of extrajudicial agreement, you'll always be the guilty one.

Kai-Uwe: Because of a measly thirty thousand?

Bernd: It won't work. You can't do it.

Kai-Uwe: So now?

Bernd: We get rid of her.

Kai-Uwe: What if I gave her the money anonymously, through that thing, what's it called . . . ?

Bernd: Crowdfunding? There's no anonymity on the Internet. Some journalist will figure it out in no time at all, and you're screwed.

Kai-Uwe: Right again. Okay, so how do we get rid of her?

Bernd: Allow me.

They return to the table, where Jens is staring nervously at his phone and Cordula stands watching the two closely, arms crossed.

Bernd: Ma'am, we have two sworn witness statements that your husband is to blame for this regrettable accident. He wasn't properly recognizable, it most likely occurred in a stretch of water that wasn't open for solo yachts, and he tried to trail my client's vessel in order to gather speed. You can find it all in the report.

Cordula: I'm familiar with that report. It's a joke. There are multiple reports that totally contradict it. Independent reports, I might add.

Bernd: Yet none of the people making those reports were at the scene, and neither were you. As I said, the witness statements carry a great deal of weight. In our opinion, the blame lies with your husband. Plus, you insulted my client in front of witnesses and tried to blackmail him—

Cordula: *I* tried to blackmail this worm?

Bernd: I can attest to that. Jens, you as well?

Jens: Absolutely.

Cordula [*wheeling around toward the bar*]: You heard everything that was just said here, right?

Bartender: I can't hear anything from back here. [*Disappears through a swinging door that reads*, Kitchen.]

Cordula: My god, what pathetic pieces of shit you all are.

Bernd: I'll ignore that now, that and your use of "worm." So aside from all that, we are currently preparing a counterclaim for damages against your husband. Firstly, for damages to the yacht . . .

Cordula: I don't believe this.

Bernd: . . . and then for the regrettable absence of his closest employee, who has been unable to work since the incident. She has been sick for well over six weeks now, and with all the projects she has . . . I have no way of telling you what it will come to yet, but it isn't going to be cheap.

Cordula: How dare you sue my husband after you tore him into pieces!

Kai-Uwe: Please, young lady, I saved his life!

Silence. Cordula stares at the three men, who stare back at first but only for a brief moment, before they drop their eyes and begin to fidget with their coffee cups and iPhones. The bartender comes back through the swinging door and cutlery clatters in the background.

Cordula: I'll say it again, with witnesses present and for the record: you're all pathetic pieces of shit. [*She storms back out of the club.*]

For a minute the silence lingers, broken up only by the coming and going of the waiter. At last he emerges from behind the bar to collect their empty glasses.

Waiter: A round on the house for the gentlemen?

Kai-Uwe, Jens, and Bernd [*in unison*]: Oh yes, please.

Outside, thunder rumbles.

IV

The following weekend. The harbor in Wedel, nighttime. The Bull Shark lies in flames. Bernd, Kai-Uwe, and Jens stand at the water's edge in the glimmering light, staring down the pier where the fire department is at work. The three men are in fancy evening dress; Bernd is dressed more modestly. An Aldi bag lies at his feet.

Jens [*shocked*]: This is a huge story, huge.

Bernd: How well is the thing insured?

Kai-Uwe: More than enough.

Bernd: That's something at least.

Jens: She really was a beauty.

Kai-Uwe: We'll all miss her.

Jens: We could make a collage maybe, the *Bull Shark*'s most beautiful trips. Or maybe just: our most beautiful memories. Or wait, wait, even better—we could crowdsource it, people who took pictures of the boat from shore or wherever.

Kai-Uwe: Not bad either.

Bernd: The one time you get tickets to the philharmonic, and then this happens.

Kai-Uwe: It was during the intermission.

Jens: And we got some good selfies with the conductor.

Bernd: I would have liked to stay till the end.

Kai-Uwe: I can't just sit around doing nothing while my *Bull Shark* is burning.

Bernd: Ah, here comes Dr. Langenbeck. [*Waves.*] Over here, sir!

Gerald walks over to the three men. He's dressed in a tracksuit and looks as though he has just showered, his hair is still damp.

Gerard: Kai-Uwe, this is just awful!

Kai-Uwe: Thank you, yes, it's horrible.

Gerald: Do they know yet how it could have happened?

Kai-Uwe: One of the firefighters said we would have to wait for the investigation, but it's probably arson.

Gerald: We'll be doing an extremely thorough investigation. If it turns out it really was arson, there will be consequences.

Jens: All the hatred toward yacht owners is getting worse and worse. And people who drive SUVs. People can barely step outside their villas anymore!

Bernd: Actually, somebody was seen sneaking around here. I already spoke with security, there's footage on the surveillance cameras.

Gerald: Excellent. We'll find him, I'll make sure of it. Kai-Uwe, I really am so sorry for you.

Kai-Uwe: I appreciate it, thanks very much, my friend.

Bernd: I think we all know who's responsible. If it was arson. Which we can only assume.

Gerald: You have a suspect?

Bernd: Last weekend Kai-Uwe received a serious threat. She tried to blackmail him.

Gerald: Who?

Bernd: The wife.

Gerald: You mean the woman whose husband . . . ?

Bend: That's her.

Kai-Uwe: I mean, maybe it wasn't a direct threat, but she was livid. She wanted money.

Gerald: Are you serious? Unbelievable! Why don't I know about any of this?

Kai-Uwe: The poor woman has enough problems as it is, I didn't have to report her on top of it all. People say all kinds of things when they're upset. But this . . .

Gerald: We'll look into it. This can't stand, grieving woman or not.

Bernd: She was quite angry because Kai-Uwe hasn't visited her husband yet.

Gerald: I see. [*Lowering his voice*] He didn't even send a card? Or send flowers to the hospital or anything?

Bernd [*upset*]: Please, sir, he saved the man's life, it's the other way around!

Kai-Uwe [*solemnly*]: I did, I saved his life. Anita too. He really has a lot to thank Anita and me for.

Gerald: Mm-hmm . . . But not even a card?

Kai-Uwe: He's had the best medical attention money can

buy. I asked about it at the hospital. And besides, why bring him a card when he's lying in a coma?

Gerald: He hasn't been in a coma the whole time.

Kai-Uwe: I saved his life. Me and Anita! Jens was there too.

Gerald [*snorts*]: All right then.

Bernd: I'm almost positive it was his wife. A highly emotional person. Quick to accuse and insult. A short fuse.

Gerald: I'll pass it along. [*Looks toward the burning yacht.*] What a waste.

Kai-Uwe: Such a beautiful ship.

Jens: We'll give it a proper send-off. I have a couple of ideas already.

Kai-Uwe: It really was a beautiful ten years together. There's no way the next one will be as dear to my heart.

Jens: Yes, she really was exceptional.

Kai-Uwe: I spent more time there than on any other ship. And all the little adjustments and changes I made, it's like a part of me is there in it. Maybe they can build another one just like it? Or is the same model even still available?

Jens: Let me check. [*Types on his phone.*]

Kai-Uwe: That woman really knows where it hurts.

Bernd [*quietly*]: Insurance will pay one way or the other, and soon you'll have a new yacht. Even if it isn't the same one.

Kai-Uwe: Cold comfort, but yes, you're right.

Gerald: I'll see what I can find out from the fire department, and my men will get the surveillance footage. I'd be shocked if we didn't come back with something soon. [*Begins to walk away.*]

Kai-Uwe [*calling after him*]: I need police protection until you have her.

Gerald [*calling back*]: You'll have it, I'll send a patrol.

Kai-Uwe: Good. Then I think I'll go home too.

Bernd: Take me with you, my bike is still outside the philharmonic. Then I'll catch a cab.

Kai-Uwe: Let's go then, I have to take my mind off this.

Jens: Oh, one other thing. What do we do about Sergei?

Kai-Uwe: Right, we need some short statement, right?

Bernd: And you should write to the family. I can draft that tomorrow.

Jens: I'll get something ready. Longtime employee . . .

Kai-Uwe: . . . and friend. Write "employee" and "friend." That sounds better.

Jens: "Like family"?

Kai-Uwe: Perfect. Anita will send you some basic info—you can text her, you can always reach her at home.

Jens: Okay, that's that.

Kai-Uwe: See you then. Let's go, Bernd.

Bernd [*grabbing his Aldi bag*]: See you in a few days! Oh, and put in the usual stuff for Sergei: "Our thoughts are with his loved ones" and so on. And make it clear we're paying for the funeral.

Jens: Maybe you could donate something? Did he have any hobbies? What did he like?

Kai-Uwe: Pff, I dunno . . . It's not like I really talked with him . . . He knew enough about yachts . . . hunting . . . Oh, I know, he spoke about his aquarium once.

Jens: An animal lover, that's good. Maybe donate something to the Tropen Aquarium in his name. How much?

Kai-Uwe: A hundred?

Jens: A hundred is good.

The three men nod their goodbyes. Bernd lays his arm around Kai-Uwe's shoulders as they walk toward the car. Jens stays to type down a couple of notes and photograph the firefighters at work.

AIKIDO DIARIES

BY BRIGITTE HELBLING

Horn

Translated by Noah Harley

"*The author . . . has considered all kinds of theories as possible candidates for understanding aikido and continuing its development. In the end, he has come to realize that in the future aikido can only continue to develop as an art form.*"
—Kenjiro Yoshigasaki, *All of Aikido*

During summer it's still light out when I come home from class. Now it's winter, dark, misty. There's ice on the sidewalk. There's construction out by the racetrack in Horn, off to the right it's wasteland, construction fence to the left, out front the traffic hums along the wide avenue. Kids hanging out by the kebab stand, whistling, laughter. It takes me ten minutes to get from the subway to my place, seven if I use the shortcut through the park. I never do, though, not in winter, not at night. "Hey, lady, wait up, would you?" Does the voice mean me? Is someone calling out for help? Give me a break. Didn't Pierre just tell us in class, "If you are attacked, always remember that the first impulse in aikido is not to resist, but to engage. Greet your attacker. Your basic sentiment should be, 'Hello, nice to see you!'"

A couple of months ago Baba gave me a book, Kenjiro Yoshigasaki's *All of Aikido*.

"I've got an extra copy," she said, "and you've got your exam coming up."

Thanks. I was happy about it. Baba is cool. I didn't say anything about the exam. Back at home I set the book down on the table. It's hefty—all the attack moves and techniques we practice in aikido are there in pictures and writing. I flipped through, then let it be. Why read about something I already don't understand in class?

Some nights later I picked the book back up. The first sentence that jumped out was the sensei discussing the new reality aikido opens up.

"All art creates a new reality," he wrote, "that isn't simply a copy of the world."

Kenjiro Yoshigasaki was Pierre's teacher. Kenjiro Yoshigasaki's teacher was Koichi Tohei. Koichi Tohei's teacher was the founder of aikido himself, O-Sensei Morihei. After an eventful life, O-Sensei underwent enlightenment in a garden in Ayabe. The ground beneath his feet began to tremble, and he was enveloped in a golden fog. Looking into the clockwork of the universe, he realized it wasn't fighting that lay at the heart of budo, the Japanese martial art, but eternal peace. *Well.* Aikido is full of contradictions like that. Victory without fighting. Strength lies in letting go. Pierre describes things simply, without making too big of a deal out of it. He's also not the kind of person who's always talking about whether aikido is or isn't suited for a street fight.

Fine by me.

Pierre hasn't ever said anything about creating a new reality, either.

Though I'm curious what that would be like.

There's a video online of Pierre in class with his sensei. Pierre is younger, eager. Yoshigasaki looks friendly, he moves like a dolphin in the water, smiling. He came to Hamburg regularly when he was still alive. I never met him, and now it's too late. He died of cancer two years ago.

I'm sitting at my desk in Horn writing this. Behind me there's a poster of Yoda, the Jedi master from *Star Wars*. Yoda was a present from Gudrun. Normally I don't see him, he watches over my shoulder on video calls. All the IT guys I work with relax the second they see him.

The IT gals do too, it's just that there are barely any in my line of work. I have to deal with so many guys on the job that sometimes I forget I'm not one myself.

Most of the old aikido teachers died from cancer. O-Sensei Ueshiba died of cancer. Liver cancer. With Yoshigasaki it was pancreatic cancer. In class we learn to focus on a point that lies a hand's width below the navel. That's the point where our body's ki connects with the ki of the universe.

Sometimes I ask myself if all this concentrating on our lower abdomen might come with drawbacks—developing cancer cells, for instance?

Something happened to me that I have to sort out. The book Baba gave me is involved. My exam. Gudrun, the thing with the janitor. Golden fog. It's not so easy to see. For the moment everything's all jumbled up.

* * *

"I don't think we can get cancer from aikido," Sam said. "We're simply not proficient enough."

Among us students, Sam is the most advanced, 2 *dan*. He takes over class once a week. He's very precise in his instructions, totally different from Pierre, who talks about body lines and extending your ki in more general terms.

The two are a perfect complement to each other, in my opinion.

We were out on the porch of the sports club where our dojo is housed, during break. Beneath us a women's soccer team ran back and forth on the field; off to the side lay the Schanzenpark with its joggers and bicyclists, and all the bushes where drunks take their leaks and drug dealers peddle their wares.

"Are you seriously worried about getting cancer from aikido?" Baba asked.

"Not really," I lied.

"It wouldn't make sense anyway," Sam said. "All the Japanese masters were chain-smokers. It was smoking they got cancer from if anything."

"Wouldn't that be lung cancer?"

Baba had asked the question. The same thought had crossed my mind, though.

During the pandemic, I started working three or four days a week from home. It felt dumb at first, but I've come to enjoy the extra time it gives me, especially in the morning. The only thing I miss is lunch with the office. It's in Eimsbüttel, on Oster Strasse, and there's a bunch of cool spots around with lunch specials. The pickings are slim in Horn. I don't like going to the bar by myself, either. These days I mostly stay at home, surviving off yesterday's leftovers and working on my scarf.

Knitting was another COVID thing. Gudrun turned me on to it after I griped one too many times about how unspeakably nervous the whole situation was making me. I laughed her out of the room at first. Me? Knitting? But then I watched a couple of tutorials on YouTube and bought some materials. The good news is that even with two left hands, you can learn to knit. You might get frustrated, but at least it's just about sticking to stitches, not masking policies. Don't get me wrong—masks are fine. But when they're constantly fogging up your glasses, they're also an issue. I may not get sick, but I can't see a thing. Can someone please tell me where the benefit lies?

In the scarf department, I set myself a goal—six feet! I've done about four and a half. The colors are gorgeous, straw-green and salmon-pink.

They're Yoda colors, okay?

"So, what about your exam?" Sam asked me out on the porch.

I could feel a slight anger rise in me. I stuffed it back down the hole it came from. Put a lid on it. Sayonara. "I don't know," I replied.

"The way I see it, you're basically there," Sam said. "But you have to be the one to say you want to do it."

"Won't Pierre tell me that I should?" I asked.

"That was before. You know Pierre, he's always changing the rules."

Sam was right.

One thing was for sure: if there was a *dan* for masking anger, I'd have achieved it long ago.

Of course I want to make *dan*. At some point. I like the idea of wearing the black belt and black robe that only the more advanced students at our dojo are allowed to wear.

The exam is just a step in that direction. No more, no less. Pretty straightforward.

That's one way of looking at it, anyway.

Not all that easy for me at the moment.

I talked to Baba after class about the pressure I always felt in the dojo whenever the topic of exams came up. I was heading to the subway and she was walking alongside me, pushing a bicycle that looks like she found it in a junkyard.

"I don't think there's all that much pressure," she said. "Exams are ridiculous anyway. How long have you been practicing aikido now?"

I counted. "Eight years."

"And this will be what, your third exam?"

"Fourth."

"So you know everything already."

"Yes, but still."

"Still what?"

I didn't know myself.

Maybe it had something to do with the enforced break during lockdown. Like everything had gone back to zero, and suddenly you were thinking twice about things.

Aside from work, there is nobody I see more often than the people from aikido. It's not like we're always meeting up, everyone has their own life outside the dojo.

It was the same with Zumba.

Zumba was Gudrun's idea. "We should do something for our mobility," she'd said, signing us up for the beginner's course at the fitness center on Wandsbeker Markt.

It was always easier to just go along when Gudrun got one of her ideas. The class had a bunch of women and one man, Rolf. Before I knew it, Rolf and Gudrun had shacked up together and were tramping about the apartment, packing Gudrun's stuff into boxes to move to Münster. Afterward, organizing my day-to-day was more taxing than I had expected. Gudrun might have gotten on my nerves quite a bit, but she also brought a certain amount of structure to my life. Maybe that's why I stayed in Zumba. It certainly had nothing to do with talent. At some point a coworker took me along to aikido, which was much more my speed.

Gudrun still lives in Münster, and is still together with Rolf. She works part-time for the municipality, takes care of her two kids, sells vegetables from her garden at the market, and writes poetry.

We talk on the phone once in a while, which always makes me happy. There aren't many people in my life I've known as long as her.

Maybe you could say that Gudrun has created a new reality? Without any sort of martial arts or other art form, just sex and biology.

She was already writing poetry.

"Aikido is an art for dealing with danger," I read in Yoshigasaki's book. Among the dangers listed are accidents, natural disasters, mental illnesses, cancer. Pregnancy isn't on the list. Ha ha. The way the sensei sees it, the point is to recognize any individual danger as part of a greater whole, a unified thing.

"That is only possible, however, if you see your life as being one with the universe. This is called meditation."

* * *

When I meditate, my head turns into a ballroom of thoughts prattling on. "Just nudge them gently to the side," Pierre says.

Sometimes I succeed, most of the time I don't.

Idiotic situation in the apartment lobby. I had just come back from shopping and was waiting for the elevator. When the doors opened, the new janitor was standing there with a pushcart. Maybe I take the opportunity to talk to him about his morning leaf-blowing routine? I mean, seven fifteen? A little early, don't you think? He didn't react but went right on pushing the cart toward the exit instead.

So I'm like, "Excuse me?" and got in his way.

Maybe it was a mistake or maybe it wasn't, but the cart banged directly into my hip. I nearly dropped my bags.

"Hey!" I yelled at him.

He stood there staring at me, then mumbled something and was gone.

The mumbling sounded something like "Sorry" or "Stupid cow." It was impossible to tell which, at least from where I was standing.

That night I discovered a bruise where the janitor's cart had bumped me. I wondered whether I should take a picture, as evidence, in case the episode repeated itself and I wanted to report him, maybe for assault or something.

I told the others about it at aikido.

"A photo won't do much," Baba said. "You fight, so everyone will assume that you have bruises anyway."

"A martial *artist*!" Hito said, grinning. He was back after a long absence.

* * *

Hito is half-Japanese. He's an actual artist, these days he's often traveling to trade fairs. He sells bonsai kits there that he designed himself, with seeds and pretty little containers you can fold yourself made from a special kind of stone paper. When he was still developing the business concept, he gave us some. I put mine to use right away, I was curious what would come of it. And now there's actually a little plant growing out of the container that looks just like it will turn into a mini-tree.

"How's your poplar doing?" Hito asks me whenever we see each other.

"Great," I reply with a flush of pride.

I always thought I didn't have a green thumb. Bonsais seem to be the exception.

My mom had a green thumb. Everything in her garden blossomed and thrived. She would save seeds from plants that did especially well for the following year. For years after she was gone, little bags of seeds with her handwriting were still popping up throughout the house in the most unlikely places.

Zebra tomatoes.

Runner beans.

Nasturtium.

I decided to call my dad.

He was in Andalusia on the coast, on vacation.

"So how's it going?" he asked, after raving about the famous ease of Spanish living.

I told him about what happened with the janitor.

"Damn," he said. "Why didn't you knock him out with your aikido?"

I had been asking myself the same question.

Not that I let on during our phone call.

"An attack forms a strong connection between two people. Accommodate by accepting the orientation of the attacker. Then surprise him with a new situation that he was not expecting, and to which he must respond. In this way, a technique becomes a sequence of acting and non-acting, control and lack of control."

That's what Yoshigasaki wrote, anyway.

What the hell was he talking about, our sensei?

"So, how's it going with the menfolk?" Gudrun. The question came up in every other phone call.

Usually I demurred, but this time, I don't know why, I told her about what had happened with the janitor.

"Sounds just like Sven," Gudrun said.

"Who might Sven be?"

"That's our janitor's name."

Gudrun may have been gone forever, but for her it's still "our" building.

"It's a new guy. And I don't know his name either, okay? Don't bug me about it."

"What does he look like?"

"He looks like Brad Pitt in Tarantino's Hollywood phase."

That wasn't actually true, but it had the desired effect. "The sexiest man alive," Gudrun had called Brad Pitt in the past—not like she was the only one, of course. She started gushing into the telephone—until, that is, she realized I was pulling her leg.

"That wasn't very nice of you, Lara," she said.

"True," I responded.

"Who knows, maybe he has a crush on you and that was his way of getting your attention," she mused.

"Ha ha," I countered, a little uncertain. "That was the first time I ever saw him."

"Well, maybe he's had *you* in his sights for a while now. He might know everything about you already. Think about it—don't janitors have the keys to all the apartments they look after?"

If she was seeking revenge, she had found it.

Did janitors keep a set of keys to apartments?

I remembered a film I had seen once where a guy stuck a hair over the closet door with his spit so he could tell whether it had been opened while he was out.

That was one way of finding out, though maybe slightly over the top, with the only basis for it something Gudrun had said in order to annoy me.

A dojo is a place of silence.

Our dojo is the opposite. Whenever we open the windows facing the Sternschanze train station, everything else comes in with it. The falafel stands, the drunks on the park bench, the street musicians who crank their amps when it's warm out. The wooden huts were back with the Christmas market. Jingle bells, jingle bells, along with the hustle and bustle of people packed in side by side.

"Listen to the silence behind the sounds," Pierre liked to say while we were meditating, while the screech of trains, the music, and all the holiday cheer continued outside.

"I don't know how I'm supposed to do that," Baba said one time.

I didn't entirely believe her. Baba has been in the club for about as long as Sam, and I suspect she was just trying to comfort those of us who couldn't hear the silence behind the sounds.

I'm not even sure if I actually want to hear the silence.

Somehow the idea is unsettling to me.

Once, during break out on the porch, I tried describing how it feels when I am supposed to listen in for the silence of the universe.

The emptiness I feel.

"The universe isn't necessarily empty," Hito said, laughing. "You're the *Star Wars* fan here."

Even if I was, wasn't that something else?

"I think that when someone like Yoshigasaki talks about the universe, he doesn't mean what we're talking about right now," Sam said. "At least not the *Star Wars* galaxy. It's more of an ever-present cosmic mind that everything comes from, and will return to. That's where the silence comes from. And since this idea of mind precedes language, you can't describe it in words. The connection has to be experienced, and everything else comes from that experience."

"And that does it for you?" Baba asked.

"Well, I'm working on it," Sam said, grinning.

Hmm.

Hmm.

Hmm, hmm, hmm.

Hmmmmmmmmmm . . .

* * *

Not long after the phone call with Gudrun, I went on lunch break. It was a sunny autumn day, so I took my pea pasta out on the balcony. I had barely sat down when the leaf blower started up in the courtyard below.

Like he had been waiting for me.

Was that even legal? Didn't Hamburg have a siesta hour? I got up and stood at the railing. "Hey, jerk! It's lunchtime, a little quiet up here!"

All at once, the noise stopped.

The janitor entered my field of vision. In the early afternoon light, he did actually resemble Brad Pitt—a little bit, at any rate. Minus the charisma of a film star, who in Tarantino's films is always pretending to be a simple driver or handyman anyway.

A Brad Pitt for the rest of us.

He stared up at me, I stared down at him. Like when kids play, who's going to look away first? He did—ha!

Then he looked back up, grinned, and threw me a kiss.

OMG.

I sat down so he couldn't see me anymore. *If you really care about me*, I thought, *keep your leaf blower off.*

Thirty seconds and the thing was back on.

It's about harmony. Avoiding resistance. Resistance means collision. Collision leads to hardening. Take the other person's perspective, and immediately things look different. An obvious example: the leaf-blowing janitor. Instead of lecturing him from the balcony like a grumpy pensioner, the next time the noise shows up I could simply go down and become one with the machine. Which then disappears from the scene all by itself.

Problem solved!

Yoshigasaki's "new reality" is a science-fiction world.

"Wrong," Baba laughed. "The leaf blower doesn't disappear from the scene. It just doesn't bother you anymore, because you've finally heard the silence behind the noise."

Great, just great.

Okay—but I could work on that, right? Like the exam everyone wants me to take. "Take your time," Pierre said the other day, though I don't think he really meant it.

The thing with the janitor wouldn't leave me alone. Every time the leaf blower started up in the back courtyard, it was personal. And it made me feel ridiculous. When Brad wasn't making a racket, he was smoking. There on the little bench by the entrance, like he was waiting for me.

I thought about complaining to the property manager. On what grounds? *Dear Property Manager, sir, I don't like the way this man is grinning at me.* Hrmm . . . I didn't have to bother sending something like that, I could already picture the response. And the alternative? Move. Eimsbüttel or bust! An affordable three-room apartment with a balcony, not too far from Oster Strasse. Sure.

Dream on, Lara.

Then one night he was standing there, in my apartment.

I hadn't let him in.

I hadn't even heard him enter.

What was he doing there?

He was babbling on about some window seal that had to be replaced.

In the dream it was absolutely clear that it was just a pretext.

A pretext for what?

And how the hell had he gotten in when my door was locked?

Enough, I thought to myself the following morning. Gudrun, that witch, had gotten to me. It was time to do some research.

"Did you lose your keys?" my neighbor asked.

She stood in the open doorway with her living room in full view, a yellow couch with fluffy pillows, a grayish-brown flokati rug, a framed poster of a rhinoceros on the wall. It smelled like smoke, cold coffee, and old-lady perfume. I shook my head.

"I don't know what your issue with the janitor is," she continued. "I say it's a step in the right direction. He's stubborn, that's for sure. The shoes, for example, I don't know if you noticed them."

"I don't have anything against the janitor," I protested. "I was only asking if janitors have keys to our apartments. As a matter of principle."

"I would tend to think not," she replied. "Property management, they'll have the keys. In case something goes wrong with the apartment. A cable fire inside the walls for instance. Or somebody dies and no one notices, then there's a corpse lying around that starts to stink. That doesn't only happen to old people, you know. You're living by yourself too, right?"

I suddenly remembered why I preferred avoiding this particular neighbor.

"A little while ago in Hammerbrook for instance," she went on. "The guy wasn't retired, he was young. He was out at night, came home, then *bam!* Dead."

"Uh-huh," I said.

"Cardiac arrest. Nobody missed him. The coworkers he

had been out with, it was days before they started to wonder why they hadn't heard from him."

"That wouldn't happen to me," I said. "And not just because of my job. Somebody would notice if I didn't log in at work."

My neighbor studied me thoughtfully. "Vacation," she said finally. "They assume you're on holiday. Everybody thinks you're spending three weeks on Norderney, when you're actually lying there dead in your apartment."

"You should write crime fiction."

"I do," she said. "Care to read one of my books?"

Before I could say no, she had pressed a paperback into my hand from a pile by the door.

Back in my apartment, I found the bonsai tree lying on the floor. It looked as though it had tried to escape its stone paper container. A single small root dangled over the edge. Bonsai on the lam.

Had I knocked it over by mistake?

Impossible.

Was it the wind?

All the windows were closed.

Poltergeists?

Hmmmm . . .

Tooth fairy?

My neighbor looked surprised to see me back outside her door so soon. "If you hear any strange sounds coming from my apartment during the day," I said, "just ring the bell. Somebody might be there when I'm not."

The sentence stopped making any sense to me the moment it left my lips.

My neighbor, I could tell, was having the same difficulty. She nodded, peering at me like I was missing some marbles.

"All you have to do is stick it back in the container, say a few nice things to it, and don't give it too much water," Hito said. "It'll be fine. Bonsais can put up with a lot. They just don't like to be drowned."

"How did that even happen?" Baba asked. "Were you playing soccer in your apartment?"

We were back outside on the porch. Beneath us a real soccer game was going on, the farm team for FC Hammonia.

"Of course not," I said, looking down at the bleachers next to the soccer field. Suddenly my heart seized.

There was a man down there, he looked like—

No, it wasn't him.

"In extreme instances, the only solution left is to kill," I read in Yoshigasaki Sensei's book.

What???

"Where did you read that?" Pierre asked.

I showed him the place in the copy of the book that we have in the dojo cupboard.

"Oh, that," he said. "That's what you mean. That's the chapter where Yoshigasaki writes about how important it is not to let resistance develop in the first place. It's quite challenging, I find. Especially when you're attacked, since the first reaction will be fear. Or anger. Both consume energy. Both mean blockage, collision, and if you don't find a way out, then very quickly someone is dead."

"Sounds like you're speaking from experience," Baba laughed.

Pierre flipped to the next page, which described a basic form. "Look here," he said, "we haven't done this one for a long time."

So then, for a whole hour, we practiced how to enter into the opponent's ki, bring his head to your shoulder, absorb the ki, and then—Kotegaeshi—extend his arm farther upward while taking a side step—Sayu Undo—and letting his body fall. Control. Non-control. Control. Non-control. Easily and naturally, the attacker disappears into the void that has opened up beneath him.

In principle.

"Not one of your strengths," Pierre said to me when we were finished.

He could say that again.

He did.

While we were changing, Sam made the mistake of asking me about the exam.

"Have you decided yet?"

I could have screamed.

I took a deep breath.

"Yes," I said.

"And?"

Greet your attacker. Your basic sentiment should be, "Hello, nice to see you!"

"I'm not going to do it," I said.

Sam looked at me. I looked at him.

"Leave her alone," Baba said. "If she doesn't want to, she doesn't want to."

Sam nodded.

A feeling washed over me like I had won some victory.

Warm, easy, free.

Astonishing.

* * *

The miracle continued as I headed to the subway. I felt as fresh as a newborn. Baba had gone the other way on her dumpy bicycle, which was just fine by me. I didn't feel like talking to anyone.

In the train I put my headphones on.

Twenty-five minutes to the racetrack in Horn.

I like my part of the city, it's a good match for me. Neither of us are particularly flashy—but functional, yes. And optimizable—who isn't?

Just before getting off, out of the corner of my eye, I saw . . .

That's right, you guessed it.

"Hey, lady!" the voice calls out behind me.

Who's the lady here?

I don't answer, I don't turn around. I just keep on walking at an even pace toward home.

"Wait up, would you?"

The grin in his voice is familiar.

Nasty.

What now?

Let's just see what happens, the new feeling of courage tells me, as I turn into the park and take the shortcut I never take during winter, and never at night. Ice lines the trampled path. The tread on my winter shoes would have worked in the Himalayas. Around me a glow—not golden, but close to it. The trick involved is not thinking about the crazy thing you're pursuing at the moment.

My footsteps in the crackling leaves.

There is nothing to hear otherwise, absolutely nothing.

Wait . . .

Is that a blackbird?

I stop for a second, listening carefully.

When the bird falls quiet, the silence that follows is borderless, universal.

I keep walking.

The street picks back up at the far end of the park, four lanes, not much traffic. There he is, leaning against an electric box, waiting for me.

I look at him . . .

Hello, nice to see you!

. . . see him as he starts moving heavily, almost running, and then—

In real life, here everyone agrees, you can forget all about the techniques that you practice in the dojo. The lessons behind them might get you somewhere. Or not.

—slips on the ice between us. What kind of shoes is he wearing? God, they're like slippers! Floundering to keep his balance, he stumbles into the street where a Golf is coming up too quickly, and while one part of me stands there, gawking like they do in movies, another leaps directly out in front of the Golf's bumper with my Himalaya shoes, the driver behind the windshield staring slack-jawed at my Kotegaeshi arm, my fingertips etching a brilliant calligraphy in the night sky, pointing out his path toward the other side of the street, where a Toyota just barely dodges it, scraping the Renault behind, before turning, shuddering, catching itself, and curving back into the right lane, its red taillights disappearing in the fog—

—and Brad, or whatever his name is, back on the sidewalk, straightening himself up in his ridiculous shoes, one hand on his shoulder, ouch, and handing me my bag with the other—

—my bag, I had forgotten it on the train—

—and looks at me, not a nasty look, out of breath—

"Hey."

"Hey, thanks!"

I wake up in the middle of the night and can't fall back asleep. I get up, take a beer out of the fridge, and wander over to the bonsai. A flower bud hanging from one of the branches. Bloodred. A blood poplar. *I have to tell Hito*, I think. I sit down, reach for my knitting, and look outside into the night, the stars, the universe bursting with life—

What a blaze of color!

The beer tastes delicious.

I knit and the scarf flows easily and uninterrupted from the needles, like a wool Yoda skin, like a living being.

Another miracle.

My neighbor's novel lies on the windowsill, the image of a gloomy, gray country road on the cover.

Sirens in the Fog is the title.

Wrong.

There were no sirens. Nobody came to collect the injured or dead, nor drove crumpled cars off to the side, nor drew chalk lines on the asphalt; no ambulances or tow trucks or police cars along the side of the road, no moans or cries or officials taking pictures, none of that—

Then what was there?

Calligraphy in the night, a ballet of vehicles, a Golf that kept on driving like nothing had happened.

Later: beer bottles on the kitchen table, the ashtray half-filled, and now . . .

"Hey."

A figure in the doorway.

Brad.

Non-Brad.

Surprised?

Not a new reality. Not exactly.

The old one can stay, as far as I'm concerned.

THE GIRL AT THE DOM
BY KAI HENSEL
Heiligengeistfeld

Translated by Noah Harley

I 'll tell you a love story. It's not a love story exactly, there's a crime at the end, though it's not exactly a crime story either. But to understand everything that came after, the person I am today, you have to . . . I have to start this a different way.

There's a fair in Hamburg called the Dom, named after a medieval cathedral that has long since ceased to exist. It takes place three times a year on the Heiligengeistfeld in St. Pauli. It's the largest of its kind in the north, though it's hardly known about outside of Hamburg, unlike Oktoberfest in Munich. It has everything you might expect at a big carnival: roller coasters, a Ferris wheel, sausage stands, shooting galleries, etc. As kids the Dom was the the city's biggest draw, all the more so in 1991, before cell phones and the Internet were around, and the year when this story plays out (though it isn't just a story, it actually happened).

That summer our family didn't manage to go on vacation; our grandmother had gotten sick. Looking back, I wonder why my parents didn't at least send me off to summer camp. My sister was probably too young at age nine, but I was already twelve. It must have been too late to sign up by the time they discovered the cancer. It was hot that summer, and all of our friends were gone on vacation. So we sat around watching TV, reading in the garden, splashing in the pool, and boring ourselves silly.

A trip to the Dom was something else entirely. Lights, laughter, loud music, the smell of grilled meat and roasted almonds. It was already packed by the afternoon, and children routinely went missing, wandering tearfully through the crowd while mothers called out in worried voices. It almost always ended with an adult hoisting the child up onto the shoulders so their parents could spot them, or with an announcement from the carousel ("Little Tanja is looking for Mommy!"). Reunion, embrace, a few tears and words of scolding, and everything was back to normal.

That afternoon I got lost myself, after about an hour. I was an independent kid, if a little absent-minded at times, and I tended to get lost. It might have been the massive teddy bears at the ticket counter that lured me off, that or the bouncy horses in the shooting gallery. Whatever it was, I suddenly lost sight of my parents and sister. My heart raced. I wasn't little anymore, but I had grown up sheltered in one of Hamburg's more prosperous neighborhoods. All alone among so many people, without my bearings in an unfamiliar place—it was a new situation.

"Looking for someone?"

The girl stood next to the Creepy Cave, a haunted house ride. She had long black hair, pale skin, and big blue eyes. She was wearing a dirty white dress and combat boots.

"Just my parents," I replied, trying to look cool.

"Scared?"

"They're around here somewhere."

To this day, I remember the gap she had between her teeth, top right.

"Come on."

She took me behind the ride and started climbing a ladder. I climbed up after her; behind the wooden walls I could hear wailing and the rumble of cars.

"Watch out for the cable," she said.

We climbed all the way up, in between the heads of two monsters. We stopped on a grating and looked around; we had a good view out over Heiligengeistfeld, out to the Ferris wheel and the roller coaster. Light bulbs were flashing next to us, while beneath us cars passed along part of the outer facade before disappearing back inside. There at the Enzian Express was my family, my sister sitting on my father's shoulders, glancing around.

"There they are!" My coolness gone, I raced back down the ladder far too quickly and ran over to them. First a hug, followed by accusations: "You can't just walk off like that . . ."

I turned around. The girl stood next to the haunted house, smirking.

The days that followed were hot and boring. My father would be at his law office, my mother visiting Grandma in the hospital or heading out to the neglected garden with the cat. After four days, I did something I had never done before: I told my sister that I was going to visit a friend, and got on the train into the city by myself. I had ridden the train alone before, but never so far, not with transfers in Altona and Sternschanze, and definitely not without telling my parents.

I found the girl sitting out behind the haunted house on the stoop of a camper van, reading comics.

"Oh, it's you," she said cooly.

Her name was Sarah and she was thirteen. I was Malte, I was twelve.

"Sounds like a kind of beer," she said.

We crossed Heiligengestfeld; she knew some of the carnies and we ate fish rolls, chocolate-covered bananas, and rode the pirate ship, all for free.

"New boyfriend?" asked the man who let the safety bar down, winking at us.

"He lost his parents."

"No I didn't," I said.

"But it looks like you did."

What did I look like? I looked good, that much I knew. Reddish-blond hair, brown eyes, and a summer tan with freckles. Unfortunately, I was also wearing linen shorts, a Marvel T-shirt, and flat cloth shoes. Sarah was wearing a checkered men's shirt with a wide belt, gray leggings, and her combat boots. Next to her I probably did look like a little kid who had lost his parents. The carts tossing us back and forth on the Voodoo Jumper made me dizzy, while she casually waved at someone she knew.

"Now what?" I asked, once we were back in front of her haunted house ride. The monsters' eyes were blinking red and a witch was swinging her clawed hand, but the carts stood still. A bloated, unshaven man crouched in the ticket booth, awaiting customers.

"Have you been?" she asked.

"We didn't get to it last time."

The truth was that our parents hadn't allowed us to. We were too young, they said. I didn't tell her any of that, of course.

Sarah pulled me over to the carts. A young man, maybe about twenty, stood at the gate chewing gum. Sarah spoke quietly to him, pointing to the ticket hut. The man nodded and we sat down in one of the carts. With a hiss, a nozzle shot out steam and we rode into the dark.

Coffins. Bones. Strobe lights and howling ghosts. A huge spider with green eyes. Prisoners reached their hands out through iron bars. More steam and bones. The tracks creaked as the cart struggled upward. Slamming doors, sunlight, a sharp curve. Outside we rode past the monsters before we were back in the dark. A skeleton shot out of a coffin, a cannibal smirked at us, lips bulging. We descended, rocking back and forth. There was a little *piff* then a *puff*, a vampire winked at us, and suddenly we were back outside. We climbed out, Sarah on the lookout again so that the man in the ticket booth wouldn't see us.

"Well?" For the first time there was a hint of trepidation in her voice.

I didn't want to be rude, but I didn't want to lie either. "The skeleton in the coffin was okay," I said, but I couldn't hide my disappointment.

The Creepy Cave wasn't creepy at all.

After that I started to visit the Dom daily. I told my mother I was going over to my best friend Friedrich's house, though he was off sailing with his parents on the Adriatic. Sarah was almost always out in front of the camper van, though sometimes she was at the entrance to the Creepy Cave with the young guy, Hanno, who was her brother. The grumpy older man in the ticket booth was their father. Sometimes he would come out cursing about something and get a can of beer out of the camper. Sarah and I killed time on the Heiligengeistfeld eating currywurst, or visiting the 3D simulation and bumper cars—there was always someone she knew. Once we had enough, we would climb up to the grating behind the monster heads and sit back to back, talking about life. Sarah knew a lot about life, nearly everything there was to know, it seemed. She had grown up at fairs, traveling from city to city ever since she could remember. She wasn't in school much—looking back, I think she was barely able to read. She could see through people and things though, making declarations like, "The government is screwing us over," or, "Hanover is awesome," revealing a world that people in Othmarschen knew nothing about. Before long, I didn't mind feeling like a little kid anymore; there was no competing with Sarah's worldly wisdom ("The blonde over at the shooting stand is a butch").

Her whole family, her father and brother—her mother was long gone—lived in the camper van. It wasn't a common setup; most of the people involved with the fair rented apartments, or at least rooms, during the Dom. But the Creepy Cave didn't bring in enough for that; in fact, it made less and less every year. Aside from the family, there was an old Polish man who traveled with them, Jakob, who helped with setup and breakdown, drove the truck, and was always repairing something in the cave. Not a day passed where he wasn't welding, soldering, taping, patching, or covering something. The Creepy Cave was old, "thirty years old at least," Sarah said. That wasn't necessarily a lot for a ride. Generation after generation, young and old had stuck to the same walls on the Rotor. The Crazy Mouse roller coaster was popular the world over, and remained virtually unchanged since the twenties. But a haunted house ride had to change with the times. The technology aged, and crowds grew numb to some of the effects. Other things, a Black cannibal with large lips for instance, were now considered offensive. A haunted house has to keep up and reinvent itself from time to time or it goes from jolt to joke, or in the worst case just annoying. Sarah's haunted house wasn't keeping up, it wasn't even trying. "We need a new ride," Sarah griped. "We could still sell the old one, Jakob says there's a market for it in Poland." Her dad didn't want to sell though, much less to "the Poles." He had spent his entire life with the Creepy Cave, and knew every last witch and ghoul. "The Creepy Cave has soul," he kept saying. The only problem was that fewer and fewer people cared to find out anything about it. Certainly, none of this was as clear to me then as it as now writing today. But even a twelve-year-old who didn't know much else about life could get the basic gist: the carts stood empty most of the time, Sarah owned practically nothing aside from her skirt, two shirts, and her comics, her father drank too much, and her brother kept staring off stonily into the empty hole of his future.

One afternoon—it was especially hot that day—we sat in the shade out behind the camper van studying brochures from haunted ride manufacturers across Germany, England, and the US. Zombie Thriller, Layers of Fear, Ghost Trip . . . elaborate rides with three or even four floors and state-of-the-art technology—Dolby Surround Sound, lasers, holograms, computer-generated animations. "Horror at its finest," promised one. "A new dimension of nightmare." Then there was the Haunted Horror Dungeon. Four floors, with hairpin turns and a "vertigo free fall." Thirty wagons that shook horizontally and vertically, ninety-five feet tall and a hundred and fifty feet across. The ride needed four entire trucks to transport it. The Haunted Horror Dungeon reigned supreme among haunted rides, nothing else compared, not in the brochures nor on Heiligengeistfeld. We flipped through the pages with bated breath, zeroing in on especially sinister details. Here a mafioso with a meat cleaver, there the withered breasts of a replicant. Our knees touched beneath the brochure.

"What's it cost?" I whispered.

"A million," she said under her breath.

A *million!* The price seemed astronomical; to this day, I don't know whether she just made that up. You didn't have to pay all the money at once, she explained, a down payment was enough. The Creepy Cave had insurance, then there was a policy for her father. In case something happened to him or the ride . . .

Suddenly a wheezing sound and steps, and her father stood in front of us, face flushed and holding a beer. "So your little friend is back?"

Sarah tried to hide the brochure under the camper van, but it was too late. He spotted it and tore it out of her hands. When he saw what we were looking at, his face got even redder and he clenched his fists. "So you're filling her head with this crap? You . . ."

The brochure was from Hanno, but what help was that to me now?

"Run!" Sarah screamed.

I sprinted as fast as I could, tripping over a cable and slipping, before pulling myself up and stumbling off . . .

Behind me her father was wagging his fist. "Don't you ever let me catch you back here again!"

"What's the matter with you?" my mother asked.

"Nothing," I said, lying motionless on my bed and staring up at the ceiling.

"Something's wrong."

"Nothing's wrong."

"I saw Friedrich's mother this morning. They got back yesterday."

"Good for them."

"You kept telling us that you were going to Friedrich's. But he wasn't even here."

"It was a different Friedrich. You don't know him."

"Are you lying?"

Silence.

My mother sighed and walked toward the door. "You know you can talk to us about anything."

"Close the door."

I didn't go back to the Dom for four days. I lay on my bed the entire time barely eating, thinking about Sarah and her father and the money—I couldn't see a way out.

Friedrich came over. We played ping-pong in the basement; when I lost, I told him the government was screwing us over. Friedrich stared at me in bewilderment, he was still a kid and didn't understand anything.

We visited Grandma at the hospital. She lay propped up against the pillows like a withered ghost; I could immediately picture where I would place her, behind the left-hand curve on the second floor, where the shock would be the biggest. My mother whispered into my ear that I shouldn't stare like that. She acted cheerful and kept saying how much she was looking forward to Christmas, when Grandma was healthy again and we were all together in front of the tree.

We watched a game show on TV, and the winner won a dream house worth a million deutsche marks. The host handed her the certificate while a small orchestra played and confetti rained down, tears of joy streaming down the woman's face. I imagined I was the host and Sarah was the winner, a gleaming new haunted house ride worth a million deutsche marks—I handed her the certificate. Ghouls howled as skull bones rained down from above, and she threw her arms around me, crying. But that was nonsense! Shows like that didn't exist. The insurance policies would have to pay for it, at least for the Creepy Cave, there was no other way. But for that to work it couldn't look like arson, Sarah had explained, somebody from the chair swing had done that in Delmenhorst, and he was in jail now. The moon shone through my attic window as I lay awake and contemplated ways of destroying the ride that would trick the insurance people. A rogue bumper car crashed through the gate, slamming into the cave . . . a kid threw up in the cannibal cauldron and a fire broke out, tongues of flames shooting out . . . It was no use, none of my plans would work. I tossed and turned, felt Sarah's hand in mine, her knee touching mine. I loved her, that much was clear. But I didn't want to love her, I wanted to *save* her.

I got to the Dom around noon on a muggy, hazy Wednesday. Everything was still closed. The door to the camper van stood open, but I didn't see anyone. I climbed up the ladder to our perch between the monster heads, where I had a view of the camper and would be able to spot Sarah without her father discovering me. I wanted to propose that she come back to my house in Othmarschen to start a new life, with school and new clothes. I wanted to tell her that if she decided against it, which I completely understood, I wanted to be there for her, that as soon as I got older I could work and earn money . . . I paused for a moment on the ladder. There were noises coming from inside, creaking and breathing. I climbed farther up to the second floor, where there was an entrance. I needed a moment to get used to the darkness, with sunlight slipping through the cracks at odd angles. Witches and ghosts hung lifeless from their metal rods, and I pushed my way through the cannibals, feeling my way deeper into the darkness. I saw

Sarah first. She was standing under a gallows, pale as an undead fairy, the hem of her white skirt lifted up. She wasn't wearing any underwear. A couple steps away her father stood gazing between her legs, one hand propped up against the executioner's block, the other moving rhythmically. Sarah saw me and cried out, letting her dress fall. Her father wheeled around, turning red then pale, then reached for the axe on the executioner's block. He stunk like booze, his penis dangling out of his pants like a broken joystick.

"You . . ." he panted. "You . . ."

Sarah grabbed hold of her father, but he shook her off and came toward me. When he swung the axe, I ducked behind the cannibals for cover. He stumbled, tearing through a bunch of cobwebs, and crashed into the gallows, which splintered and broke, then smashed his head on the tracks to the ride. He straightened himself up, blood dripping from his temple, before sinking back down to his knees, clutching at his stomach and penis.

"Get out of here . . ." he panted. "Everyone . . . get out . . ."

He didn't look so much dangerous as sad, burping and bleeding next to the collapsed gallows. Sarah was trembling.

"You can't tell anybody," she whispered.

"Your father can't do that kind of thing to you."

"My brother will kill him."

"It'll harm your growth. You have to see a counselor."

Her father slumped off to one side, and a few seconds later he was snoring. We looked at each other. We couldn't leave him lying there like that next to the tracks, the ride would be starting soon. We would never manage to get him back down the ladder.

"In the coffin," I said.

I cleared the skeleton out of the coffin, then we grabbed

hold of her father by his hands and legs and maneuvered him in.

"The booze!" Sarah yelled.

She brought over the half-empty bottle and we stuck it in the coffin, closing the lid. Sarah went to get a toolbox from downstairs and we set the gallows back up, fixing it with some fabric and positioning a steam nozzle so that passengers wouldn't notice the spot later on, we hoped. Her father grunted and rolled in the coffin. We stapled the cover shut and draped the skeleton over it. It wasn't a real coffin, just thin plywood—it would be easy for him to get out later. For the time being, we hoped that he would get a couple hours of rest. We heard the bottle tip over in the coffin and a trickle of booze began to form a puddle at the head; Sarah wiped it dry with her sleeve. Jakob called up and we climbed down the ladder. He grinned when he saw us, sweating and flushed—he was picturing something else.

"What about your father?" he asked.

We shrugged, we hadn't seen him. He muttered something about alcohol wrecking your brain, pressing some knobs and tugging levers. Moments later the light bulbs flared up, and howls and the sound of chattering teeth came pouring out of the loudspeakers. The Creepy Cave had lived to see another day.

Wednesday had a reduced price for families (and still does to this day). The Dom filled earlier than usual with young families. I ran through the stalls blindly, feeling numb. The scene in the Creepy Cave was still pounding through my head: I saw Sarah with her skirt raised and her father in front of her, rubbing himself between the legs. She needed to see somebody right away; I did too, probably. But what I really needed was money. I had to buy the Creepy Cave, it was the only hope. I used all the money I had—about six marks—on a game, but only won enough tokens for a lighter in the shape of the Eiffel Tower. I could give it to my grandma; she could use it to light the candles on the tree when she was back home for Christmas. I kept running around, totally disoriented, until, an hour or two later, I was back in front of the Creepy Cave.

Business was better than usual. Carts rumbled, doors clattered, teenagers hooted, kids snuggled down into the arms of their parents. Jakob sat at the ticket booth, keeping a worried lookout while Hanno alternated between looking after the carts and the control booth; today of all days, they could have used the father's help.

I didn't see Sarah anywhere. I was on my way to the camper van when I heard screaming coming from up above. A cart with two kids clinging to their parents came through the doors; everybody looked horrified. A second cart followed with teens hooting and jeering, "What a sick ghost!" The door opened again, though this time it wasn't a cart but a zombie, the likes of which the Dom had never seen. His hair was caked in blood and sweat and one eye was swollen over. Drool came from his mouth. His undershirt was torn, his penis dangling from urine-soaked trousers. He stumbled across the tracks to a chorus of "oohs!" and "aahs!" from below, but there was no railing. The next cart came out and rammed into the zombie from behind, derailing. Sparks flew, screams erupted, and the zombie braced itself against the cart, cursing and drooling. Another cart came through the door and there was another collision. The zombie raised its first, lost its balance, then tipped over the tracks and hit the pavement with a thud.

I remember absolute silence, though that isn't possible—

the music from the other stands and rides must have kept going. The frozen feeling I remember must have been my own as well. The crowd swelled, curious onlookers streaming in from everywhere. I caught sight of the father for a fraction of a second, his cracked skull, a sea of blood, before I was pushed back. The entire scene—from the moment he appeared on the tracks to the moment he crashed onto the pavement—couldn't have been longer than thirty seconds. In my memory it lasts an eternity.

I didn't run. I stood there in the crowd getting jostled back and forth; before long, I heard sirens and an announcement over a loudspeaker. My hand wrapped around the Eiffel Tower in my pocket. I knew what I had to do. And I knew I didn't have much time.

For days after I lay in bed with a fever, breaking out in fits of sweat and heart palpitations. "Summer flu," my mother declared, and made me nettle tee and warm compresses. In truth, I was waiting for the police to arrive. But they didn't come. What came instead was a wave of reports in the evening newspapers, on the radio and local TV: tragic accident at the Hamburg Dom, the father an alcoholic, child neglect, a call for donations . . . The cameras showed the burned-out Creepy Cave—the police were calling it an electrical short circuit. My mother clapped her hand over her mouth. "My god, that's exactly where we were trying to find you!" Nobody had seen a twelve-year-old boy in shorts climbing up the ladder to the Creepy Cave shortly before the fire broke out.

I felt better after a few days, and could get up and go out to the garden. But I resolved never to feel happy again for the rest of my life.

The fair ended, vacations ended, Grandma died. My sister and I stood at the coffin. "Have you ever seen a corpse?" she whispered to me. I quickly shook my head.

The new school year started. Friedrich and I were back to playing ping-pong, and I won just as often as before. The teachers were pleased with my work, commenting only that I seemed absent at times, as though I wasn't focused on things but hovering above them. I turned thirteen, fourteen, my placid sense of stoicism proving a source of wonder, even confusion, to my parents and classmates alike. Nothing upset me, I seemed to float permanently a couple of inches above the hustle and bustle. No signs of hormones or rebellion; the doubts and crises of my friends all fluttered past me. It was as though I had left everything they were suffering through long ago.

I turned fifteen, sixteen, I didn't go to any protests, didn't get into graffiti, drank only out of politeness, didn't take any drugs. At seventeen I got my first girlfriend, Christina, and it was at her urging that I returned to the Dom for first time since the summer of '91.

It was December, the winter fair. It's traditionally somewhat larger than during summer, with mulled-wine stands and additional rides. I didn't think back much to what had happened; my memory had sequestered it all in the realm of the unreal. We walked past the shooting stands and candy stalls—they had barely changed with the years. For a moment I thought I must have dreamed it all.

Then my heart stopped.

It was the Haunted Horror Dungeon. The ride was larger than just about anything else at the fair. Four floors. Long lines waited outside the ticket booth, and every few seconds a cart rushed inside.

"Should we go?" Christina asked.

"A haunted house, I dunno . . ." I responded, hoping she wouldn't hear the shaking in my voice.

"It must be really good."

"Why don't we—"

"Oh come on!"

How could I deny her? I got in line, drawing nearer and nearer to the little booth where a young woman sat in a white jacket, pale, with long black hair and blue eyes. My heart beat faster with every step. I wanted to run away or find some excuse: *I'm sorry, Christina, let's go on the Ferris wheel, the roller coaster, anything you want . . .*

"Two tokens, please."

I pushed a ten-mark bill under the glass. Tokens at the ready, the woman glanced at me and froze for an instant . . . then slid the chips under the glass, along with the ten-mark bill. Fingers trembling, I gathered everything up and tried to stammer out a thank you, but she was already looking past me to the next customer. I walked back to Christina, hoping that she hadn't noticed anything. We climbed up a set of stairs and got into a cart. A crew of young men were helping people in and out and lowering the safety bars—it was an actual business. I didn't see Jakob. Hanno, now with a full beard, kept watch from behind a pane of glass.

We entered the darkness. Christina pressed herself against me, and I wrapped an arm around her. The cart swiveled left then right, up and down; ghosts leaped out at us as we drifted up to the second, then third floor, a hairpin curve, vertigo free fall, Christina let out a whoop . . . I pulled her toward me and kissed her like I had never kissed any girl before.

"I love you," I whispered to her, her face flashing green and blue in the light of a hologram. "I love you . . ."

* * *

That was all more than twenty-five years ago. Christina and I are long since married; we rarely fight. Our kids are well-adjusted and the pride of their grandparents, who visit regularly. We built our home on my grandmother's property—a large, spacious compound with a pool—at precisely the right time, when interest rates were low. My father has retired from his law practice, which I run now along with two partners with similar values. Sometimes, when I'm facing an important decision, I take out my wallet, where I keep the ten-mark bill that I would never think of spending or exchanging for euros. I grip the bill between my fingers, sensing its voice, its force. *Trust yourself*, it usually says. And most of the time, it's right.

Even now I come across as a little absent at times, somehow above it all. During those moments, my life feels like one long, cheerful epilogue. As though everything important lies behind me, and I already fulfilled my primary life goal in the summer of 1991. It seems as though anything good that I've experienced since then has come as a reward for the one right decision that I made at the time, a twelve-year-old kid in shorts with a lighter in his pocket.

Is there anything left to wish for? Maybe at best that my kids experience something similar. Not that it's likely—a father can't do much about that. It was a gift then and would be today—a gentle push from some higher, benevolent power.

Last year Christina and I took the kids to the Dom. Our youngest—named Friedrich, like his godfather—was eleven at the time, and sometimes a little absent-minded. We hadn't gone more than a couple hundred feet when suddenly he was gone. Christina fell into a slight panic—"God, where's our son gone? What if something happens to him?"

"Don't worry," I said, handing our daughter some money for a candy apple and slipping my arm around Christina, "he'll come back."

EXPROPRIATION

BY ROBERT BRACK

Ottensen

Translated by Geoffrey C. Howes

Klara writes: Tuesday, November 28, 1922. I will join the Communist Party to atone for my guilt. I will fight against the oppressor to exact revenge. I will fight until I have cleansed not just myself but the whole world of the stigma, the mark of Cain, which blemishes everyone . . .

She wipes a tear from her face and continues writing: I no longer feel anything, my heart has died, my soul is frozen.

The table in her garret room just barely fits next to the bed. To open the wardrobe, she would have to put the washbowl on the floor. A nail on the door awaits her coat. Cold air seeps in through the hatch, along with the screech of the wheels on the first junction line, rattling from Altona to Hamburg.

Lying next to her diary are a cigar, a cigarette, and a box of matches. She reaches for the liquor bottle, takes a gulp, can't help coughing, and writes: I ought to stick a fuse in this, it should be a firebomb, a signal! For . . . No! I won't write your name again. Maybe I should erase it from what I've already written.

From time to time, flashes flicker across her ceiling. Then a tram crosses the nearby intersection. Morning is breaking. Soon the steam and smoke from the industrial railways will waft over the roof. Steps can already be heard on the sidewalks in the winding streets. Often they sound metallic, as if the passersby have nailed rivets into the soles of their shoes. She, too, is supposed to go to the factory. "Just like every day, for all eternity, amen." That is what she said to Hedy the first time she linked arms with her. Laughing.

Klara wrote: Wednesday, November 1. What good luck I've had. They believed me when I said I was eighteen years old! And why shouldn't they? I feel grown up, it's only a couple months away. Now I'm going to be a worker. Not a little shrew like the woman I've left behind in that sad, stuffy town. Work makes the man. So why not the woman too? The workwoman! I like that word. I found this room on a tip from the newspaper lady on the main road. I asked her what newspaper the workers read. She showed me the "People's Daily" and the "Echo." I picked the "Echo." Then I asked her where I could find a room. Her eyes narrowed: "You new here? No dough? But respectable?" I nodded. "If you read the 'Echo,' you gotta go see Stühr." She named an address. "He's a stogie roller!" I didn't know what she meant by that, but I didn't dare ask.

With my knapsack on my back, I trudged on my way. My god, what a hubbub there is in this Ottensen place! The neighborhood is nothing but industry. Little freight trains rumbling down the streets, the tram gets in your way, the wagons block you off. Before you know it, a barrel is rolling over your foot, or there's a crate full of stinking animal hides in your face. Phew!

And all the streets and alleys are crooked! The huts and stalls get in each other's way. She's sent me on a wild goose chase. It seemed like the address was wrong, but people knew the name Stühr. "Hedy lives back there," someone said. Next to a low passage there was a sign: "Retail sales through the gateway."

Then I was at a sliding window. A woman of indeterminate age, wearing a lot of skirts, eyed me. All of a sudden I had a bad conscience, heaven knows why. She interrogated me: "Where ya from?" A different city. "By yerself?" Yes. "Got work?" Not yet. "Money?" I want to work. "Hmm." Incidentally, she sold cigars. Those were the "retail sales." I showed her the "Echo": "The newspaper lady said because I read this, I should ask here." "Is that right?" She was skeptical. Then she said, with a crooked grin: "The papers have only interpreted the world in various ways, ain't that so?" So I replied: "The point, however, is to change it." She nodded earnestly and led me up a steep stairway to the attic. It was divided up into little cubbyholes and one bigger room full of men crouching close together. One of them was talking incessantly to himself. Only later did I notice that he was reading to the others from a book. It was cold up there. The wind was blowing in through a hatch in the roof. Even so, it smelled of men's sweat and some spice I didn't recognize. The old lady introduced me briefly. Old Stühr was the only one who looked up. She said a few words I didn't understand. He nodded slightly. That's how I got in with the cigar rollers. The spicy smell came from the tobacco leaves stacked in a corner.

My little digs are across from that room, under the gables. It's so cramped, and the slanted ceiling is so low, that right away I picked up two bruises and a goose egg on my head. But I've got a feather bed, a jug, and a washbowl. Ain't I the lucky one? To get set up so quick?

Mrs. Stühr wants the money up front, for a week. "Just don't put it off," she said, "'cause it loses its value so fast."

In the evening I met Hedy, and I'm nuts about her. ~~But psst! Don't tell anyone~~! She has skin like porcelain, with tiny freckles, brown eyes, and curls that shine like fresh chestnuts. We could almost pass as sisters. Her slender hands really know how to swiftly roll a "stogie" from leftover tobacco. I'll take up smoking yet, because of her.

Hedy (I really like writing her name!) laughed when her mother told her about the thing with the "Echo": "With me, you'd be better off showing the 'People's Daily'!" She's sticking with the Spartacists, but her parents think she's on the wrong track.

Klara wrote: Thursday, November 2. Hedy (again!) took me to the factory the next morning. They hired me right away. "I wouldn't have recommended it to you if you weren't class conscious," Hedy said. "There's probably going to be a strike." Hoo boy, I thought, have I made a mistake here? Chosen an incalculable risk for the sake of a pretty face? But aren't things tough all over? And the workers' struggle, isn't it inevitable?

Hedy (oh my!) gave me a precise explanation of what's at stake: the Karlmann cigarette factory wants to exploit the inflation to push down wages. Quite simply, by not raising them. If they did that, they would be driving their workers into destitution—and most of them are workwomen. Hedy stands by the machine and makes sure that the tobacco is "flowing." I'm a rookie, so my job is sorting and packing. It's a sweat-drenched mad rush because the machines set your pace.

And on top of that, there's getting to work! It takes us an hour on foot. All the way to Bahrenfeld. A military barracks there was converted into a factory. We're being drilled on the parade ground of capitalism—that's how Hedy put it.

Which is why I'm now endlessly tired after my workday. The thick down duvet is waiting for me. I hope my cold feet will warm up quick. Where does Hedy sleep?

* * *

Klara wrote: Sunday, November 5. My head is spinning. Too much has happened. This city is my destiny, but I don't like my destiny anymore. I was able to play guardian angel even though my intentions were diabolical. I wanted to throw myself away. Instead, I picked up another person. You might even think there's someone up there, steering my fate. But in my favor?

Should I have asked her? I had such an urge to! On Saturday, the shift ends an hour earlier, so it was still light when we set off for home. Unfortunately, we were getting drizzled on by rain that felt like it wasn't just made of water, but of soot as well. It clung smudgily to our skin. The gasworks aren't far from here.

The question was on the tip of my tongue. I'd tried it out again and again while sorting out the damaged cigarettes, a job that brings you to tears because you have to pay such close attention. The question: "How would it be if we spent a nice evening together?" Or: "Haven't we earned ourselves a nice evening?" Or: ~~"Take me out, Hedy!"~~ (Oh, that would be so wonderful!)

I almost said it. Because she was paying so much attention to me. She was asking me questions. She wanted to know something about me. "Where are you from?" Makes no difference. "Is it far from here?" Infinitely far. "Did you run away?" I fled! "Why?" Because of the goddamned boondocks, it was so dreary, so cramped, so narrow-minded. And I was fleeing from . . . "From who?" That man! And then she laughed: "One man or more of them?" All of them! "What do you have against men?"

What was I supposed to say to that? Especially when she came at me with Edgar. "A person does need at least one of them, doesn't she?" How can she look at me so mischievously while asking that question?

"I dunno," I grumbled.

"I dunno."

"I dunno."

"I dunno."

And that's why I headed out that evening. Alone.

Yes.

All you have to do is cross the border, then you have all the freedom. In the area dedicated to St. Paul, even the streets are named for freedom: Kleine Freiheit, Grosse Freiheit. Little Freedom, Great Freedom. They've hung so many colorful garlands of lights over the street that just looking at them makes you woozy and your heart beats faster. But of course, the pictures and posters with the beautiful women are painted for men. You have to round three or four corners just to find the "Ladies' Club" on a side street. The address was in the "Girlfriends' Guidebook." No sign over the door, no pretty women in the display window. But what about inside?

Oh my god!

I didn't even have enough money! One glass, and it would be gone. And that's what made me . . . I just had to . . . that's when I became . . .

First, the thin woman with the feather boa and the endlessly long cigarette holder. When I told her I stuffed those things, she laughed snootily. Then the gaunt one with the riding crop. She was practically tripping over her patent-leather boots. The plump one with heavy breasts under a sailor's sweater got into rough seas after her third rum . . . That's when I skedaddled . . .

And in that goddamned darkness I lost my way. Suddenly I was at the water's edge. Cargo barges, stacks of wood planks, and once again those crates full of rancid animal hides. Those are my curse! I just puked my guts out.

You've got to go downriver, I told myself, that's the right direction . . . then up a stairway, then another, and higher . . . and then he was lying there, moaning to himself.

I leaned over him and only recognized him when he mumbled her name.

He groaned. "Hedy?"

Her father. Collapsed. Feeble. He wasn't all there. I helped him up.

"Hedy?"

"Come on, I'll take you home."

He hung on my shoulder like a sack of potatoes.

"Hedy, I had no choice . . ."

"Hush now, I'll take you home."

"They pay in dollars . . . This is our chance . . ."

"Please walk! Let's go! Get moving!"

"Hedy . . ."

"I'm not Hedy!"

Even so, I had to listen to his confession: "Mother will understand . . ." The confession of a man who's turned smuggler in hard times and is ashamed of it.

In the rear court he came to and was surprised to see who was escorting him. He led me to the window to Hedy's quarters and knocked gently. She said: "Edgar?"

He groaned: "It's me . . . Father."

That got her moving. She came out and looked at me, bewildered.

"I found him. He was lying on the street . . ."

"Phew! He reeks of booze!"

"Hey, it's me!" (So direct, my god!)

She stared at me. And I stared back. She was wearing a white nightgown.

I said: "A specter is haunting Altona—the specter of beauty."

She snorted a laugh and hauled her father inside.

I staggered up the steps and fell into bed.

Dreamed that she came in and covered me up and ~~breathed a kiss onto my forehead~~.

In the evening: I spent Sunday in bed with Goethe's "Werther." I found it on a shelf over where they roll the stogies. Because on Sundays it's quiet up in the attic. That's when the smoothing board and cutting machine are idle and no one's stirring the tobacco glue. The wrapping forms and shaping presses are arranged neatly on the shelves, and the work aprons hang limply from the hooks. No coarse, hairy men's hands are separating the stems from the leaves, spraying them with mist, cutting oval wrappers and filling them with fine-cut tobacco, while condensation drips from the fogged-up panes of the ceiling hatches. No hefty male bodies are squatting side by side, wrapping and rolling their stogies, whose value goes up in smoke day after day after day.

And I'm amazed that a man can write about another man who harbors emotions that only a woman can feel toward another woman.

Klara wrote: Wednesday, November 8. Isn't it practically a betrayal if a woman turns her attentions to just one man? Wouldn't it be better if the collective of lovers made no distinctions? Especially since he's a Communist. Edgar. If love were free association, then everybody would be Communists. But something has been forgotten in the course of history . . . the freedom of love. What a feeling! If it were spread all around, it would surely bring down the walls of every fortress. But Edgar talks of nothing but the class struggle. That's all right with me.

Maybe we'll go on strike. So that Karlmann gives us more

money for our drudgery in his "butt shop" (as Edgar calls it), because its value goes up in smoke day after day after day. I'd like to singe Edgar's hair off so that his blond head stops infatuating Hedy. Poke out his eyes, which shine so blue blue blue. Mangle his mouth with its charming grin, the scoundrel. Isn't he just wonderful? Oh, Hedy, you're the one that's wonderful! All *he* is is a stupid guy.

Except that he really does know a lot. For example, he knows the factory is supposed to be getting new automatic machines that will replace us. Because Karlmann has made some capital. Abroad. He's sitting on mountains of dollars. Did some spectacular speculating on the New York Stock Exchange. That's going to cost us dearly. What happens to the workers when a machine can stuff the tobacco into the papers better than we can? Then all we'll be doing is packing and stacking boxes—until a machine can pack and stack even better. And who's going to smoke the stogies when we can't afford to buy them anymore? Then there'll be a machine for that too. We'll build a factory dedicated to consumption instead of production. And woe betide you, Capitalist, when that machine goes on strike. Like we'll be doing . . . soon!

The stogie rollers can't go on strike. They are their own exploiters. And yet they're threatened by the same fate. That's what Edgar says. That's what Hedy's father says. You can read it in the "Echo." In the "People's Daily." Because the huts and shacks and cottages and sheds, and the busy rear courtyards with their retail sales, are set to disappear. Karlmann is buying up the neighborhood. Karlmann has big plans. Cigarettes bring in money, but cigars bring in much more money. And that's why the stogie rollers are going to be put on the assembly line as well. And the place where their booths stand is where a big factory is supposed to go

up. Right next to the train station, so they can ship to everywhere in the world—or at least to the harbor. The Haddock
Line is going to become the Cigarette and Cigar Choo-Choo.
That's what Edgar said. Because till now this little train has
been running from the harbor through a tunnel to the freight
yard, loaded with crates full of fish. And returning empty.
But once Karlmann has laid down his industrial line from
Bahrenfeld to the train station, and once the former cigar
wrappers and rollers, now subjugated, are sorting their cigars
on the production line at his factory, then the Haddock Line
can make itself useful on the return trip as well—"Karlmann's
Tobacco Products Conquer the World!" Because, Edgar says,
it does no good if you earn a couple of bucks smuggling at the
Free Port, you've got to sell the merchandise wholesale to
the whole world . . . spectacularly speculating on the future
exchanges.

But to tell the truth, I can't stand Edgar. Whenever he
talks that way in front of the factory, the women hang on
his every word. Hedy thinks he's stupendous when he speaks
about the revolution. I'd like to knock him off his pedestal,
that hero of lower-class women. Because sometimes they
gape at him like his leaflet is just a fig leaf. They tear it from
his hands. They want to see him stripped bare of it. But he
will fall and fall and fall and hit the ground and his plaster
head will shatter, and his torso will break, and the rest of him
will . . . turn to dust. That would be nice, Klara my dear, but
how do you propose to make it happen? (Psst! Nobody can
read this!) (~~Oho! I'm not to blame, I'm only in love!~~)

And what does Hedy's father, the chief stogie roller,
have to say about that? "You cannot industrialize that kind
of handicraft!" Hedy replies (she picked this up from Edgar):
"But you can buy a neighborhood like this one with foreign

currency. Especially when the politicians are on your side. The Social Democrats have wedded themselves to the Liberal Democrats . . . and they're polishing up the golden calf, which, unfortunately, you can't eat, which is why the working class is starving."

"Hey, I'm not working class, I'm an artisan," Hedy's father heatedly objected. "We're collecting money, we're starting up a cooperative in our houses!" Edgar had a fit. But Hedy glared at him. He immediately stopped and got deadly serious.

Then something dawned on me. Not only his torso and what's below it is interested in her—no, that plaster head harbors feelings, and there's a heart beating in his chest, for her. I hate that heart. It should be surgically removed and pickled in formaldehyde at the pharmacy. Then she can visit it from time to time and gawk at it. (That's very wicked. I'm sorry. No, actually, I'm not.)

Klara wrote: Tuesday, November 14. I'm lying in my bed and scribbling, scribbling. The candle flickers because they've opened their roof hatches over there. Well, thanks a lot for the draft too! They're rolling and wrapping their stogies in the dim glow of petroleum lamps late into the evening. They need the paper with numbers on it, more of it all the time. And even now someone over there is reading, while I'm snuggling under the downy duvet: "Buddenbrooks." They're hoping they learn something from it, those poor, valiant stogie rollers. Incidentally, they've gotten away from collecting funds. Who's going to have any money in these times, if it wasn't manufactured in America? They save up the dollars they've smuggled for themselves at the Free Port. But to collect as many dollars as Karlmann has would take them a thousand years.

Forgive me, Edgar, I was being unfair to you. (It's a good thing you don't know.) Because she's the one I should hate (if I could, yes, I would!). Hedy, the floozy. And worse yet: the traitor. Edgar, Edgar, you haven't the faintest idea.

We had a general meeting in the cigarette factory. Of course, the boss said that was forbidden. But when the shakos from the barracks were moving in, they told Karlmann Jr. that it was the "certified right of the workers to assemble." Some of the cops are Socialists, oh my goodness! ~~That cracks me up.~~

Karlmann Jr. (the words fop, dandy, and boor were invented for him) took it with a sense of humor. He put up his umbrella (it was raining again, and an icy wind was blowing, blowing) and looked around, sizing up his female workforce with a crooked grin. I stuck my tongue out at him. Then his gaze fixed itself on Hedy.

I jabbed my elbow into her side and spit, indicating that she should too. And what does she do? Stares back at me. I step on her foot. She pushes me away. Well then. So I listen to Edgar, who's standing on a stack of crates and ranting about exploitation and speculators. And calling for a strike. And for supporting the stogie rollers. Solidarity in our struggle, etc. There's a little bit of clapping, but people's hands are numb. One woman calls out: "We want money, that's all!" Then he starts again from the beginning and explains the mechanics of capitalism. Some were already leaving. I found it exciting. So much so that I forgot about Hedy.

When I turn around, she's standing there under Philipp's umbrella. (That's Karlmann Jr.'s name.) She's joking around with him. Leaning against the factory wall and showing some knee. She even lets him stick a ciggy in her mouth, the floozy. And I shout: "Hedy!" And she casually waves, like she's trying to shoo a fly away. "I'm standing in the rain and you're under an umbrella!" I yell, because I can't think of anything better to say. But women have no power, not even over women. Yet men have power over men.

To be specific: Karlmann Sr. comes to my aid, fortunately. His Daimler stops outside the gate and honks. The old man shakes his index finger, and Junior has to sprint. In doing so, he steps into a puddle that's sooo deep I have to laugh. And Hedy laughs too. And it's all very well for her to laugh, because she's still holding his umbrella. And Karlmann Jr. now realizes that. He turns around briefly, but then gestures dismissively with his hand—back through the puddle again? Bah!

Hedy's standing in front of me, and I scold her. "Traitor! Slut!" I point at Edgar, but he isn't even there anymore. Only the crates are still lying around. And Hedy laughs. I get mad as all get-out and say weird things like: "You showed him your knee!" "Is that being a traitor?" she asks coquettishly. "You bet it is! We're talking about strikes and wages, and you cozy up to the enemy class! You're betraying your boyfriend . . . and me!"

When I realize what I've been saying and how I've said it, I start feeling odd. Because Hedy is smiling like she's never smiled at me before, and she says: "You're such a cutie, you know that? The man who gets you someday can count himself lucky!" "But I don't even want a man," I whine. And then she leans down to me and gives me a kiss on the cheek.

I freeze. She turns around and struts away, under her umbrella. And sways her hips, and I know she's making fun of me. And then I get furious and think: If I was a man, if I was a man, what I'd do to you . . .

But I'm not.

* * *

Klara wrote: Friday, November 17. Maybe I am after all! It's only a question of courage, right? Power? Bah, a guy like Philipp has no power. He has something more like will. But so do I. Today Hedy wanted to go upstairs to the business office during lunch break, to return the umbrella. I said: "Have you gone crazy?" She asks: "What do you mean?" I say: "The way you're throwing yourself at him." She: "Who do you mean, he's not even there." Me: "How do you know that?" She: "I haven't seen him, anyway." "Well then," I say, "in that case just keep the umbrella." She looks at me doubtfully: "As security?" "No, as an umbrella," I say. Then she looks all pensive. Runs her fingertips across my face. I don't know for how long, it seemed like a long time to me. My face was naked before her gaze. I shuddered. The siren howled and the break was over.

All the crooked, poorly stuffed, torn ciggies that got weeded out today—they all came from me.

On our way home, the Daimler pulls up next to us. "Oh no," says Hedy. She holds the umbrella over both of us.

"That's a nice umbrella you've got there, miss," Philipp Karlmann says.

"'Cause it's raining," Hedy replies.

"Where did you get it?" he asks.

"Stole it! From a thief!" I cry. Maybe a little too shrilly.

"Then I guess I have to call the police," he laughs.

Now we just stand there. Stupidly.

Hedy says: "It's not proper for a gentleman to take an umbrella away from two ladies when it's raining."

"In that case, get in the car, both of you."

"That wouldn't be proper either, Mr. Bourgeois," Hedy says, and my ears prick up.

He laughs again. I step up and say: "They're exploiting us, Mr. Bourgeois, and they're making fun of us too!"

"Would you just get in the car?" He opens a back door.

Hedy folds up the umbrella, tugs the car door open wider, and tosses the umbrella onto the backseat.

"I prefer to go to the factory without an umbrella," Hedy says, and turns away.

"Just like every day, for all eternity, amen," I say, linking arms with her, and we stride off.

"Maybe," she says.

When we got home, we were soaked to the bone. Hedy's mother fixed us two grogs and we wrapped ourselves up in blankets and sat in front of the stove. When my hand stole through a slit to touch her skin, Hedy jumped up and ran away.

Klara wrote: Saturday, November 18. She left for work before I did, and at the factory she kept her distance. When lunchtime arrived, she had already disappeared. Was it a mistake to play the man? Is that even what I did? During the break I saw her with Edgar. They were standing close together. How come a man gets to play the man, yet a woman doesn't?

But I've been deluding myself about everything.

There is a class of people who have everything taken from them, over and over again. If you belong to that class, you have no chance. You'd do well to keep this in mind.

Men or women, it makes no difference, it all depends on class.

Which is to say that it's come out that the buildings we live in have actually been bought up. By an American company. And guess who this company belongs to? The folks in that Daimler. Now word is going around among the stogie rollers that they've been expropriated. "Oh, if only our houses belonged to us ourselves," they lament. "Oh, if only . . . oh, if if if . . ."

Now Edgar is sitting over there with them in the attic, and they're yammering and jabbering and pissing and moaning, and at some point he shouts: "Come on, do you just want to putter around in a shack in an allotment garden, you petit-bourgeois daydreamers? We're striking for you, but you need to do something too."

Then it quiets down and they're whispering to each other.

I tiptoe over and eavesdrop.

"Don't get duped," I hear. "Don't capitulate . . . resist . . . a fight to the death . . . an answer . . . kidnapping . . . If you have nothing, you have nothing to lose!"

This last sentence came from Edgar's mouth. Courageous. Decisive.

And then he knocks on my door. Steps in, head high, and collapses, suppressing a sob.

"Klara," he says, "help me." And shoves his hand under my blanket. (Luckily, I'm dressed under it.)

"I can't," I say. "Never. I really can't."

He takes my hand. I scoot into the farthest corner. He looks up in surprise, laughs bashfully, and says hoarsely: "It's her I want. Do you know where she is? Did she say anything to you? I beg you . . ."

I give him my hand. He's desperate.

"Why me?"

"She tells you everything, doesn't she?"

"Me?"

"Come on, tell me!"

"I don't know a thing," I say.

"Where'd she go with him?"

"What do you mean, with who?"

"Philipp! I saw her get into his car."

"What?" I feel cold, stiff, speechless.

He spits out words at me . . . talking about immorality, taking liberties, corruptibility, whoring, weakness, deceit, bondage, Sodom and Gomorrah—but all he means is the entitlement of men . . . blah blah, spit spit, sob sob.

I don't say a word. I look past him, into space. Until he finally leaves.

Klara wrote: Sunday, November 19. She says all she did was give him back the umbrella. In return, he invited her to a restaurant. He brought her back before midnight. Nothing happened, she says.

"Really, nothing?"

"Klara . . ."

"Really? Nothing?"

"Klara . . ."

"Really? Nothing?"

"Klara!"

She gives me a piercing look. (Ooh, her eyes!) I want to believe her.

Klara wrote: Thursday, November 23. We shut down the conveyor belts, stopped the machines, silenced the tools, and entrenched ourselves in the factory. The stogie rollers and their wives brought us provisions, blankets, and newspapers. We said: "We're fighting for you." The "Echo" said we were illegal because we weren't cooperating with their union. The "People's Daily" cheered us on. The Spartacists handed out flyers: "Down with the Tobacco Baron!" "Expropriate the Expropriators!" "Our only demands: more money, and let the stogie rollers keep rolling their stogies." For that we stayed overnight.

Where was Hedy? Edgar was looking for her. I was looking for her.

Klara wrote: Friday, November 24. The Daimler pulled up. Sitting in it are Junior and Senior, a "shyster" (as Edgar calls the lawyer), and a "heister" (as Edgar calls the trade unionist). They tell our committee we broke the law, depriving Karlmann of his property. We say he cheated us out of our wages because his money is worthless. We want dollars! He's got enough of them. They fetch the shakos from the barracks. Now they too are saying we're thieves, we've stolen Karlmann's factory from him. And then they raise their cudgels and cudgel us out. I've never seen so many shakos. Where was Hedy?

We all have bruises and lacerations, we're limping and stumbling on the long path from Bahrenfeld back to our wretched shantytown. We're furious. No wages due to criminal property damage, they say. We gather in the rear courtyard at the Stührs'. We get some soup. Then everybody goes home. Only Edgar and I are left. He asks: "Where's Hedy?" And I say: "Is that all you can think about right now?" And he says: "But she's cheating on me!" Me: "How can she be cheating? Did you pay her money to stay true to you? Dollars?"

I am so angry: "Everybody's taking everything away from everyone and claiming it's their property!" He: "Don't you have any feelings at all?" And me: "My feelings are none of your business, just like Hedy's feelings are none of your business!" He: "When the Karlmanns came, she suddenly vanished." Me: "She can go wherever she wants to." He: "No she can't. She's betrayed us!" Me: "No, it's just the opposite. You want to take away her freedom, that's what I call betrayal! You're fighting against property, and you want to make her your property? Wise up, man! The slavery of women should be preserved, or what?" He: "Is that her freedom, going with Karlmann?" Me: "If that's what she wants, let her do it." (Saying this almost makes me sick to my stomach, but I look at him defiantly.) He: "So, you do know that's what she's doing." Me: "It's her business what she's doing." He: "And you, are you doing it too? Do you have a swanky new dress?" Me: "What I'm doing is my business." He: "You were with Karlmann too!" Me: "Even if I was, what business is it of yours?" He: "You're all a bunch of whores." Me: "At least they get paid for it. They rent themselves out. Other people sell themselves for nothing. Guys like you are robbing women." At this he turned and left.

Klara wrote: Monday, November 27. Freezing rain, the factory is still closed. I'm lying in bed. Across the hall, the reader is mumbling about the Buddenbrooks . . . Hanno's been disinherited, the fortune is dwindling . . . while the hands of the stogie rollers glide over the smoothing boards, press the tobacco into the molds, cut the leaves, and puff fine mist on them. Now they want to make luxury goods. Production only for the rich. The best tobacco. That brings in ten times the profit, they say. But the money has become ten times less valuable, gentlemen! You folks need dollars. You can live off those.

The tramping of boots in the courtyard. Shouts, screams. The boots stomp up the steps. What's going on? The shakos!

They rammed the door open, stormed inside, tore the blanket from my body, searched under the bed, knocked the basin off the dresser, and rummaged around. A confusion of shouts: "Where is he?" "Was he here?" "Have you seen him?" "Do you know him?" "Where's he hiding?" They found the green bills under my pillow. "What's this? Where'd you get these, you tramp?" "Who do they belong to? Did he give them to you?"

"No, that's money. It belongs to me." "An honest thief stole it for me!" I don't say that last part, because they wouldn't understand. They stomp back out. I smooth out the bills and stick them back under the pillow. My fingertips glide over them and they crackle.

Then came the scream. Mrs. Stühr screamed through her open window out into the courtyard. Shrieking, shrill. Then the window slammed shut. A door banged open. Footsteps. I ran downstairs. On the table in the kitchen is a copy of the "Echo" with "Brutal Murder! Spartacist Terror!" on the front page. "Son of Tobacco Tycoon Murdered . . . Body Found in Haddock Line Tunnel. The victim's body blocked train traffic . . . initially an accident . . . but strangled . . . apparently thrown onto a railcar to cover up the murder . . . perpetrator from Spartacist circles . . . threats to honorable Altona family . . . investigation into . . ."

Edgar.

"Where's Hedy?"

She's run away. <u>She</u> was the one who screamed, not her mother.

"There!" Old man Stühr holds out a sheet of paper. Edgar's handwriting: "When you read this, I will be no more . . . Nothing makes any sense, NOTHING!"

"Look for her, please," old man Stühr says. "Bring her back, as fast as you can!"

I take off and don't find her.

I go out again and don't find her.

I come back and grab the green bills.

St. Paul, do you know where she is?

Great Freedom, Little Freedom, no freedom, no Hedy.

Klara wrote: Tuesday, November 28. A shako found her. He saw a shadow that wasn't supposed to be there. Behind the frosted-glass pane in Karlmann's factory. The shadow was moving. The morning sun fell through the skylight and cast the shadow on the glass. It was swinging back and forth on a rope.

"Suspect Takes Her Own Life," the "Echo" writes.

"Victim of the Class System," the "People's Daily" writes.

The Stührs weep. Everyone else is silent.

How can you take your own life and lose it at the same time?

ALL IS LOST!

That's not true. Edgar still exists. Without a purpose. He turned himself in. Now he's cowering in a cell in the barracks, with the shakos.

I say nothing. I write. (Please excuse the damp spots on the paper.)

[This is a postscript; the agreement was unilaterally suspended.]

Klara wrote: Saturday, November 25. Edgar came back on Saturday. Around noon. Came thumping up the steps, tore the door open without knocking, and screamed at me: "Is she here?" "With manners like yours, all that's missing is a shako on your head," I replied. Then he started roaring: "You're in cahoots with her!" Then came the insults. I glared at him. Then he turned around and stomped over to the stogie rollers, roaring at old man Stühr: "Where's your daughter, that floozy? Where is she, that bourgeois whore?" Then the men stood up and flung him down the stairs.

Later, when I told Hedy about this, she said: "Serves him right." (He was unhurt.)

He loitered around the courtyard for a while more, then he disappeared.

Hedy came early in the evening. Snuck up the stairs. A cardboard box under each arm. She deposited them in my room. "Don't open them!"

At dinner, she reassured her parents: "Don't worry, I'll find work." Well, all right. They were letting me eat with them, and it was better not to say anything. Her parents were silent. What are you supposed to talk about when your days in your own house are numbered, with no prospects of anyplace else to stay? Hedy was shooting glances at me that didn't quite fit in with her parents' worried expressions. It was almost childish, like we were sisters or something.

And then she did say this, when we were upstairs, taking the clothes out of the boxes: "I told them I'm taking another one for my sister, she's the same size and build as me. My twin sister."

That was the moment when all became clear. We put on the clothes and acted like we were stuck together like Siamese twins. The coats weren't all that stylish, and neither were the shoes, but we felt as sophisticated as Asta Nielsen.

When an opportunity presents itself, you go for it, right?

And the two of us went for each other, but only later.

For now, we snuck out of the house.

Took the tram that brought us to the realm of St. Paul the Unsaintly.

Little Freedom, Great Freedom.

The lively bars, the cabaret, the midnight dance café.

I didn't ask her where all those green bills in her purse came from.

She said: "Wherever we stand in the light, a shadow falls on us." She meant other people's gazes. Siamese twins are hardly welcome anywhere. For such peculiarities of human existence, little freedom is allotted. Especially since top hats and caps, tailcoats and frocks can't be put in a box. We made a rhyme!

We even wondered whether one of us should come wearing a top hat next time. "Then we can stuff the rabbits into it and make them disappear," Hedy said, "one after the other, till they're all gone."

The light was too bright. We went where it was dark.

The movies.

The film was short, and the last kiss came too soon.

And then the lights were on again.

"I know a place where there are no rabbits," I said.

"An island?" Hedy breathed apprehensively.

"Exactly."

I took her hand and led her to the club.

Green bills, great freedom.

We joked with Feather Boa, took the riding crop away from Patent-Leather Boots, comforted Sailor Sweater, and danced the worst tango in the world. A bottle fell on the floor and spun around. Her mouth was the loveliest deposit return in the world.

Klara wrote: Sunday, November 26. Morning was breaking but it didn't break us up. We took a room next door. The wisp of gauze that still floated between us disappeared and we stuck to each other like Siamese twins.

We stayed there all day long and all night. The green bills worked wonders. We were treated like ladies, and food and drink were brought to us.

"From now on I'm never going to drink anything but champagne," Hedy said.

"I'm never going back to the factory," Hedy said.

"It's very simple," Hedy said, "because the people who have money don't pay much attention to what they have."

I said: "A specter is haunting this room, the specter of beauty."

She said: "And the specter of freedom."

"No beauty without freedom" (I said).

"No freedom without . . ." (she paused).

(green bills) (nobody said that).

That's how I found my Hedy and hid her from the others. Two nights and one day.

Klara wrote: Monday, November 27. She screamed and ran away. Why didn't she come to me? What does it have to do with us if a Spartacist strangles a capitalist? If a man strangles another man? And what does the factory where you hung yourself up have to do with it? Did you feel guilty? Because he thought you had been with that pathetic umbrella? That you'd let yourself be paid by him? Nonsense! You stole from him. You were with me, not him. But in doing your deed, you denied me. You obliterated yourself and me as well. And that's why I will no longer speak your name. You do not exist, you did not exist, you could never have existed.

Klara reads: "Tuesday, November 28, 1922. I will join the Communist Party in order to atone for my guilt." She reaches for a cigarette and lights it. Watches the blue haze rise to the ceiling. Smokes. Grinds out the butt on the back of her hand.

She tears the pages out of her diary and stacks them on top of each other. Picks up the cigar and lights it. With the glowing tip, she ignites the pyre on the table. Watches the sheets blacken, the writing disappear, the words crumble into ashes. Then she picks up her knapsack and leaves the room.

About the Contributors

INGVAR AMBJØRNSEN was born in 1956 in Tønsberg, Norway's most pub-filled city, grew up in Larvik, and has lived in Hamburg since 1985. He published his first book in 1981, following an unfinished gardening apprenticeship and jobs in various fields including psychiatry. Since then, he has published numerous novels and received several awards, including the Brage Prize, the German-Norwegian Willy Brandt Prize, and the Norwegian Booksellers' Prize. Ambjørnsen attained world renown with his Elling novels, which have been translated into thirty languages; the film adaptation, *Elling*, received an Oscar nomination in 2001 for Best Foreign Language Film. His most recent novel is *Echo eines Freundes*.

ZOË BECK was born in 1975 and studied in Germany and England. She is a writer, translator (Amanda Lee Koe and Sally Rooney, among others), publisher (CulturBooks, with Jan Karsten), and dubbing director for movies and TV series. Beck has been awarded numerous accolades for her crime novels, including the Friedrich Glauser Prize, the Radio Bremen Crime Fiction Award, and twice the German Crime Fiction Award. Her most recent book is *Memoria*.

TIMO BLUNCK, born in 1962 in Hamburg, is a musician, singer, composer, producer, and author. In 1981 he became the bass player in the internationally successful avant-garde punk band Palais Schaumburg. At the same time, Blunck cofounded, with Detlef Diederichsen, the band Die Zimmermänner, with whom he is still active today. In 2001, following stints in England and the US, Blunck began running the Hamburg-based company BLUT, which produces music for films, events, and advertising. His debut novel, *Hatten wir nicht mal Sex in den 80ern?*, which was accompanied by a solo musical album, was followed by the novel *Die Optimistin*.

ROBERT BRACK, born in 1959 in Fulda, has lived in Hamburg since 1981. Starting in 1988, he has published crime novels with political and/or historical themes, among them *Und das Meer gab seine Toten wieder*, about a 1931 police scandal in Hamburg that led to the dissolution of the female criminal police unit, and *Blutsonntag*, about the dramatic events that took place during a Nazi march on July 17, 1932. In his novel *Unter dem Schatten des Todes*, Klara Schindler, by order of the Communist International, travels to Berlin in March 1933 to investigate the backround of the arson attack on the German Reichstag building. Brack was awarded the German Crime Fiction Award and the Raymond Chandler Society Award. His most recent novel is *Schwarzer Oktober*, about the 1923 communist uprising in Hamburg-Barmbek.

BELA B FELSENHEIMER, born in 1962, is a musician, actor, author, voice actor, and audiobook narrator. Formerly a comic book publisher and radio show host, he is best known as a member of the iconic punk rock band Die Ärzte. As an author, he has published several short stories and a debut novel, *Scharnow*, which reached #2 on the *Spiegel* bestseller list and was showcased in two sold-out reading tours across Germany, Austria, and Switzerland. His second novel, *FUN*, was published in January 2025.

FRANK GÖHRE was born in 1943, grew up in the Ruhr area, and lives in Hamburg. The author of the now legendary Kiez trilogy, Göhre has been awarded the German Crime Fiction Award three times, most recently for his novel *Verdammte Liebe Amsterdam*, for which he also received the Stuttgart Crime Fiction Prize. He has reissued the complete works of Swiss author Friedrich Glauser and written his biographical novel *Mo*, in addition to working with Alf Mayer to publish books about Ed McBain and Elmore Leonard. Göhre's screenplay work includes *Abwärts* and *St. Pauli Nacht* (winner of a German Screenplay Prize). His most recent book is *Harter Fall*.

Noah Harley (translator) lives in New York's Hudson Valley, where he divides his time between translating things of various shape and size from German, writing and performing music under Noah B. Harley, and wandering through the beautiful and rocky Catskill Mountains. His work has been published by Akashic Books, *Harper's Magazine*, the MIT Press, the National Gallery in London, and once, proudly, in the *Guinness Book of World Records*, for most dominoes toppled in a single go.

Brigitte Helbling, born in 1960, has worked since 1987 as a freelance culture journalist with a focus on comics, literature, and essays. As a playwright, she has been responsible for around two dozen screenplays since 2000; the pieces are mostly developed in collaboration with the independent theater collective Mass & Fieber/ Mass & Fieber Ost. Helbling has published three novels to date, most recently *Meine Schwiegermutter, der Mondmann und ich*.

Kai Hensel was born in 1965. After graduating high school, he initially worked as an advertising copywriter, then as a comedy writer and screenwriter for numerous TV series and movies. His plays *Klamms War* and *Which Is the Best Drug for Me?* were performed on a variety of German stages and translated into numerous languages. He has also written travel essays on Russia, Mexico, and Iran. Hensel has received the German Short Crime Fiction Award, the German Youth Theater Prize, and the Schiller Förderpreis; his novel *Sonnentau* was nominated for the Glauser Prize.

Geoffrey C. Howes (translator) is Professor Emeritus of German at Bowling Green State University in Ohio. He was coeditor, with Jacqueline Vansant, of *Modern Austrian Literature* (1999–2005), and was on the editorial team of *No Man's Land*, a journal of German-language literature in English translation (2016–2022). In 2020, he was a judge for the PEN Translation Prize. He has translated texts by over thirty authors, including Robert Musil, Peter Rosei, Jürg Laederach, Gabriele Petricek, Doron Rabinovici, and Margret Kreidl.

Jan Karsten is the publisher and editor of CulturBooks, an award-winning independent publishing house based in Germany that specializes in contemporary international literature and crime fiction and has twice won the German Crime Fiction Award. Karsten also translates literature from English, including works by Keith Gessen, Carl Nixon, and Kathryn Scanlan. He lives in Hamburg.

Nora Luttmer, born in 1973, studied Southeast Asia with a concentration on Vietnam, in Passau, Hanoi, and Paris. Today, she lives in Hamburg and works as a writer, journalist, and facilitator of cultural education for children. Her first crime novels, about the Hanoian Inspector Ly, take place in Vietnam; *Schwarze Schiffe* was nominated for the Glauser Prize in 2014 in the debut category. She is currently writing a new crime series set in Hamburg, her second for Rowohlt Verlag. For her short story in this book, "Ant Street," she revived the bistro owner Aunt Lien from her crime novel *Dunkelkinder*. Her most recent book is *Schwarzacker*.

TILL RAETHER was born in 1969 in Koblenz, grew up in Berlin, and works as a writer and freelance journalist in Hamburg for *Brigitte Woman, Merian,* and *SZ-Magazin,* among others. He studied American Studies and history in Berlin and New Orleans and served as deputy editor in chief of *Brigitte*. His crime novels about the highly sensitive Commissioner Adam Danowski, the latest of which is *Sturmkehre*, have been critically acclaimed and nominated several times for awards. His most recent book is *Die Architektin*.

JASMIN RAMADAN, born in 1974, studied German Studies and philosophy in Hamburg. In 2009, she achieved her breakthrough with her debut *Soul Kitchen*, the prequel to Fatih Akin's film of the same name. This was followed by numerous short stories and four other novels. In 2020, at the invitation of Philipp Tingler, she opened the competition for the Bachmann Prize with an excerpt from *Auf Wiedersehen*. Ramadan is a freelancer living in Hamburg and writes the *taz* column "Einfach gesagt." Her most recent book is *Auf Wiedersehen*.

KATRIN SEDDIG, born in 1969 in East Germany, has lived in Hamburg since 1994 and published six novels as well as various stories and essays in anthologies, newspapers, journals, and magazines. She has been a columnist for *taz* since 2013. She has received the Hamburg Literature Award multiple times, along with the 2020 Hubert Fichte Prize and the Calwer Hermann Hesse Prize. Her most recent novel is *Nadine*.

TINA UEBEL, born in 1969, is a writer, freelance journalist, traveler, literary organizer, and comanager of the Nochtspeicher club in Hamburg. Since 1993, she has published numerous short stories and travel features, as well as five novels and three expedition reports. She was awarded the Hubert Fichte Prize in 2012. Her most recent novel is *Dann sind wir Helden*.

MATTHIAS WITTEKINDT was born in 1958 in Bonn and grew up in Hamburg. After studying architecture and religious philosophy in Berlin and London, he worked as an architect, director, and author of theater and radio plays. His work has received the Kurd Lasswitz Award and the Berlin Architect Prize. Since 2011, he has focused entirely on his critically acclaimed crime novels, twice winning the German Crime Fiction Award. His most recent book is *Hinterm Deich*.

PAUL DAVID YOUNG (translator) is a playwright, critic, and translator. In 2022, Seven Stories Press published his translation of Stefan Koldehoff and Tobias Timm's *Art & Crime*. He has written criticism for the *Brooklyn Rail, Art in America,* and *Hyperallergic*, in addition to *PAJ: A Journal of Performance and Art* (MIT Press), which also published his book *newARTtheatre*. His 2019 play *All My Fathers*, praised as "hilarious" by the *New Yorker*, was presented by La MaMa Experimental Theatre Club in New York, and directed by Evan Yionoulis, director of drama at Juilliard.